BURN

BLOOD BROTHERS
BOOK ONE

HEATHER LONG

ISBN: 978-1-956264-91-3

BURN

WHAT LINES WOULDN'T YOU CROSS FOR THE PEOPLE YOU LOVE?

My name is Grace Degas Black.

Years ago, I made a splash during a charity fashion show where an agent "discovered" me. My work led to the glitzy world of haute couture, perfume ads, and more. I was living my best life, traveled the world, and the only thing that would have made it better was if my twin would have come along for the ride.

My other half. My best friend. Then one day, she disappeared.

I couldn't escape that sinking feeling of something being terribly wrong. Then the nightmare came for me. I woke up in hell's waiting room.

Chained.

Taken.

Moved from one location to another, I could only struggle to survive amidst the suffocating fear. Then just as abruptly, salvation came from the most unexpected place. Salvation and retribution.

I wanted my sister back.

But my saviors had no intention of letting me go—not when someone continued to hunt me.

Was it me they were hunting? Or my sister?

I didn't care what I had to do, but to find her, I would make the world burn. These men were going to help me, they just didn't know it yet.

To all the women who were told they were "too much" — here's to you. May your "too muchness" continue to make everyone uncomfortable, while you thrive in the glow of your undeniable awesomeness. Keep being extra—it's clearly working.

FOREWORD

Dear Reader,

Welcome to the first book of a brand new series. Blood Brothers will be five books total. I am super excited to be sharing these characters with you. They've been living rather rent-free in my head for over three years. You see, many moons ago, Blake Blessing and I were in Seattle for a week long writing get away and hanging out with our friend Sara.

At the time, we were wrapping up a book in the Cardinal Sins series and Blake was working on plotting out a new book and series that would come out a couple of years later. The name of that series Bastard Brothers of Carnage. As we threw the ideas back and forth, I said rather "randomly" I want to write Grace's story. She said, *yes!*

Yes, Grace Black, the fmc of this book is the identical twin of Amorette Black, the fmc of Bastard Brothers of Carnage. While we collaborated on their backgrounds, and their flashbacks, everything else is independent. They are written specifically so you do not have to read one series to read another. Obviously, we won't tell you no if you want to read any of the books in either of our respective worlds (and shared ones), but we love making every series accessible to new readers.

I've literally had these characters in the back of my head for over three years. When I sat down to write Burn, the characters, the words, even the situations just *flowed*. I am already eager to dive into the next book and I can't wait to hear your thoughts.

Please be aware this book contains content with dark themes and intense situations intended for mature audiences only, including but not limited to: sexual assault, dubious consent, physical violence, emotional and mental abuse, as well as kidnapping, stalking, manipulation, and other potentially triggering topics.

And now, as always, the housekeeping notes:

For those of you who have never read a why choose, or reverse harem before, first let me thank you for picking this up and giving it a shot. Second, the heroine will not make a choice in this book or any other between the guys in her life. It may take her a while to reach that conclusion, but it's the journey that drives it. There are many ways to frame this kind of relationship, currently why choose fits it very well.

I'll see you on the flip side.

xoxo

Heather

PROLOGUE
GRACE

The hand wrapped around my throat tightened, threatening to squeeze off what little air I could inhale through my nose thanks to the meaty hand plastered against my mouth. The only thing I could smell was the stench of sweat, feces, and urine. The room reeked. My eyes watered as I fought to keep my breathing shallow. An impossible task with my heart desperately sprinting as if it would get us to freedom.

"Gracie!" Alphabet's voice rang out of the darkness. "Come on, Gracie. I know you're pissed. I'd be pissed too. But this isn't the time to play these games."

A whimper of sound scrabbled in my throat and the hand fastened over my mouth went even tighter. The pressure dug his fingers into my cheeks, as if burning their imprint into my face. I jerked my gaze up to the dark eyes of the man holding me.

He was a giant. Bigger than Voodoo and Bones. I twisted, trying to kick him again. The fact he held me off the ground with only his hand on my throat gave me desperate little in the way of purchase. Twice I connected with his leg, but he barely even flinched.

"Gracie," Alphabet called again, the coaxing note in his voice almost sweet. "C'mon, I promise, I'll pin the dickhead down for you and you can pummel him."

The tears spilling out of my eyes redoubled at the kindness in that offer.

Spots danced in front of my eyes as the amount of oxygen I was even able to suck in through my nose seemed to be too thin. I'd gone scuba diving once. The mix had been a little off. I'd gotten lightheaded and sick. Thankfully, the diver with me had recognized it almost immediately. It could have gone so much worse.

My captor shoved even closer to me, like he wanted to cover me with his whole body. With his stench. The smell alone was nauseating. Combined with the smothering effect of his grip, I fought to maintain my awareness. His face was so close to me, all I could see were his dark eyes and the scar that bisected his eyebrow.

I wasn't going down like this. I wasn't going to die, in the dark, covered by the smell of someone who had spent too much time with corpses. I wasn't dying *here*...

Raising my hands, I dug my fingers into his wrist. I needed something to hold. Something to tear into with everything I had. I worked my way up to his thumb. With both of his hands on me, he couldn't go for a gun or another weapon.

"Gracie..." Alphabet's voice was drawing mercifully closer. I managed to get a grip around my captor's thumb. The shift in his grip freed up my jaw for a split second and I bit down into the meat of the man's palm.

He jerked and slammed my head back against the wood. The spots dancing in front of my eyes threatened to black me out as I slid down the wood. I needed to yell. His hand was off my mouth but the grip on my throat had tightened completely, shutting off my air.

Then he had a gun in his hand. The barest flicker of light gleamed off the weapon. A footstep with a familiar drag just outside the barn door. That was right, I was in a barn. The world spiraled as my lungs caught fire. I couldn't breathe. I needed air.

Fighting harder, I clawed at his arm, at his hand and flailed with my feet, but he only knocked me against the wood again and as everything went black, the gun went off.

A crack of fire in the darkness that swallowed me whole.

ONE

GRACE

The car picked me up at four in the morning to get me to the shoot before sunrise. The perfume campaign was kicking off with a series of print ads, billboards, and eventually commercials. My agent was up my ass about setting up a "publationship" with someone in the sports or acting world. It would raise my profile and set the stage for making the leap from modeling to acting.

Possibly.

Course, I wasn't totally decided on making that leap. Not that my agent wanted to listen to me on the subject. Modeling was a challenge that *also* required a solid bit of acting to deliver the mood, or not deliver it, as required by the job. Five years in the business and I still enjoyed what I did.

The air was crisp when the driver opened my door. I was more than capable of doing it. This early, however, I would absolutely let them spoil me.

"You made good time," Nancy, my manager's assistant and also mine for shoot days, said as she met me with a stay-warm tumbler. The flat white was the perfect temperature, likely made in the past five minutes. My driver probably kept them alert to when I was arriving. The unsweetened oat milk added a creamy texture while the non-dairy helped prevent bloating.

It was the only indulgence for the long shoot in front of me. While I preferred to limit those when working, it was too damn early in the morning and the day promised to be brutally long. I deserved the coffee, particularly since it would just be water after this. I'd add electrolytes to the rotation at lunch because food wasn't on the menu until *after* we finished.

"Madeline and Louise are already here," Nancy said as she walked with me toward the trailers that were set up. The whole shoot was on location with a full crew from the photographer, the product company, *and* the marketing company. "Eleanor is still on her way."

Nancy climbed the three short steps ahead of me to the prep trailer and opened the door. The warmth inside flowed out to wrap around us.

"There she is!" Louise hustled up the aisle to me. "Good, you have your coffee, come sit, sit. Let's make you more beautiful."

From the moment I arrived, I relaxed into the moment and just sipped my coffee while Louise and Madeline debated the hair, the makeup, and the look they were going for. Since we would have several styles for the day, they had to go with what the photographer and marketing rep had agreed on first. All I had to do was settle in and let them play like I was the dress up doll.

The next ninety minutes passed swiftly. I finished my coffee, then took a moment to clean my teeth before switching to water and they resumed working on my hair.

Ringlet curls were the style for the morning, it would be easier to start higher and tighter, then loosen it up as the day went on.

Eleanor arrived just as Nancy unzipped my first outfit. I was dressed in a lace thong and nothing else when the chilly air flooded in with Eleanor's arrival. Dressed and made up with near flawless precision, Eleanor exuded all the style and class of Anna Wintour and the warmth of an ice queen.

As she often said, Eleanor was here to make money, and negotiate business deals. It was better for people to fear her and even better if she left them unsettled. I liked her. Ballsy bitch terrified me when she'd taken me on as one of her "girls." Then I'd seen her take down a man, twice our weight and standing nearly a half-foot taller, using an umbrella and wasp spray.

Her absolute irritation at having broken a nail may have contributed to her making sure he was unconscious after he was down. Eleanor would back you all the way to the wall and come out swinging on your behalf. By the same token, she would also tell you if you were full of shit.

Frankly, beyond my sister Amorette, Eleanor was one of my favorite people. We disagreed. Hell, we even fought, Eleanor and me, but she had my back and not once did I doubt it.

"You look too skinny," Eleanor said as she stepped inside. "And you need to make an appointment for a spray tan. Nancy, take care of that." She set aside her massive purse and untied the scarf from around her neck. "Also, who signed off on this? You look like one of those cartoon creations where they hyper sexualize all the doll-like features."

I lifted a shoulder. "I think the ladies did a lovely job,

Eleanor and you know they always want me overdone so they can airbrush it down."

With an indelicate sniff, Eleanor gave me a once over. The coolness in her eyes warmed a few degrees. I could practically see the question burning in them. Was I really fine with this?

"Hopefully, I'll be a little more warmly dressed, at least until we get to the water shots." The northern coast this time of year was definitely not pleasant and one of the shot series involved me on rocks and the waves splashing in.

I was going to be frozen to the bone.

"Never say I don't take you to exciting places." Eleanor's droll tone shifted as she removed the schedule from the mirror.

"I would never make that mistake."

The corners of Eleanor's lips twitched at the comment and the rest of the room remembered to breathe again. The first outfit was a simple white shift. The butter soft cotton would not obscure much of my figure and my nipples were definitely going to be on display.

This, however, was the look Lloyd wanted, so this was the look he'd get. At least I had slippers to wear to the actual site, because I'd be barefoot after that. The sunrise was a ribbon of orange in the distance, a promise of pink and red at the very edge of the horizon as Eleanor, Nancy, and I made our way down toward the rockier shoreline, where the dark water rolled in and the air held a briny freshness, even with the breeze nipping at my nose.

Lloyd was already there, along with Jock and his people. They were scouting the area for the best angles and spots. There were rock markers set up in a few locations. It was all designed to get me where they wanted me *before* the sun came up. Exterior, environmental shoots were among the most difficult.

Limited time made for shorter tempers and brusque comments.

"I had a call from Maurizio," Eleanor said as she lit a cigarette. The crisp burn to the tobacco scene was as familiar as her perfume. "He's increased the offer to one million, but he needs you there all week."

"I already said no," I told her, arms folded. I had a robe on over the shift as a concession to the temperatures. My legs were bare though and at this rate, the laser appt was going to have been for nothing because I'd be sprouting new leg hairs in the cold.

"That was to a quarter of a million," Eleanor reminded me like I'd forgotten. "This is for a whole million and I promise, it's not about sex."

"It's always about sex," I said, unimpressed.

"Five minutes, sweet one," Lloyd called.

I lifted my chin toward him, a thank you as much as anything.

"Not this time," Eleanor said. "In addition to the standard NDA, I had them add a clause that if he or any of his people propositioned or made any sexual advances on you, the contract would be null and void."

I slid a look toward her. "Seriously?"

"He wants you there because he wants one of the most beautiful women in the world on *his* yacht for the whole week. Your presence will bring more A-listers out to join him, not to mention improve his stock with the ladies. After all, just because you aren't fucking him doesn't mean others won't think you are."

Wrinkling my nose, I shook my head. "I don't care what

he offers. I have plans and I'm not changing them. We had this fight last week when you booked *this* shoot, *this* week."

"Your sister is just a few hours away and I'm sure she'd understand…"

I raised my hand. "I don't care if Amorette understands. It's not about understanding. She and I haven't had time together in over a year. We have plans and a place on the Outer Banks, that's where I'm going. No yachts. No paparazzi. And no billionaires with delusions of grandeur. Just, Am, me, and some wine with greasy food and terrible choices in bad movies."

Eleanor sighed.

"I know you like money, but not everything is about money." Even if most things were. Five years ago, I would have leapt at the offer and made my apologies to my sister. We'd both done that, in the pursuit of our careers and our dreams. She never failed to support me, even when she didn't get it, and I wouldn't fail to support her now.

She was in the process of saving a woman named Irena from her vicious ex and taking him for everything he had. Not all heroes wore capes…

"Grace, darling," Jock called, snapping his fingers. "Come. Now."

I shed the robe, letting Nancy catch it, as I strode forward. My nipples were hard as rocks before I even took three steps. The sun was climbing relentlessly higher. The rocky shore hurt the bottoms of my feet, the thin slippers proving to be little protection against the sharper stones.

"Beautiful," Lloyd said as he caught my hand. "We're going to have to move fast. We'll be doing topless as well at least for the sunrise. One arm across your breasts…"

"I remember," I assured him. Lloyd and Jock preferred to cover all their bases. They also loved the more artistic shots. Working with them was always a blessing and a challenge. They would push me, but it wasn't about sex for them. Did sex sell? Absolutely. But making sensual poses look sensual in places like this was all about the angle of the camera, the eye of the photographer, and my ability to project the image they wanted.

The first few shots were static, then they waved me toward the water.

"Walk along the edge," Jock said. "Let the water stroke your toes."

I didn't snort, though I was almost dead certain Eleanor had. Maybe I imagined it. She was a dozen feet away, sunglasses on and cigarette lit as Nancy spoke to her. They were probably handling emails and messages.

Barefoot, I padded down over the rocks and ignored where they stabbed at the soles of my feet. The first rush of water over my toes was brutally cold. The second helped to numb the ache. A breeze picked up and I raised my arms as if imagining I could fly with it.

It was cold as hell and it pressed the cotton shift so tightly against me, I didn't have to imagine it highlighted my whole body.

"Perfect!" Lloyd called. "Keep moving. Just—play with the water. Kick it up…"

Every instruction added a fresh layer of hell to the morning, but I didn't let it disturb my zen. When Lloyd called for a smile, I smiled. When he said glare, I glared. When he told me to play, I danced like it was raining. When it came time to let the shift go, I walked with my arms wrapped around my upper half, just enough to hide the curve of my breasts.

We'd gone almost a half-mile by the time the sun was up hovering above the horizon and the light stretched out with almost insubstantial fingers to stroke over me. The wind redoubled and tossed my hair.

"Spin!" Jock said. "Arms wide!"

A laugh escaped me. These images would be all whimsy and seduction. A temptress of purity on the warm shores as the summer waves came in.

The absolute absurdity of it all captured for the masses who couldn't feel how frozen I was or how cuts on the bottoms of my feet stung. They wouldn't know the frostbite I courted with my nipples or how today was anything but a warm sunny day.

That was fine, after all.

I traded in dreams and mystery. My job was to put on the show and make them believe in the magic.

And I was *damn* good at my job.

TWO

GRACE

The shoot went until past midnight, but Lloyd and Jock were enthusiastic about the number of photos they got. They'd brought out part of Jock's crew to process the digital images, it let them review during outfit and location changes. In the end, it also made a long day even longer while also making sure we maximized our time on location.

It meant I received not only the bulk of my shooting fee, but it doubled when we went over eight hours, then tripled when we got close to midnight. Either way, it was a tidy sum and made me even happier I turned down the yachting offer. Eleanor and I parted ways as my driver returned me to the city. It was almost three am by the time I'd showered, moisturized, and fallen face first into bed.

I slept in until almost noon. Eleanor and Nancy had both left me messages, including Eleanor telling me that the offer had gone up to two million. She sounded almost mournful in her voicemail, but she was already turning it down. Good, I wasn't going to have the debate again.

Nancy had sent over tickets for Paris, which I was due to

be in a couple of weeks, as well as reservations at my favorite spa in the whole city. Making sure I updated my calendar with the reservation numbers, I finished going through the messages. The only one who hadn't responded yet was Amorette.

It was the middle of the day and she'd had court this week. When she was deep into a case, particularly one that meant as much to her as Irena—fuck I couldn't remember her last name. The client was important. If I hadn't heard from her before I left the next day, I'd send her a message to remind her about our girls weekend. The case was important, but so was time for us. It was why I rented us a place on the Outer Banks.

As much as I wanted to stay in bed, I needed to go to the gym, then shower, then get my nails done before I packed. Thankfully, my building had a gym and since the building was secure, only residents could use it. Helped me to avoid guys trying to hit on me or pick me up. It had become such a nuisance at my last gym that when I moved, I paid extra to make sure I could work out in the building.

Twenty minutes and a protein shake later, with my headphones in and workout mix chosen, I was running on the treadmill. It didn't need to be a long run today, because I also had weight training. But there was something just mentally cleansing about the ritual. I'd only started running in high school because I'd been dating one of the guys on track. Kept running when I was dating a football player, then hockey, and eventually when I came to New York—running went everywhere.

I kept running cause I liked maintaining my physique. Thin was a requirement of the job, but I didn't want to be so skinny, and lacking in muscle, because that would make me frail. I also liked food, so I split the difference. After my run,

I switched to weights. The workout wasn't pushing me. Today was about toning and burning some calories.

After barely eating the day before, though, I didn't want to make myself sick. Once the workout was done, I grabbed a shower, changed, and got another protein shake. The rest of the day went smoothly. I got a massage after my nails were done, then an early dinner with some friends. Grilled salmon and quinoa with a glass of white wine.

It was a good evening. I made it an early night rather than heading out to go dancing with the others. As much as I enjoyed the club scene, I wanted to leave early the next day since I planned to drive to the Outer Banks. My work phone would be staying here and I'd just be taking my personal phone with me. Five days away. One day each way on the road, and three days with Am.

It sounded like heaven. Particularly since I would be leaving for Europe not long after I got back. As much as I loved the travel, the culture, and visiting the sites in so many interesting places, it was still work. It would still put me out of reach for months. I hated being in a completely different time zone from Amorette. It made keeping in contact challenging, but we'd managed it all the way through her schooling and we'd manage it now.

Maybe I needed to show up for her closing arguments in the case. A plan formed that made me grin as I curled up in bed. I'd fish for the case schedule and see if there was a chance for me to be there for her closing argument. I wanted to cheer her on, and granted, I wouldn't be whistling or throwing confetti or anything—but Amorette never missed me competing as a cheerleader or performing at a game.

She'd show up warm or cold, dry or rainy, and she even brought her homework, but when I looked up in the stands,

I'd see her smiling back at me. The idea of being able to do that for her in the courtroom?

Oh yeah.

I was so down for that.

THE DRIVE the next day was actually kind of perfect. I didn't leave as early as I originally planned but the traffic via the tunnel was also nowhere near as bad as it could have been earlier in the day. I split the time on the drive between jamming to music and then listening to an audiobook. I actually started and stopped a couple of different audiobooks. Being a mood reader was a pain in the ass but if I could lose myself in a book, it was a nice break.

The first one was a faerie book. Brand new from one of my favorite authors. Okay, well maybe not totally brand new. New to me. As much as I loved her, it just wasn't grabbing me. I'd save it for later. I needed something with a lot of action. The procedural didn't work even if it was from one of my favorite series. I finally chose one at random rather than trying to figure out what to listen to.

The book opened with a casual assassination followed by a fun conversation with someone in a gunfight. Right, this was *exactly* what I needed. The drive flew past. I stopped once for gas and to stretch my legs, but otherwise I kept on the move. The book proved to be the perfect length.

It finished just as I got to the grocery store. I wanted to stock up on food and wine. I sent Amorette a message but she hadn't read the last one I'd sent. Frowning, I pressed call. If she was with her client or in court or on the road— well, she wouldn't answer. Her voicemail greeting was so sober and serious it made me grin even wider.

"Yes, sister mine, I would like to leave you a message. This is your favorite sister, the gorgeous one, and I am standing in the parking lot of the grocery store. I am heading inside to pick up all of our favorites, as well as some wine. This is your not so gentle reminder that if you are on a special diet or want to be a picky eater, now is the time to answer me or you're going to be stuck eating what we ate in high school."

Laughter escaped me.

"Actually, I'm thinking even more junk food than what we ate in high school. You get the theme. Anyway, call me, and I'll see you hopefully sooner! Love you."

Ending the call, I shook my head. Depending on how deep she was in the case, I may not see her until late tonight. Fine, I'd get all the things. I had so many bags of groceries when I returned to the car. I'd settled on just six bottles of wine. Two for each evening was usually about right for us and if we indulged more? Who cared?

GPS got me to our rental. The instructions with the code were in my email. Twenty minutes after arriving, I'd stocked the kitchen, dropped my bag in a room, and changed into something comfortable before coming out to sit on the deck. The breeze off the water was heavenly, and I put my feet up and just soaked up the vibe.

An hour later, Amorette still hadn't answered her messages. It didn't mean anything, she could be with her client, in the office, doing research, working on her closing argument. She'd vanished into the law library for three days before finals once, and I'd been camped out in her apartment when she finally came home.

It had been almost funny at the time.

Almost.

Still, our weekend didn't officially begin until the next

day so I opened a bottle of wine, heated up a microwave meal and then settled back out on the deck with the second audio book playing on my headphones.

I was still thinking about the story when I went to bed a few hours later.

The next day dawned kind of gray and rainy. I went for a run on the beach before I had a shower and then settled in to wait for Amorette. By mid-day, I was getting antsy. By three, I'd started calling her..

I kept getting tossed into her voice mail. It annoyed the hell out of me, but all I could think was something had gone wrong with the case. It was the only thing that would make her blow me off. Or forget about me.

The only thing.

A little before five, I called her office, but they were already on their answering service. I didn't leave a message there. At this point, unless she'd broken her phone, she was already going to run into a tsunami of messages when she checked in.

The guilt would probably get to her. I'd finished the second book by bedtime and I turned on a reality show while I waited for her. I skipped the wine, but I fell asleep on the sofa. When dawn came, there was still no sign of her and no message.

I called her apartment. The landline was there for emergencies, but she would answer it if I called. No one picked up. I went digging through my phone, I had a list of contacts for her, in case of emergency. One was her new boss, but I'd never met him and I didn't want to introduce the idea of a panicked sibling.

Her property manager also didn't answer. The new boss was next, and I left a detailed message. I'd never called so many people without getting a single person to pick up before. Granted, I preferred text messages too but come on. It was late afternoon when the property manager called me back. He didn't know what her plans were and he'd seen her a couple of days before on her way to court.

With a casual assurance that Amorette was fine, he dismissed me and hung up. Now, I kind of hated people. The agitation was getting to me. Amorette would have called by now. She wouldn't have been so caught up she utterly ignored me.

That wasn't us.

Ever.

I sacked up all the supplies and put them in the garbage, cleaned up what little mess I'd created and headed back to the car with my bag. I was a lot closer to Amorette's place than I was mine *and* I had a key. Keeping my nerves in check, I used the audio book to distract me as I drove.

It was late by the time I got there. I found a place on the street to park. I'd have to move the car before six in the morning, but that was fine. The lack of responses from Amorette on the drive had my teeth on edge.

Key in hand, I went to open the lobby door but I didn't even get the key into the lock. Something dark yanked over my head as a chemical smell invaded my mouth and nostrils. I couldn't breathe or scream.

The plink of the key hitting the ground seemed to echo forever. As the world spun away. It was almost like being high, but not in a good way. I couldn't focus and even as I tried to fight, my grasp on consciousness slipped away entirely.

It was darkness.

Then nothing.

CHAPTER

THREE

GRACE

The sound of crying and skin slapping against skin woke me. The pounding in my head began to drown out the other noise almost immediately. My mouth tasted like ass. The sliver of light cracking my eyes open admitted drilled into my brain with fresh agony.

I tried to roll away from the noise. How much had I drunk the night before?

Sobbing penetrated the haze and I pressed my hands against the... floor? The cold cement against my hands finally made it past the fog of sleep. This was more than just tiredness. I'd been drunk enough to know the difference. This was more like someone slipped me a mickey.

More crying pulled me to the present and I made it to sitting upright and stared out into a nightmare. It had to be one, right? There were men pumping away between the legs of nearly a dozen women in similar situations to mine.

The smell of sex, urine, and sweat filled the air with a rank kind of miasma. The sobbing came from the girl closest to me. She had her head turned away from the man raping her.

Oh, fuck no.

I didn't care how bad my head hurt. I pushed to my feet and lunged forward. He wasn't looking at me—only a chain snapped taut as I made it a couple of steps and I fell.

My knee protested slamming into the floor. Worse, it sent a jarring pain all the way up to add a new turbulence to my headache even as the world swam around me. My stomach rebelled. I wanted to vomit.

Laughter drifted through the nightmarish sounds surrounding me. The sound jarred. Amusement didn't belong in this house of horrors. Some distant part of my brain was desperate to believe I was locked in a bad dream and I'd wake up any minute.

Just too many dark books and wine. I knew better than to go to sleep after too much alcohol. Not even squeezing my eyes shut broke me out of this hell.

A masculine voice I didn't recognize said something in Spanish. It wasn't Castilian. I didn't even think it was Andalusian. It was closer to Argentinian. Maybe.

Either way. I understood what he said.

"The beautiful doll is awake."

Why wasn't there something closer I could grab to throw at the asshole still pumping away on the poor girl? A hand grasped my chin as a scent of too strong cologne threatened to suffocate me.

I jerked my face away from his touch. Or at least I tried. He tightened his fingers, the force of them biting into my flesh as he forced my head back to look up at him.

The man wore a five-thousand-dollar suit, a silk tie, and had on Armani cufflinks. Disgust curled through me.

"Tell Ignacio," the man continued in Spanish, as he rubbed his thumb over my lower lip. "He claimed her for himself." Then he smiled at me. "But I plan to fuck this mouth after he's sated himself."

"*¿De verdad?*" I asked. Maybe it was the desire to throw up or the vicious pounding in my head. It could just be that I'd woken up in some inner circle of Dante's hell surrounded by demons. Then the man smirked down at me and thrust his thumb into my mouth, I reacted.

I bit down so hard on his thumb, I drew blood, and I punched him right in the dick. He went from a shriek, to choking as he fell to his knees. I fisted his tie, pulling it taut and spat his blood back out at him.

His gasps turned to gargles and then he was trying to grab my hair. I jerked away from him. Even with the chain on my ankle, I managed to get behind him and I still had a hold of his tie.

A boom of laughter ripped through the air. The man who'd been raping the woman next to me suddenly headed for us. But rapid-fire Spanish cut him off as an arm looped around my waist.

It dragged me back against a hard chest and I yanked the suit with us. He fell backwards. There was something satisfying about him hitting the ground. Unfortunately, it also jerked his tie out of my hands.

Dammit. I wanted to scream.

"Such a beautiful fighter," the man holding me said, his English lacking any kind of accent. He stroked my hair like I was some kind of cat. I couldn't see him, but I had a front row seat to the suit climbing to his feet. Rage vibrated off him and slapped against me like angry waves.

Blood spattered his already reddened face as he pulled his tie from his neck. I hope it hurt like hell. Violence wreathed the air around him as he stalked forward.

"Stop." My captor pivoted to the left, putting me out of reach from the man reaching for me.

"She—" He spit the pronoun out like it was a dirty thing and blood struck me from where he waved his hand. "Filthy *puta* bit me."

"You shouldn't have touched her." The man holding me responded in an even tone. His absolute lack of accent threw me. I didn't think he was American. The dialect was too flat. It sounded like he wasn't a native English speaker, yet I couldn't place what his first language could be. "I told you, this one is mine."

He stroked my hair again. While I couldn't place his origin, there was no mistaking the danger in his voice.

The prick in the suit glowered at me. You know what, fuck you buddy.

"He said he planned to fuck my mouth after you were done with me."

"Did he?" A shiver of apprehension went through me at the silken menace underscoring those two words. He snapped out something in—a language I didn't recognize but the suit did. Whatever it was had to have been bad because he paled.

The shackle on my ankle was removed and my captor continued to pet me as the man's suit was stripped off and he was lashed to a post.

"Do you think ten is enough, pet?'"

"Ten?" Ten what?

"Hmm, you're right. Make it twenty." He snapped the fingers of his free hand and kept me right there with a front row seat to the whipping the suit took. Not once did he scream nor did he look away.

The pure malice in his eyes promised me a brutal

retribution. Reading people had always been something of a hobby. With men, it was as much a business advantage as it was self-defense. They were bigger and they were stronger, if I could charm them, I stood a much better chance of surviving.

Bile coated the back of my throat as blood flecked his chest and spattered around from the heavy strikes of the whip against his back. Only when he sagged from the abuse and the twentieth lash landed did my captor turn me away.

His path gave me a full view of all the women. There were so many. They were all shackled and naked. Some huddled with their arms around their knees. Others still screamed and fought.

I wanted to help them but at the moment, I wasn't even sure I could help myself. By the time we exited that hall and the door closed on the horrid sounds, I'd made my peace with the fact this was all really happening.

The man continued up a darkened hall. He moved like I weighed nothing at all. I still couldn't get a look at him. Another man straightened at our approach, but my captor only said two words. I had no idea what the words were or what they meant but the man waiting merely nodded then opened a door to let us into...

My stomach dropped.

It was a private room. There were chairs, a sofa, and on the far wall a bed. There was also a door that opened into what looked like a bathroom. It wasn't opulent, but it was a damn sight cleaner than the main warehouse. It also smelled better too.

Setting me on my feet, my captor wrapped my hair around his hand. "You will not try to assault me, pet, do you understand?"

The inflectionless English just made my skin shiver. I couldn't even say why.

I swallowed hard. "I understand."

Not agreeing was a challenge, because if there was a snowball's chance in hell of getting out of here, I needed to take it. He turned me by my hair and I looked up to meet his gaze.

His eyes—well his left—was a pitiless kind of dark. The other was milky white. An angry scar bisected his eyebrow and across his right eye and down to his cheek. He'd lost his sight, but I had to wonder how he hadn't lost his eye totally.

"You are as beautiful as all your pictures," he said, stroking his fingers through my hair.

"Thank you?" I wasn't really sure what to do with that compliment. "I don't really feel beautiful at the moment." There was a faint sourness in the air that was *not* coming from him and sweat had soaked through my shirt.

"No?" He canted his head and there was something unsettling about being under the focus of his attention. It was like he stared right through me, all the way down to my bones.

"No," I said. I licked my lips not that there was an ounce of spit in my mouth. "I smell. I'm sweaty. I feel kind of disgusting after—" I had no idea what the other man's name was. "Well, after he touched me."

My captor nodded slowly.

"I don't suppose I can have a shower?" Maybe he'd be sympathetic. He seemed that way. Or maybe that was just his pure possessiveness. Men like him did not share. They took what they wanted and to hell with everyone else.

"What would you give me for a shower, pet?" He spread his fingers and combed them through my hair. There were snarls here and there. Instead of just tearing through them, he was slow and methodical.

I licked my lips again and his gaze dipped, his attention shifting my eyes to my mouth. He wanted to fuck me.

Men.

So predictable.

My heart pounded a little harder. Adrenaline dumped into my system. Fear was a powerful motivator. So was surviving. I'd fucked men before to get what I wanted. Scratch their balls and they'd scratch my back.

"I have wondered what it would feel like to fuck this sweet body. You are smaller than I thought you would be." Well, that was direct.

"I'd be happy to show you," I said, letting that hang there in the air between us.

His nostrils flared and his pupil dilated a fraction. Arousal was swift, because he was already turned on.

"After I shower," I added slowly. "With your permission, of course."

Lips pursed, he inspected me. "Take your clothes off here. I wish to see all of you."

He released my hair and took a step back. It was a test.

Of course it was a test.

I was basically offering myself to him and he wanted me to prove it.

Moving to a chair, he took a seat and studied me.

"Now." The single syllable snapped out of him, the demand unmistakeable.

I reached for the hem of my t-shirt. The casual clothes tickled a memory in the back of my head, but I left it alone for now. It was just a body. I'd been nude on plenty of shoots with far more people around than just one man.

Whether I did it for money or art or survival, it was just a body. I didn't bother making a production number out of it. The cool air against my damp skin was welcome.

The bra, jeans, and panties followed in rapid succession. I had no shoes or socks on. No jewelry either.

Once I was naked, he steepled his hands together and studied me. I debated whether he wanted me to pose.

"Turn around."

No comment. I pivoted in a slow, deliberate circle. The moment my back was fully to him, I braced for him just grabbing me and getting to business. Nothing happened, however, and my heart slammed against my ribs like it was determined to crack them.

Once I faced him again, he nodded.

"You may shower. There is a hair dryer in there, make sure your hair is dry when you come back, I want to feel it on my skin and in my hands when I take you."

The words "thank you" seemed glued to my tongue, but I managed to squeeze them out. His nod was magnanimous. The shower was fully stocked and the water was warm.

Unfortunately, there wasn't much in the way of weapons and there was also no way to close the door. Awareness of him observing me the whole time didn't go away, either. I made quick work of the shower, and washing my hair, rinsing away the sour odors of fear and pain.

Once I was done, I toweled off, then hooked up the hair dryer. It would take a minute. He had no product here for me, so whatever I ended up with was going to probably frizz.

Well, frizz was still soft. The minutes of freedom between stepping into the shower and finishing blow drying my hair passed too quickly. Once I was finished, I took a deep breath and returned to the room.

The man still sat in his chair, his head tilted back and

his left eye open. The scar seemed to glow despite the shadow cast by the chair's winged back.

"Where do you want me?" I was proud of how steady the words came out.

"Is your cunt as smooth as it looks?" The question had me glancing down.

"Probably," I said. "I get lasered regularly."

It slowed the growth to almost nil. It didn't get rid of it entirely. He curled his fingers, a single beckoning gesture and when I reached him, he traced his fingers down my abdomen toward my pussy. He paused to trace his fingers over the bare mound, then deeper along the seam of the lips.

"Foot here," he commanded, patting the edge of the chair next to him. I raised my leg, baring myself to his inspection. The way his lips parted and the swift breaths he took said he very much liked what he saw.

The gentle probing of his fingers as he stroked from my clit to my entrance seemed utterly at odds with the situation. At least until he thrust a finger into me. I wasn't quite wet enough for that and there was some pain associated with the resistance.

"Don't worry, pet," he said in a low croon. "We have all night." He stroked his thumb against my clit. The dryness made the friction uncomfortable. Course, when he pulled his hand out and spit on his fingers, I tilted my head back.

I needed to think of something I enjoyed or this was going to be even more uncomfortable.

"Would you like me to touch you or do I have to wait?"

He rubbed his spit against me and I tried to ignore where the moisture came from. "You will be touching me soon enough, pet. But I have plans and we're going to do this my way, since you are being so sweet and cooperative."

Eventually, my body softened. It knew what to do and the more he circled my clit, the more moisture gathered between my legs.

"Play with your breasts," he told me and I raised my hands to cup them.

Pinching and rolling the nipples until the tautness stretched to my belly. He had two fingers inside of me thrusting as he worked my clit.

I might just come like this and, right now, I was fine with it. One step at a time. As a shiver went through me, he pulled his hand away abruptly and a sound escaped me that could definitely be a complaint.

His low chuckle wrenched me to earth and I looked down at him.

"You are a good pet, and I am going to enjoy the next few hours." After he licked his fingers, he unzipped his pants and opened them to free his large, bulbous cock. "Now ride me, pet."

Survival, I reminded myself. He was hardly the first dick I mounted to get what I wanted or needed. I slid a knee on either side of his thighs and reached between us to fist him. His swift indrawn breath had me stroke him once or twice.

He was rock hard and not small. Probably why he'd worked so much spit into me. If he went in dry that would definitely hurt.

Still, I didn't give myself time to think. I lined him up and plunged downward. He gripped the arms of the chair and not me as he blew out a breath.

Right.

He wanted me to ride him.

I slid a hand into his hair and began to roll my hips. It wasn't the most comfortable of positions or even giving me a lot of pleasure but I could get him off.

That was what mattered right now.

FOUR

GRACE

There was no rest. There was barely any water. My captor seemed to enjoy ordering me around even more than just using my body. As grim tasks went, it could be worse. The first time he came, he wanted to come *on* me.

Fine.

The second time, he splashed it all over my face. So fucking gross. I'd never been fond of facials. The third time, he wanted me to swallow. That I hesitated on. These guys apparently like kidnapping and raping women. There was no guarantee he was clean.

Not that he gave me a choice though. At my brief show of resistance, he'd fisted my hair and shoved his cock so far down my throat, I choked. Then he finished there, and gagging or not, he wouldn't pull out until I swallowed.

After, he was all soothing sounds and petting. Then he shackled me to the foot of the bed and went to take a shower himself. When he came out, he nodded to himself and then pointed to the pallet at the foot of the bed.

"You will sleep there. If I summon you in the night, you will kneel and say, 'what pleases you, sir?'"

I stared at him.

He gripped my chin, much like the man in the suit earlier. There was nothing soft or gentle about this man. As long as I cooperated, he didn't use his strength against me. But I didn't mistake that for any real kindness.

He expected me to serve him.

"I understand," I said, pushing the words out past the sour taste he'd left in my mouth. "May I have a drink of water?"

Not answering for a long time, he skimmed his hand down to my breasts. He hadn't really fondled or touched me anywhere except my hair and my cunt.

The fact he pinched one nipple and twisted it brutally was unexpected and I went to my knees at the sudden sharp pain. It almost felt like he was going to twist my nipple right off, and the act shed a light on a fear I hadn't even known I possessed.

Kneeling didn't free my breast, if anything it made the bruising force even worse. His dispassionate stare filled me with dread. Finally, he released me and the sudden rush of blood to the abused area just aggravated everything.

"When you wish to make a request, you will assume a proper posture. If you want something from me, pet, I expect you to beg for it."

Not for the first time, I wished I had something—anything—a book, a bottle, a stick. Since all I had was the blanket I currently knelt on and the short chain attached to the shackle on my ankle, I had to suck it up.

Nodding my head once, I debated whether I should keep staring at him or lower my head. "Do you wish me to look at you when I ask you questions?"

Neutrality was getting harder to hang onto. My breast really fucking hurt. I had to fight against the urge to make sure my nipple was still there.

"Your eyes are exquisite, pet, I would prefer you look at me. Unless others are present. Then you will look down. Tomorrow, when you demonstrate your sweetness in front of others, you will look down."

Demonstrate.

Gross.

"Thank you," I said, then tacked on, "sir," at the end. "May I have a glass of water?"

"You may." With that, he disappeared into the bathroom then returned with a cup full of tepid water. It wasn't great, but it wasn't horrible. It washed out the taste of him and I'd take it.

"Thank you, sir." The words scraped against my throat on their way out. His nostrils flared each time I said sir. Good to know. When I finished the drink, he held out his hand to take it back.

"Sleep," he ordered before he disposed of the cup and then climbed into the bed. He didn't give me any more time before the lights went off and the room plunged into darkness.

I had no idea what time it was, where I was, or how long I would be here. What I did know was that I would survive. With that in mind, I made myself lay down and pulled the blanket up over me. He hadn't allowed me to shower and rinse off the stickiness he'd left all over me.

In the dark, I used the edge of the blanket to clean my face as much as possible. The smell was right there though. It wasn't long before his breaths grew deeper and more even.

It wasn't until I was absolutely certain he was asleep

that I let myself think about how I got *here*. Even if I didn't know where *here* was. I'd been going to Amorette's place. I'd been looking for her.

That much I remembered. Then...

Then nothing.

Had they taken Am too? Was she somewhere here? This man knew who I was, so why had he gone to Amorette's to get me?

My stomach bottomed out. The possibilities were terrible on all fronts. Amorette didn't show up for our weekend. She didn't answer her calls. She never left me unread.

Never.

I squeezed my eyes closed as grief wrapped around my throat. The man in the bed kept talking about *me*. What if they took Amorette first thinking she was me? What if...

No, I couldn't think like that.

It didn't matter how much I tried to push it away, the dark thoughts continued to swirl with all the terrible possibilities. Sleep seemed elusive, yet I must have passed out at some point.

Between one blink and the next, there was light in the room and the blanket was pulled away. "Get up," my captor said. Dressed only in pants, he tugged me up from the pallet. My sleep-fogged brain fought to catch up to where we were.

"I'm sorry," I started to say. He'd said he would call me and I needed to kneel, but he only shook his head and gave me a shake.

"Silence. I am taking your shackle off, you will come with me and stay with me, do you understand?"

Not even a little bit. Rather than argue, though, I just

nodded. He moved to where the shackle locked around my ankle and he unlocked it.

"Dress." He pointed to my abandoned clothes. "Now." The snap got me moving. I managed to get the bra, panties, and t-shirt on, before he gripped my arm and hurried me to the door leaving my jeans behind.

Well, at least I had panties on.

When he opened the door and let more light spill in, two things hit me at once. He had a gun in his free hand and there were shouts coming from down the hall.

Shouts and—

The pop-pop-pop sound echoed toward us. Ice then heat flashed through me. The guard who'd been out there the night before was gone. Instead of heading back to where the beds, women, and men had been, my captor hurried me the other way down the hall.

His grip on my arm had more iron than the shackle that had been around my ankle. A string of invectives left him. At least I thought they were, I didn't understand the language. The tone, however, was *very* clear.

More than once, I banged my toes off the uneven cement pavers. Gunfire carried up the hall, then something whistled past and slammed into the wall. Every muscle in my body locked up as a hole appeared in the wall just ahead of us.

Not seeming to realize I'd stopped moving, my captor hauled me along. Then he pushed me toward the other wall as he turned. I'd seen guns before. Even held one in a couple of shoots.

I'd never been right next to one when it was fired. The sound from down the hall had nothing to being right on top of it. The bangs were loud, and seemed to redouble in the narrow hall.

I followed his aim to see who he was shooting at. It wasn't quite real. There were actually people shooting at *us*. One man went down when half of the back of his head painted the wall. Another doubled over. There was a grunt from my captor and I swung my head back to see a red stripe across his shoulder. There was a second along his ribs.

"Come," he ordered, dragging me again. This time it was real dragging. I couldn't seem to get my legs to work. I kept staring down the hall at the pair of men who weren't moving anymore.

He'd killed them.

Shouts carried toward us. More were coming.

My captor hauled me closer, then gave me a hard shake. "Run."

I wasn't even sure I could run.

One glance behind us showed more men approaching. If I said nothing, would they kill him? Would they kill me? What I wanted to do was get away from all of them.

His gun roared again. Then there was plaster from the wall splintering. Something hot scraped against me and it burned. The grip on my arm vanished. It took a moment to sink in that my captor was retreating down the hall ahead of us firing back at the men who were running toward us.

As much as I wanted to do something, anything, I didn't move. I just *stood* there.

Two of the men ran past me, shooting after my captor. The roars of the guns made my ears hurt. Another man skidded to a halt in front of me. Then he said something in garbled language.

His mouth moved, but no sound registered. Was he actually talking to me? Why couldn't I hear him? His scowl deepened and he caught me with the back of his hand.

Honestly, it was a relief when my head hit the wall and darkness fell like a curtain.

The next time I opened my eyes, it was to darkness, a dank smell, and the sound of breathing around me. Low voices called out to each other. A mixture of Spanish and English. Enough that I could understand.

There was an old man. A young boy. A woman. A different, second woman. A third woman said something but she wasn't speaking Spanish, it was French. More like Montreal French rather than Paris.

I cataloged the different sounds and accents. The voices in the dark told me a few things. The primary one was we were definitely not in the warehouse anymore. The second was we were moving. The third was someone had to relieve themselves and they'd made use of a pail.

It sounded awful. With care, I pushed myself up and tried to take a mental inventory. I hurt, but I still had on my panties, bra, and shirt. Nothing hurt any more than it had already.

My breast was still bruised and my head was stuffed with cotton and it ached. I was cold and hot at the same time. There was sweat on my arms. It was so humid in the truck. But the metal was cold against my legs.

Had all of that really happened? Had some other circle of hell come to take me from another? Where were we now? I had a thousand questions, and no answers.

Worse than all of that, my skin was still sticky. I leaned my head against the side of the—whatever we were in, a truck I supposed. The sound of the tires on the asphalt had a kind of soothing rhythm.

One of the kids started to cry and I closed my eyes. One of the kids. There were more kids on here than just that little boy. Had they also been in that warehouse? That image was too horrible to comprehend.

It was all just *horrid* period. I had no idea how long the truck moved, I was pretty sure I dozed off and snapped awake. My inner body clock was completely shot. I didn't know what day or time it was.

The sudden application of the brakes jerked me out of the doze and to awareness. Eventually, we came to a complete stop. Were we at a gas station? Somewhere else?

Should we shout? Let someone know we were here? Even as these thoughts tumbled one over the other in my head, I swallowed back any sound as the other passengers began to hush each other.

I strained to listen. Were those voices? I wasn't sure.

The sound of gunfire, however, registered clearly and I jerked with each shot that was fired.

I shoved a hand against my mouth to stifle any screams clawing their way out. Were we being stolen by someone else? What fucking twisted world had I fallen into? Was there a way out?

The sound of the latches going echoed through the container. Then a chain slid loose, and one of the huge doors creaked open and let light into the darkness. A light that blinded and I wasn't the only one raising a hand to shield my eyes.

Fresh air rushed in, and it was cool against my sweat drenched skin. The flashlight was wielded by one of the men and he skated it over all of us. It gave me my first look at the other people on the truck with me.

Men. Women. Children.

All of us shackled and chained to the walls.

"Keep it together, Hawk," one of the men said as he studied us. The disgust on his face wasn't vicious. If anything, it was pained. The one without a flashlight climbed inside. He had keys that jangled.

Some of the women pulled back and worry rippled through the container. Fear was a sour taste in the back of my mouth, but I didn't take my gaze off the newcomers.

Instead of attacking anyone, the newcomer knelt down and unlocked one of the older men's chains. Then he gave him the keys and motioned to the rest of us.

With that, the newcomer leapt out. They were letting us go?

I really had no idea what they were doing, but the old man began to release us one by one. His shuffling steps were painfully slow, but I didn't look too closely at this freedom.

Not yet.

I didn't dare.

FIVE

GRACE

T he next few hours raced past as more men appeared in addition to those who'd opened the truck. One by one, the older man freed the passengers, including me. I found myself searching every single face aboard the back of the trailer.

I didn't recognize anyone from where I'd been. That didn't mean they hadn't been there. Honestly, I didn't even know how long I'd been on the truck or unconscious before and after. Not to mention I had no idea of the name of my captor or any of the others involved.

If waking up in that warehouse had been a nightmare and the next day a descent into one of Dante's nine circles of hell... I didn't have the words for this. The men who'd freed us were rough, hard spoken, and full of violence except when they spoke to one of us.

Then they deliberately softened their voices, pitching them lower and kinder—especially for the kids. They also made a concerted effort to not loom over anyone. When more men arrived, they were joined by a doctor.

El medico. He spoke passable Spanish and despite the

wariness in everyone, he was allowed to ask some questions. Water was drunk down thirstily and blankets passed around. I waited until the kids had one before I got one.

It wasn't even until the blanket was around me and cut off the wind that how chilly I was hit me. Food arrived with another group of men. There were hushed conversations. I caught snippets here and there. They needed to get us out of here, but no one wanted to suggest we get back on one of the trucks.

Good. I didn't want to get back on one.

"*Hola*," the doctor said in a gentle voice as he approached. "*¿Hablas ingles?*"

I debated it. Did I?

"*Poquito.*" It wasn't the whole truth, but it wasn't a full lie, either.

He nodded, then motioned to my leg. "May I look at the wound?" The Spanish was a little rough. He knew enough to get by, but he wasn't totally comfortable speaking it. That was fine.

"*No duele*," I said with a shrug. It didn't hurt. I had bruises everywhere. The largest one on my heart. At the moment, I'd rather no one else touched me if they didn't have to. I still didn't know if these guys were on our side or not.

Despite the relief in the air, no one had fully relaxed. How could we? I'd gone from one set of captors to another. Was this just a third set? Irritation scraped through me like sandpaper.

What I needed was to get out of here, regroup, and then find my sister. Maybe I should ask for a phone and call the cops. The problem was, I didn't even know *where* we were.

"If it doesn't hurt," he said, not taking a step toward me

or trying to touch me. "Does anything else? I promise no one here wants to hurt you."

I'd take it under advisement.

With another shrug, I shook my head. "No."

The doctor exhaled a long, slow breath before he glanced at one of the men who'd opened the doors in the first place. He had a lovely face. Probably could have been a model. But the rest of him was hard as stone.

"She's not going to let me examine her. None of these women are going to want to."

The other man nodded. "I can't say I blame them, Doc. One look in there just makes me want to kill the people who put them in chains. Do what you can. We've got a bus coming to pick them up. Then we need to see where we can place them."

He frowned.

"It's not your fault, Milo," the doctor said. "It's not on you or Jasper. You guys found them and got them out. We'll take care of them from here."

"How the fuck are we going to do that?" The man—Milo—said. "We have so many damn problems right now, Mickey. How are we supposed to take care of these people?"

"Easy," the doctor said, gripping Milo's shoulder. "We'll figure it out." Then the doctor spared me a glance, I cut my gaze away. I could retreat, but I also wanted to know what they were saying. "Look, come on..."

The pair walked away to continue their conversation and I huddled into the blanket. The bottoms of my feet ached. So did my ankle. Frankly, everything hurt. I took another drink from the water.

We spent another agonizing hour on the side of this empty road. It could have been longer or shorter, but either way, it felt like forever. Then, as the man Milo had said earlier, a bus appeared.

It looked like a converted school bus and it had a church name on the side of it. With care, they shuffled all of us toward the bus. The doctor even picked up one of the kids who was asleep and carried him aboard.

I moved with the crowd, but kept my distance. It was hard to trust anything these people said. If there had even been the suggestion of a convenience store or a gas station, I'd have just headed for that.

Instead, we were leaving the middle of nowhere aboard a nondescript church bus. The kindness being shown was hard not to just fall for, because the men were being very kind.

That said, it was equally difficult to trust. I found a seat in the middle of the bus. Like me, the other former prisoners kept their distance. They huddled together in smaller groups. Some chose to sit alone. Our rescuers came through again with more blankets, fresh bottles of water, and what smelled like burgers and fries.

As much as I wanted to turn my nose up. I had a specific diet I was supposed to eat, I didn't dare. Particularly after my stomach rolled over itself and cramped when the first scent hit me. The burgers were small and plain. The french fries were hot and salty.

Instead of devouring either as I wanted, I took my time. The last thing anyone needed was for me to throw up. Eventually, the bus doors closed and with the doctor and a couple of the other men aboard, we pulled away from the rigs. I studied them as we drove past.

We'd been in the back of some 18-wheeler. The harshness of that reality left me cold. It was too dark to make out the landscape. The accents said we were still in the States. But were we? I had no idea.

The one good thing about the shadowed interior of the bus was I didn't have to pretend any feelings one way or another. I couldn't see them and they couldn't see me. My heart could break a little as I tried to imagine Amorette right now.

Where was she? Maybe they'd grabbed me and not her. That was a hope, right? The man before seemed to be very clear on the fact he wanted me. I spilled some of the water onto my hand and used it to wipe at my face.

While they'd grabbed me near Am's place, maybe they'd been watching for me to visit. As hollow and fragile as that line of thinking might be, I couldn't resist keeping my mental fingers crossed. Am might be calling the cops and the FBI right now.

If she got ahold of Eleanor, she'd pick up the torch and they'd both be burning everything down. A smile tugged at the corners of my mouth. Am had been born a crusader. No way she'd give up on me.

Unless...

That insidious little voice crept out of the corner of my mind. Unless they'd already taken her. Unless she'd disappeared into this gaping maw of despair. The only thing I knew for certain was she wasn't on *this* bus. She hadn't been on *that* truck.

With how many had been in that warehouse... My stomach dropped. She could be anywhere.

Exhaustion and grief weighed down on me, even as I pressed my forehead against the cool glass of the window. I needed to keep it together. Though I'd thought staying awake would be a battle, I had no trouble keeping my eyes open.

The last time I'd closed them, I'd found myself some-where else entirely. I couldn't escape if I didn't stay on top of all the opportunities. Eventually, we followed a stretch of highway toward a city rising in the darkness. The lights of it shone like a beacon. More, there was a sunrise coming up.

We were near the coast. I could see lights on those huge, super-cranes that were found in ports. So we were definitely near the water. That was something. New York was near water.

Manhattan. Brooklyn. Queens.

The city ahead of me was none of those places. I didn't catch a sign welcoming us to wherever. We trundled through the slowly rousing city. There were coffee shops, and diners that began to do a brisk business as foot traffic entered and left with their tall cups.

The number of people in suits suggested it was a week-day. Which one? How long since I'd drive from the Outer Banks to Am's place? Was my car still parked there?

I hadn't woken up with my purse or phone or anything else. Depending on when my disappearance was reported, the car might have already been towed. I didn't have a pass for parking on the street there.

So my car could be sitting somewhere, unclaimed and unwanted, another clue in the mystery of my whereabouts. The only question I had though, was who would be looking for Am if I wasn't there?

The more my thoughts whirled around, the more nauseated I became. All I wanted to do was find a phone, call her, and have her answer. I wanted to hear the profound relief as she heard my voice and knew I was okay too.

Then I would make arrangements to fly to her and we could wrap each other up in a hug. After I told her what happened, she'd be on fire to take down all of these monsters.

But I had to call and she had to answer.

The bus trundled into a pot-hole filled parking lot behind a clinic. The doctor rose as we slowed and he raised his hands. In careful, but still somewhat broken Spanish, he said, "This is my clinic. You will all be safe here. There are bathrooms. There are showers. We will get you clean clothes. Then we will work with you to get you home—"

A surge in the voices behind me suggested that last part wasn't welcome, but Doc raised his hands to quiet them.

"If you don't want to go home or can't, we will find a place for you. I know you have no reason to trust me, so just be patient, please. We want to help all of you."

He made good on that word as the doors opened and the passengers filtered off. I was one of the last. I wasn't too proud to admit that I'd waited to see if there was a trap closing on all of us.

The doctor was right there as I descended the steps. Before I could step all the way down, he held up a hand. I hesitated. Was the trap closing right here?

"*Zapatos*," he said, holding up a pair of flip-flops. They were the cheap kind but they would definitely protect my already sore, bare feet.

"*Gracias*," I murmured. He set the shoes down on the last step so I could step into the first one and then the other. He didn't try to touch me or anything else. Then he backed up so I could descend the last step.

"There's more food inside, and clothes." It was a mixture of Spanish and English, but I still appreciated the effort. I followed his instructions and crossed the cracked and broken blacktop to the door to the clinic.

It was a rear door but it was wide open. There were more people inside and not just the other survivors. A woman—clearly a nurse—was speaking rapidly to one of the other women. She was offering to look at any wounds or issues.

Another woman offered me medication, and an exam. She also asked me if I needed a morning after pill. Well, that was something. I didn't think I would, but I also didn't turn it down.

She didn't bat an eyelash, she provided the medication with more fluids. Then she offered an exam, blood work, and any other tests I might need.

Bloodwork was fine, but I'd wait on the pelvic until I got home. I went upstairs to wait for a shower to be free. There was a community center up here. It was nicer than I expected. Where the downstairs had that definite medical feel, this was a little warmer and more open.

Eventually, it was my turn. Another woman was up here and she'd brought clean clothes, including underwear. I could have kissed her. The shower was lukewarm, but I didn't care.

I scrubbed every inch of myself, twice. There wasn't much in the way of product for my hair, but I made do with the basic shampoo and conditioner. Afterward, I braided my hair back from my face. Then I was dressed, I sacked up my soiled clothes and carried it out with me.

It wasn't until I made it to the big room with all the chairs that I realized there were more newcomers here. A pair of men were speaking to a mother and her child, well, one of them was. They hadn't been with Doc or Milo or any of the others downstairs.

The second of the pair turned and met my gaze. He

looked like he'd just woken up, his hair was disheveled and stubble decorated his cheeks. His eyes were an icy kind of blue, but despite their paleness, they weren't cold at all.

"Hello there," he said with an open smile. "We're just telling your friends how this is going to work."

"Dude," the other man said. "Ease up."

"What? I'm being nice." He took a couple of uneven steps toward me. "I'm Alphabet," he said, introducing himself.

Alphabet.

His name was *Alphabet?*

Despite the disbelief his name generated, it was hard to deny his charm. He held out his hand to me.

"Hey," the other man said, gripping Alphabet's shoulder. "Remember what Doc said."

"She's not the first wounded woman I've met," Alphabet said in a low voice, sending a cutting look at his companion. "It's better to be normal. Respectful. Also, I'd like to know her name beyond the fact she's beautiful, you know."

The man with him, dropped his chin and shook his head. Like Alphabet, his friend was tall and broad-shouldered. He also had blue eyes. But his eyes were a deeper blue, and from there their appearance differed.

The second man had short, neatly clipped brown hair. A beard decorated his chin with a carefully groomed mustache on his lip. Where Alphabet was dressed in jeans, a t-shirt, and a jean jacket, the other man had on suit pants and a button down. They were a study in contrasts.

"Just leave her to catch her breath," his friend said, meeting my gaze briefly.

Alphabet huffed. "Fine, you talk to her. But if you get her number first, I want it."

His friend waited a beat as Alphabet limped over to one of the others.

"Sorry about him," the man continued in English. "He means well."

I still hadn't said anything, nor did I pretend to understand him. Sooner or later something would have to give, but I wasn't comfortable with even more strangers.

"Hey," the man continued, narrowing the gap between us but managing to not loom over me. It was a definite talent. "I know you."

My heart stopped.

"You've got an unmistakable face."

Fear was an icy coat over my too hot skin.

"We're going to make sure everyone gets home, including you."

I glanced to where Alphabet sat speaking to a woman. She'd relaxed gradually. When I looked back at his friend, the man also glanced to Alphabet before he looked at me again.

"You don't want anyone to know. I won't tell."

I had no idea how I was supposed to believe him.

"Right, you need us to prove to you that you can trust us." He nodded. "Take a seat, and hang out. We're going to take the first round here in a few. You can go with us. See where we take everyone."

A frown tightened my brow.

Why? Why couldn't I just leave?

"We don't know everything about the people who had you," he continued as if I'd asked the question aloud. Then again, maybe it was an obvious question. "To make sure you're all safe, we want to get you home and to safe ground before we leave you."

Still not a reason to trust them.

"You're right," he continued almost conversationally in a low voice that said it probably didn't carry. "You have no reason to trust us. It's why I want you to see how we handle everyone else. If you decide even after that—well, we'll take you to an airport. I'll even buy you a ticket."

"Why an airport?" I asked the question in English without giving a thought to the slip. The man seemed to understand that I understood him.

"Because airports have security checkpoints. Harder for someone to reacquire you there. We'll have to get you some ID but we can do that."

Oh. That made a lot of sense.

"You in?"

I blew out a breath, then glanced to where the woman wept openly on Alphabet's shoulder and he offered her comfort without touching her. Just like the man talking to me. They weren't invading anyone's space.

Maybe they really did know.

"For now," I conceded. Since he mentioned it, I didn't want to be reacquired by anyone. I had to get home. I had to get home and see Am.

If she wasn't there, then I had to be the one who went to find her. None of that could happen if I didn't make it.

"All I'm asking," the other man said. "I'm Lunchbox, by the way."

What kind of names were these?

"I know, it's weird. But it works for us." He gestured to the chairs. "Want to take a seat? I can grab you some coffee if you want? We still need to talk to a few more so we can work out how we are going to move everyone out."

"I'm fine," I murmured and retreated to a chair away from all of them. Instead of following me or pushing me for more, Lunchbox left me alone as he went to speak to one of the other survivors.

Alphabet and Lunchbox.

Definitely weird.

SIX

ALPHABET

It took us a solid thirty hours to get the majority of these people to the various shelters, homes, and more. Human trafficking was the purview of dirtbags and scum. People were not property, nor should they ever be bought and sold like they were.

They'd been hauling men, women, and children around like cargo. It disgusted me. When Doc called and asked for a favor, the last thing I was going to do was tell our old companion "no." Bones had been finishing up a job and we just had to wait for him and Lunchbox to return. Voodoo had put together a list of supplies and gone to pick up transpo.

It was pure dumb luck we'd been down the coast when Doc called us. Then again, it wasn't the first time dumb luck saved our asses. Once we got there, we made quick work of sorting through the people who could go and the ones who needed more medical care.

For those that would need more time, Voodoo reached out to a couple of shelters a few towns over. They worked with the displaced. Not everyone on that truck had been illegal, but some had been. Those who needed legal assistance would get it.

Those who just wanted to go back to where they'd been taken from, well we'd get them there too. It was just a matter of resource management. Voodoo would take care of that. Bones was going over security with Doc. Some of the survivors were going to have to stay here. We'd rather leave one of us with Doc, but he said he had it.

Lunchbox took in all the details with me. He identified who would need new identification. It helped that he was good with people. The pixie in the corner hadn't said a word since she'd retreated. If she told Lunchbox her name, he hadn't deigned to share it yet.

No matter who I was speaking to, though, my attention return to her again and again. Something about her was off. I couldn't put my finger on either what it was that was off or why it was off. I worried over it like a hangnail.

Eventually, we were ready to take a trip. Voodoo was also back with a tour bus. An honest to god tour bus. I stared at it and then at him. "Do we want to know where you stole this?"

"Acquired," he informed me. "And no, it's fully loaded, and comfortable. We've got a place in the back we can crash when we need if we take it in shifts. There are places for them to ride and spread out. It also has a bathroom. Say thank you, Voodoo, and get your ass onboard."

"Thank you, Voodoo. Get your ass onboard." I deadpanned the delivery and he just smirked at me. The sound of soft laughter came from behind us, but when I turned, I couldn't see who had found the comment funny.

It aggravated me a little that I couldn't identify where the humor came from. These people were so browbeaten and gray with exhaustion, that a little laughter would go a long way.

Switching to Spanish, I invited them to come aboard. "We're going to be on the road for a few days. We will make stops for food, drink, and to stretch your legs. Some of you will be home sooner than the others. But if you trust us a little longer, we'll get all of you there."

The weight of the pixie's stare settled on me like a heavy cloak. I didn't see her right away as the survivors began to climb aboard. They were all swaying from the exhaustion. Lunchbox had scooped up one of the kids from his mom and carried him for the fatigued woman.

Bones was right behind him with another. Voodoo had circled around all of them and gone to the backdoor to speak to Doc. It was late into the night again, a good time to leave under cover of darkness. I wasn't sure how much sleep any of these people had gotten.

There she was, moving quietly behind the others, she drifted up toward the tour bus door. We were taking seventeen passengers with us. The others would need more time. If Doc could place them before we were done, he would.

If not, we'd come back. Then Pixie was the last one at the door. She glanced at me, her thoughts an utter enigma behind the shadows moving in her eyes. She was so damn beautiful it kind of hurt to look at her. Despite that, I didn't turn away.

"You ready?" Bones said from behind me and it tugged her gaze from me to him. For the first time since the accident, I found myself almost resenting him.

"Just need the pixie aboard," I told him. I made a point of keeping an eye on her from the periphery of my vision. She frowned at the description, or maybe she was frowning at getting on board.

Right, time for backup. I whistled. Goblin had been parked up in the truck with the window open while we got all these people moving. Not everyone was comfortable around dogs.

He leapt out of the open window and raced toward me. The pixie swung her gaze around as Goblin slowed to a trot. His tongue lolled with his open mouthed grin. I raised the fingers on my right hand at his approach.

It was a signal to halt. He stopped. When I curled my fingers, he sat then looked from me to the pixie then back.

"Good boy," I murmured.

"Is he friendly?" Three words in beautiful unaccented English. I kept my comments to myself. Dogs worked their magic every time.

"He is," I told her. "Goblin, come."

Goblin trotted toward me.

"Goblin?" Surprise popped through both syllables.

"It fits him." Not crouching, I made a circle motion with my index finger and Goblin pivoted. "Friend," I told him, then held out my hand for hers. "Just place the back of your hand against my palm."

She gave me one wary look then obeyed. I lowered our hands together and Goblin gave her hand a thorough inspection and sniff before he licked it.

"Friend," I repeated, then glanced at her. She was wholly enthralled. "You can pet him if you want."

It was the closest to relaxed I'd seen her since we arrived. The tension in her body eased and she crouched slowly. The clothes were far too baggy and oversized, especially around her torso and waist. The t-shirt hid her silhouette and the sleeves dropped down to her mid-forearm. Even as she lowered herself to meet Goblin, the hem of her shirt was nearly to her knees. From a distance, she looked more like a child wearing her parents' clothing than an adult woman. The pair of flip flops revealed her pale pink toe nail polish and tiny delicate feet.

When she was at eye level with Goblin, I said, "Easy." It was a release command. He hurried forward to greet her, tail wagging. He didn't jump. Instead, he just sat there in front of her while she stroked his head. He leaned right into the contact.

"He's sweet," she said, the faintest of tremors in her voice. "Yes, you are." No longer paying any attention to me, the pixie seemed to relax for real. Finally.

"If you want, he can sit with you." Goblin usually stuck close to me, but I was doing okay right now. She needed the comfort and the support.

"Really?" She met my gaze briefly, not stopping her petting of Goblin.

"Yep." Then I held out a hand to her. "Come on, let's get you two on board and comfortable."

She stared at my hand for a moment. Considering the circumstances, this might be pushing it. If she refused, I wouldn't take it personally. After a too long moment where I almost lowered my hand, she gripped it lightly and I gave her a gentle tug.

Once on her feet, she released me and I took a step back. She glanced down at Goblin. "Want to sit with me?"

Goblin wagged his tail, he looked between us again, always checking with me first. I lifted my chin and motioned to the stairs. "Up you go."

He dashed up the three steps to the inside and she followed along, still slow, but I didn't think her movements had anything to do with reluctance now. After a beat, Bones descended.

"They're in the second row," he said. "You good?"

"I'm fine," I told him. "She needs Goblin and he's helping. I'll stay near the front." That way if I started to slip, Goblin could warn all of us.

Bones took me at my word and clapped me on my shoulder. With everyone on board, we got moving. Doc waved us off and by the time Voodoo turned the tour bus out of the lot, the pixie was sound asleep, curled up under a blanket with Goblin stretched out against her lap.

It was sweet.

Over the next seventy-two hours, we returned several of our passengers to their home cities or to relatives. We checked each place before we left them. I made arrangements for papers as needed. Voodoo provided them with funds, and a card. If they needed us for any reason, they just had to call.

It wasn't until our pixie was the last one left that she admitted her name and her address.

Grace Black. Manhattan.

She was the farthest away of all our passengers. Driving, it would take us another couple of days yet. "New plan," Lunchbox said. "Two of us take Miss Black home and you two take care of the tour bus."

"I could just go to the airport," she offered, all the while she was petting Goblin.

"You could," I told her. "But then you'd have to say goodbye to Goblin a lot sooner and that might break his heart."

A smile flickered over her lips.

"We don't mind taking you home," I said, lifting my chin to Lunchbox. Thankfully, she didn't take a *lot* of persuading. The wariness in her eyes had seemed to grow heavier with each passing day. I wasn't the only one who'd seen it. Instead of being relieved to be farther and farther away from her captivity, she seemed to worsen.

Bones and Lunchbox seemed equally as puzzled. The one thing that settled her was Goblin. So, we would let Goblin help take her home.

An hour after that conversation, she was posted up in the back of the four door SUV Voodoo picked up for us. It wasn't the best gas mileage, but it would be comfortable. Instead of driving all night though, we stopped at hotels out of the way.

Never hurt to play it safe. We gave her her own room and took the one next door then spelled each other out for watch. Goblin slept in the room with her. I kept waiting for her to open up more, to say more, but she didn't.

The last night before we were going to get into Manhattan, she was glued to the news on the television. Every single channel. If Lunchbox knew what she was looking for, he didn't share it.

It was closer to four days later that we pulled up in front of her brownstone. Lunchbox pulled into an empty spot across the street. It had limited parking but we wouldn't be here that long.

"Stay," I told Goblin as I eased out of the front passenger seat before I opened the back door for her.

"You don't have to walk me in..."

"Just going to walk you to your door and make sure you're inside and safe," I told her.

She hesitated, standing there next to the car with a lost look on her face.

"Problem?"

"I don't have my keys," she admitted. "I don't—I don't have anything."

I pulled open the door to the front seat and took the kit Lunchbox tossed me. "Do you have an alarm?"

"Yes," she said, then gave me a mystified look when I held up the pouch. "But I am going to have to call someone for a key."

"Or not," I said. "I'll get it open, you take care of your own alarm."

When she blinked at me, that puzzled look back in place, I motioned to the building.

"Come on, you want to go home, right?" It was a lot like coaxing a wounded animal. There was something so fierce and vital about her but it was coated in a miasma of—darkness. I had no other word for it.

Frankly, I didn't fucking like it but no one asked me.

She gave Goblin one last look before crossing the street with me. The slow pace she set was easy to match, but it was like watching someone heading to a firing squad.

I wanted to tell her something, anything really, to make this easier for her but I had no idea what that could be.

At the front door to her brownstone, I pulled out my tools and went to work. Not all locks were easy to pick. If there was an inaccessible deadbolt on the inside, this definitely wouldn't work.

The first tumblers gave, then the second. I freed the top lock then went to work on the handle lock. Four minutes later, I opened the door for her.

An alarm buzzed a warning and she hurried in three feet to turn the alarm off. Four minutes. I was getting rusty.

"Thank you," she said, turning to look at me and then past me to where Lunchbox was in the SUV.

"You're welcome," I said, then I pulled out a card. It had our number on it and I'd already written down my private number on the back. "Here."

She took it for a moment then stared at it before she looked at me again.

"Anything happens, even if you just want to talk—call. I'll always answer the number on the back. The number on the front means you have to leave a message and that could take a little time to get to us. So for an emergency, always the number on the back."

With a slow breath, she nodded. "Thank you—again."

"You're welcome, Gracie."

She frowned a little as she split her attention between me and the card.

"Close the door, Gracie."

"Oh." Another flicker of a smile and as much as I didn't want her to vanish, I waited as the door closed. Then one by one, the locks turned.

"Good girl," I murmured before making my way down the steps and heading toward the SUV. My leg was aching, but I ignored it. It was a very familiar feeling.

Once I returned to the SUV, I climbed into the passenger seat and closed the door. Lunchbox didn't pull out and I didn't say anything.

We just sat there.

After a couple of minutes, Lunchbox asked, "How long?"

"Let's give it an hour?"

"Done."

CHAPTER

SEVEN

GRACE

Standing in the middle of my living room was surreal. Nothing here had changed. A book I'd been reading sat on the coffee table. It was an old favorite, the spine long since cracked and even the pages had an almost cloth texture to them.

Three magazines lay fanned out. I was on the cover of one of them. It was a glossier one for fashion, but it was a nice image and came with a tidy paycheck. The colorful blanket lay over the back of the sofa where I'd pushed it after I made myself get up and go to bed.

Everything in the room was almost too white, too pristine, too—too sterile. The only splashes of warmth seemed to exist in that colorful blanket and the photos on the mantle. The blanket was one *Maman* had knitted when Am and I were little. We shared the blanket. A few months with me. A few months with her.

I should have taken it to our weekend and handed it over for her turn. At the same time, I was so damn glad I didn't. It would have been sitting in my car after I'd been taken. Maybe it wouldn't have survived.

The thought nauseated me.

"Come on," I said, my voice unnaturally loud in the silent place. Why was I just standing here? I needed to do something...

Glass broke somewhere and I turned toward the doors that led to the kitchen. On lead feet, I made it two steps before a masked man appeared in between the sliding barn doors that separated the living room from the dining room.

Shock rolled through me.

Shock, and then hot on its heels, pure fury.

"Get out," I yelled, as sound and color rushed in, puncturing the bubble that had kept me so separate. I reached for the first thing in range—a vase and I threw it. The book next. A crystal glass bowl. Everything was a weapon.

That was what self-defense class taught. I even threw my book. The projectiles barely seemed to slow the masked man down as he advanced toward me. I retreated.

A lamp became my next weapon. Then a fake plant. Then an old clock, it was heavy as hell and he was right there. So I just bashed him with it. The blow staggered him.

But he jerked the clock out of my hand and threw it. Parts went everywhere as it smashed against the brick. He fisted my hair and yanked me forward. I tried to slam my knee into his junk, but he avoided it—narrowly.

A whistle cut through the chaos and my captor jerked his head up. "Catch," Lunchbox said as he launched something. The grip on my hair fell away as the air fryer from my kitchen slammed into my assailant's chest.

"Come on, Pixie," Alphabet was just there. "Time to go."

"No..." I didn't want to go. The man on the ground was getting up. But Lunchbox was already there and he delivered four hammering blows and the man collapsed.

"It's better to go," Lunchbox said. "There were four

others. We took care of them. But sending a five man team for you means they aren't giving up. They know where you live."

The explanation made sense and at the same time— we'd just gotten here. Alphabet clasped my hand. "Come on Pixie-girl. Goblin's waiting and we can grab some food on the way back."

Back where?

Before he could tug me another step, I yanked away and grabbed two of the photos from the mantle. One was of Am and I, the other was us with our *Maman*. I grabbed the blanket next.

If I was going, then I wanted things with me. The wreckage of the room around me registered then. There was a splintered french door leading into the kitchen.

There was another body there too. Maybe we should go out the front.

"Nope," Lunchbox said, hooking my arm and turning me around. "Back door is better." Then without waiting, he just picked me up. The man was a full body shield, my feet didn't even brush the floor. "Lots of broken glass, I'll put you down outside."

Alphabet wasn't waiting for us. He led the way and it was like walking through a war zone. I hadn't even heard this fight. Had it happened while I'd been screaming and throwing things?

My whole world was turning upside down. They'd found the narrow alley behind the buildings and diverted down it. True to his word, Lunchbox put me on my feet. With one hand against my lower back, he ushered me toward the SUV.

The vehicle was parked exactly where I'd left them. Goblin was in the backseat, tail wagging as soon as I climbed in. "Buckle up and then keep your head down." Lunchbox didn't wait to see if I obeyed, he was already closing the door.

Alphabet was in the passenger seat. There was a slide and rasp of a gun being checked, then Lunchbox was in the driver's seat.

"Chances for a backup team?"

"Not even going to risk it." Lunchbox already had the vehicle started and we were pulling away. "Head down, Gracie."

The snap in his voice had me pulling the seatbelt across me even as I slid my head down. Goblin sprawled on the seat next to me then moved to settle against my lap and I was laying against his back.

It was—nice.

"Three cars back," Alphabet said.

"I see 'em." He shifted lanes. Manhattan wasn't a great place for car chases, but they didn't seem to be slowing down much.

"Dry river?" Alphabet said.

"Not in the city," Lunchbox replied. "Too many civilians."

"Could be a combo dry river with a little Pride and Prejudice."

It was like they were talking a completely different language.

"Going for Dale Earhardt right now. Get Bones on the line. If we're going to be on the run, I want to at least have friendlies on their way to us."

The two went quiet for a moment, then Alphabet said, "Hey, we ran into a problem with the last delivery. Porch pirates tried to lift it before we'd even left."

Silence.

"We cleared the building, but it's going to need maid service—sooner rather than later. Might need to make sure there's an exterminator with the maid. At least one of the pests was still breathing."

My place. He was talking about my place.

"We're playing follow the leader at the moment, and trying to get out of the conga line. How far are you guys from Manhattan?"

More silence.

Lunchbox turned left abruptly and if not for the seatbelt and bracing, I'd have flung off the seat. Goblin made a little whining noise. Yeah, he wasn't a fan either.

"Sounds good. We'll be there." A pause. "Do you care how we deal with them?" Pause. "Good. Talk soon." He ended the call.

"Head to Jersey," he said to Lunchbox. "I'm going to make our friends a cocktail or two. It's a little early for happy hour, but we should be ready by the time we're out of here."

Alphabet climbed between the seats. He slipped through like he wasn't six foot plus, with broad shoulders. It was more like watching a contortionist as he seemed to shrink himself down, ducking his head to avoid the roof of the vehicle, while elongating his limbs to get past the tight squeeze. He might have been a bit clumsy in the execution but there was a kind of ease to it too. "Hey Pixie-girl." The wink did not settle my nerves. "Goblin's good for hugging, isn't he?"

He paused to scratch Goblin's ears, then he reached over into the backseat and pulled a case up.

"Need Goblin on the floor for a couple," he said and I loosened my hold. Without complaint, Goblin slid down into the well. There he sat and pressed his head against my leg. It was nice to just pet him.

It also left me alone on the backseat with Alphabet as he popped open the case. I still had the blanket and photos so I pulled them to me and hugged them in lieu of Goblin, even if I kept one hand on him.

"What are you doing?" I asked. He had a glass canning jar, like *Maman* used when she made preserves.

"Putting together a little cocktail for our friends. They're being very pushy. They need to understand that we are not that into them."

"In the tunnel in three," Lunchbox warned. We were slowing down, but still moving. I swore my stomach fell to my feet. At this rate, the people following us would be able to run up to the car. The lights helped, but it still felt ominous and oppressive.

When he was done, Alphabet closed the jar and sealed it. "Think you can hold this for me?" He held it out to me and I stared at it. Then I wrapped a hand around it. It meant letting go of the blanket. "Thank you."

He twisted to put the case behind the seat again and stared out the rear window. A muscle ticked in his jaw that was utterly at odds with the casual tone he'd been using. We slowed even further.

"Dude," Alphabet warned.

"I know," Lunchbox said. "I don't have much choice. There's a bit of traffic in here, but we're close to the exit."

The thud of my heart echoed in my ears. Was I going to get these guys killed? I'd seen bodies in the warehouse. More outside the truck. Then the ones in my place. How many bodies were going to fall?

"Deeper breaths, Pixie-girl," Alphabet said as Goblin

whined. The dog was leaning all of his weight against my leg. The pressure helped. The shallow, sharp pants hurt my chest. It was harder to make them deeper. "That's it. Just take them nice and slow."

"Don't worry, Gracie," Lunchbox said over his shoulder. Unlike Alphabet's shaggier look, Lunchbox's hair was closer clipped, though it had a suggestion of curls to it. Maybe he had to keep it short to avoid them. The color was more burnished copper than brown, but that could also be the way the sun hit it. "This is just a little snag in the plan. We're going to be in Jersey soon, then we'll be able to shake them."

My mouth was so dry, but I got my breathing under control.

"Get back up here," Lunchbox ordered, then Alphabet grimaced.

"Hang onto the jar a minute longer," Alphabet said. He had a little bit of a harder problem getting between the seats on the way back. When his leg got stuck for a second, he swore and bumped his head on the roof. The messy blond hair kind of stuck up in the back anyway. Still swearing, he yanked it forward and sat.

When he reached back for the jar, I passed it off. Goblin returned to the seat and crawled into my lap so I was laying over him and hugging him.

Eyes closed, I rubbed my cheek against Goblin's fur. The sable and white dog with his short, square muzzle and rose-shaped ears that perked up kept me sane as we suddenly emerged into the daylight once again.

Gradually, we began to speed up. But not too fast.

"On our right," Alphabet warned.

"Yep." Lunchbox hit the gas and we accelerated as he

began to weave in and out of traffic. "Come on, take the bait."

Take the bait? They were insane.

Certifiable.

"You want them to catch up to us?"

"In about five minutes," Lunchbox said, then we were taking an exit and he increased his speed. "This is the fun part."

The fun part?

I squeezed my eyes shut and concentrated on breathing.

"Here they come," Alphabet said, his voice a steady contrast to Lunchbox's lighter-hearted tone. "Left lane."

"Already planned on it."

A moment later, the window on the passenger side opened.

"Five," Lunchbox said. "Four..."

Three...

Two...

I cracked my eyes open in time to see Alphabet toss the jar of liquid out. A moment later there was a bright flash, a whoosh of fire and I sat up abruptly. What the hell was that?

The car that had been pacing us suddenly veered hard right with a squeal of tires and slammed into the concrete barriers that kept the lanes defined.

Fire plumed up from the engine along with smoke.

"Nice," Lunchbox said, a deep compliment in his voice. "I love it when you pay attention."

"Yeah, fuck off, I wanted to make sure they didn't keep following us."

My mouth was open as I stared from one man to the other. Unhinged. Insane.

Absolutely fucking crazy.

"You had me holding a bomb."

"Not a bomb," Alphabet said over his shoulder, shooting me a grin. "It's a Lunchbox cocktail, kind of like a molotov but with a little zest."

"I was holding it," I repeated.

"Yes, you did." He winked. "Excellent assist." Then he straightened to look forward and sighed. "Back roads?"

"Yep," Lunchbox said, and we were already leaving the highway. We were in Jersey. We were still in Weehawken, maybe. Or maybe not.

I stared out the window for a moment, but continued to pet Goblin. I wasn't sure who I was trying to soothe, the dog or me.

"They were going to kidnap me again, weren't they?" The men in the house. Then the men in the car. That was a lot of people.

"That seems the most likely scenario." Lunchbox glanced back at me.

"Why?" The man in the warehouse—the one they'd said wanted me specifically. He even told me he'd coveted me. But I didn't know him. Did he command this many people? What about the people who broke into the warehouse when I was there? The men who'd driven the truck?

None of this made any sense.

None of it.

"No idea," Alphabet said, this time there was a rough sympathy in his voice. "But you're safe for now. We'll rendezvous with Bones and Voodoo. Then we'll assess and make a new plan."

New plan.

I leaned my head back.

Something dug into my hip and I shifted to pull the framed photograph out. Am stared up at me from where we stood, arm in arm. It had been her graduation from law school.

"I need to call my sister."

The guys didn't say anything.

"Please," I said. "I just need to call her and make sure she is all right."

"We'll take care of it, after we're secure," Alphabet said. "I didn't see another team, but that doesn't mean they aren't out there. Running silent and fast is the best thing we can do right now."

"Is your sister in New York?" Lunchbox asked.

I shook my head. "No." I wasn't sure where she was, that was the problem.

"Good, then we don't have to worry about her going into your place."

"If someone is after me..." That meant they could be after her too. Or they already had her. More and more, that reality settled into my bones and I wanted to cry.

The more the tears burned in my eyes the angrier I got. Am had to be all right. She just had to be.

"No ifs," Lunchbox said and I caught his gaze in the rearview mirror. "Don't know why, but you were definitely the target. We'll get you secure, don't worry. Then we'll reach out to your sister. If necessary, we'll pull her out too."

If necessary...

Then what? What were we supposed to do? Just stay with these guys? I didn't barely knew them. They barely knew me.

And they still came in to save me.

An immutable fact. They could have just left after they dropped me off. They didn't.

They'd gotten me out. They dealt with the pursuers. Goblin bumped his head against my hand and I glanced down at him.

Fine, I would trust them for now.

"How long until we get somewhere secure?"

EIGHT

LUNCHBOX

At some point, mercifully, our passenger fell asleep. The shadows under her eyes and the pallor to her skin couldn't diminish her beauty. If anything, the smudges and lack of color, gave her a more hollowed out look, yet the tarnish couldn't reduce the shine.

Grace Black was a stunner. More than that, she had a million dollar smile who lit up every campaign she'd ever been a part of, from fashion to cars to perfume and more. I still couldn't get past the fact she was found on a truck of trafficking victims.

In no way did she fit that profile. If anything, she was the farthest from it. She had a high profile, recognizable, and was even featured in some memes the last time I checked. She may not be Gigi or Bella Hadid famous yet, but she was well on her way despite her small size. Most models were a lot taller than her what? 5'2? 5'3?

Maybe not a household name *yet*. But if I recognized her, well, she couldn't be far off it.

"She still out?" Alphabet asked in a low voice and I nodded.

"Hopefully she sleeps the rest of the way to the rendezvous. I don't think she's slept once since we met her." The wariness in her killed me. I wouldn't call her wounded, but I didn't doubt the wounds were there.

Then I kept circling back to her expression when we came in. She'd been fighting. There'd been a cold kind of rage in her face and a fire in her eyes. From the destruction around her, she'd been throwing everything at the guy. It wasn't going to help much when he had an easy seventy pounds more muscle on him.

Still, had to admire her. I'd wanted to kill the guy because as soon as the fight was over, all the fight bled out of her. It was like someone just cut her strings and she sagged.

"Who the fuck are these guys?"

"No idea. Did you get anything we can run?" I should have, but I wanted her out of there before the shock really set in. She'd been so quiet and withdrawn on the ride into the city. It didn't surprise me she was shutting down.

Once in the car and with Goblin resting against her, she'd succumbed to sleep pretty swiftly. There was a picture she was holding close. Two girls in it. One of them was her and the other a mirror image.

Her sister was her twin—either identical or so close it didn't matter. That would add another wrinkle to the problem.

"Fingerprints. Phone. Don't worry, it's off. And a wallet. Nothing in the wallet but some twenties and singles. I left them in the wallet. I might be able to get prints off them once I get back to my equipment."

"That works," I said, rolling my head from side to side. The sun had gone down a few hours earlier. According to the GPS, we were about an hour out from where we'd meet Bones and Voodoo. "How's the leg?"

"Fantastic," Alphabet lied even as he rubbed at his thigh. "I could probably run a marathon."

"Glad to hear it. I'll make sure to put money on you next year in Boston."

He snorted. "You need sleep," he said. "Your jokes are weak."

"Fuck off," I responded and he grinned. The smile didn't last long though. I wasn't the only one who was tired. Once we had backup, we'd move to a safe house for rest. If necessary, we could find an off highway hotel to hunker down in.

A solid eight in the rack wouldn't kill either of us. I still had a few more hours in the tank, but I didn't want to risk another fight while running low.

Alphabet glanced in the back. When we'd stopped for gas the last time, he'd called Goblin up and out so the dog could relieve himself and have some water. I'd gotten her more comfortable and tucked her blanket around her.

"We'll figure it out," I told him. It was what we did. We were problem solvers. Whoever was after her, we'd deal with it and them. Grace Black was not the type to disappear without speculation or investigation. She had ties—a sister for example—business associates and I would imagine boyfriends.

Bones texted that they'd arrived at the rest area meetup we'd scheduled. Alphabet messaged him back that we needed sleep and Grace needed somewhere safe. Voodoo joined the conversation with an address.

It added another fifteen minutes to the drive, but it was definitely off the interstate. Bones was outside when I pulled in. He strolled down from the porch to meet us. The house wasn't huge, but it was tidy and set back from the road. There were huge trees cutting the visibility.

I didn't like that for sight lines. We'd have to check them later. But Voodoo wouldn't have sent the address if it wasn't secure. So I left it for now. Goblin hopped out to follow Alphabet. The fact he limped wasn't lost on me or Bones.

"Hit the rack," Bones told him. "Six hours, minimum." You could take the captain out of the army but you couldn't take the captain out of him.

The fact Alphabet nodded and Goblin trotted after him immediately told me all I needed. The lack of argument said he was definitely hurting.

"No injuries that I know of," I answered Bones' unasked question. "But it's been a lot of driving, sitting, and it was five to two. Not really a fair fight for those guys."

With a snort, Bones moved to the back door of the SUV. Gracie hadn't so much as twitched. Her breathing was so deep, it worried me. I didn't see any wounds on her and the guys might have had drugs, but they hadn't had them out.

"What is she? A buck and change?" Bones shook his head. "She seems almost too fragile for me to pick up."

"She'll be fine, you should have seen her throwing shit at the guy who closed in on her. She tried to bash his brains in. She might be tiny, but she's feisty." I couldn't quite keep the grin off my face and Bones just shook his head before he reached into the back.

He bundled her up into the blanket and lifted her out with care. As soon as he cleared the door, he headed up to the house. I grabbed our gear, and snagged the pair of framed photos. They were the only things she'd brought with her.

Guilt scraped against me. She'd been damn upset about

leaving. I'd half expected a raging fight or a total denial, but she'd suppressed her reactions so damn ruthlessly, I wasn't sure it was healthy.

Course, the past few days couldn't have been the best for her mental health so she got a pass. After I locked the car, I headed in. The interior had low lighting. It was pretty basic, but comfortable.

It seemed to fit our basic needs, it was clean, had enough room for us and I hoped hot running water, because I was showering before I crashed.

Voodoo leaned against the counter in the kitchen where a coffee pot brewed the standard black. His neutral expression betrayed nothing. Then, he was cagey like that.

"You already assign rooms?" Since he called the place, it gave him the pick of rooms.

"I'm on the sofa. Bones is in the master with the client. Alphabet's in the back on the left. There's two more rooms on the right. Shower on the left. Supplies are in there."

I set the photos down in the kitchen and the bag on the counter. "Clothes?"

"Yep." He pointed to the duffels in the living room. Go bags we kept when we had nothing else. "Anything we need to know right now?"

"Two five man teams. One in her place. Second in a vehicle that tried to tail us. We took their vehicle out with a cocktail. Not sure if we got any of them, I was more interested in securing Gracie than going back to scout the targets."

Voodoo nodded.

"She know why they are after her?"

I shook my head. "I don't think so. She was a little shocky earlier and more than a little lost. I don't know how a girl like that ends up where she did."

"Girl like that?" Voodoo raised his eyebrows.

"Google Grace Black. We'll discuss tomorrow."

"Got it." He pulled out his phone. "Get some sleep."

I headed for my go bag then straight to the bathroom. Ten minutes later, showered and teeth clean, I hit the double bed in the room I'd picked out. Alphabet's snoring was audible through the door as I passed it.

Stretched out diagonally so my feet didn't hang off the end, I dropped an arm over my eyes and tried to quiet my brain. Sleep was discipline. Rack time was also important and I hadn't slept in the past thirty-five some odd hours.

The moment I tried to sack out, I replayed the arrival of the five man team. They pulled up in a van and parked a half block down. What caught my attention was the military boots they were wearing with their suits.

One of these things was not like the other. They also didn't move like business men. They moved with precision. When they cut down an alley to head to the back, Alphabet was already pushing out of the car.

By the time we reached the back of her place, they were already inside. Fuckers were not moving slow. The team had a kind of lethal efficiency. Their biggest problem was not expecting an assault from their flank.

They hadn't left anyone on watch. Even then, it took a minute to get through the four in there before I made it to the living room where Grace fended off her attacker. I replayed each moment after I cleared the doors and hit him with the air fryer.

It had been handy and it made a satisfying thunk against his chest. He'd had a hand in her hair. He wasn't touching her anywhere else. What I focused on was how he'd gripped her hair, the way he kept her still, yet despite her blows—he didn't hit her in return.

That bothered me. Not that he didn't hit her. I didn't want anyone striking her. It bothered me that his *reaction* was contained even when she was trying to do him bodily harm.

I kept circling back to that choice. When I took him down, he'd let her go rather than drag her down with him. He'd been trying to contain her, not *harm*. Was he following orders? The specificity in the targeting made this an entirely different kind of threat.

It wasn't about wanting a beautiful woman. It was about wanting a specific beautiful woman.

Violence threaded through me as I did another replay of the scenario. Nothing about it changed. Those men had been there to take her. If I had to place a bet, they'd come to collect her.

But the guys the Vandals took those victims from were not former military. If anything, they were more street level. So how were the two tied together?

I was still chewing on that when I finally let myself go to sleep.

Tomorrow would be here soon enough.

NINE

GRACE

My eyes were gritty and my mouth dry as awareness trickled back in. As bad as I felt, I didn't want to wake further. The moment I did, I'd have to deal with the reality of where I was and what I was doing. Instead of forcing my eyes open, I burrowed against the pillow and pulled the blanket tighter around my shoulders.

The lack of sound around me was even more telling than the fact I was in the bed. We weren't in the car anymore. It must mean we'd arrived at our destination. They hadn't been particularly forthcoming about where, except it was far away from Manhattan. From my place.

From the men who had come to get me.

A shudder rippled through me and sleep fell away like crumbling earth from beneath my feet. When my eyes snapped open, the last thing I expected to see was a man sitting in a chair, half-sprawled as he read a book.

He wasn't Alphabet or Lunchbox. Though he looked to be about their size with how he dwarfed the chair. Dark hair fell over his forehead. It wasn't as long as Alphabet's nor as clipped as Lunchbox's.

I frowned as I stared at him and he lifted his gaze from the book briefly to glance at me. His expression arrested me. For a moment, no emotion seemed to exist there, his eyes seemed pale but it could just be the way the light hit them. The absolute neutrality was more unsettling than a scowl.

"Boom?" I tested the syllable. That wasn't right. "No... The witch doctor is the other guy. You're...*Bones*."

They had such weird names and at the same time, I kind of liked them. Bones straightened slowly as he studied me and lowered his book and emotion seemed to bleed back into his face.

"You're Grace Black." The deep, even voice offered no clue to his actual mood.

"Yes." No point in keeping that a secret. "Where are we?"

Rather than answer my question, he asked one of his own. "How are you feeling?"

Exhausted. Everything hurt. My muscles. My bones. My heart. "I'm fine." It wasn't totally true, but at the moment, my complaints were a lot less than they had been.

"Miss Black, you and I will get along much better if you don't lie to me." Pale gray eyes seemed to bore into me as though he were capable of reading my mind.

"I don't know you," I said rather than try to argue that I wasn't lying. I sat up, preferring to face him on a little more even ground.

"You know my guys though," Bones countered.

"Lunchbox and Alphabet?" At his nod, I ran my tongue over my lower lip. "They're your guys—how? They work for you?" Was this kind of mafia? I hadn't really been able to parse the dynamic at the clinic.

The doctor had been straightforward. The men who pulled us out of the truck, they'd been rougher. Not as refined. Alphabet seemed—I wasn't even sure how to describe it. A little more laid back, but Lunchbox had been more formal. More direct.

Bones?

I really had no idea what he was at the moment, other than intense.

"They're my guys, my brothers," Bones said, offering even less of an explanation. "They've also offered you protection, which means I have. What one of us commits to, all of us does."

Pulling my knees to my chest, I frowned. "I'm not holding any of you to this. They got me out of a bad situation—after getting me home." I sighed.

Home. Then I looked down at the knit blanket that was laid over me, I'd been wrapped up in it. My pictures were missing, but whoever brought me in here had made sure to bring the blanket.

Waking to a strange room was becoming a bad habit. The blanket helped.

"Anyway, I'm not holding anyone to anything. I'm out. If you can get me to law enforcement, I can file a report. I can reach out to my sister." I still hadn't called Am. I glanced toward the heavily curtained window. The blackout drape kept the time of day a mystery. "I need to call her anyway."

"You don't have to hold us to it," Bones said as he rose. "They gave you their word. Now I'm giving you mine. We'll make sure you're safe. We'll find out who is after you. Then we'll deal with it. Until then, you stay with us."

"No," I argued. "I have a life and a sister. I need to get back to them."

"Right now, you have a life because your captors put you on the wrong truck. I don't like coincidences. I don't like blind luck. You've benefited from both. If the boys had left after you got home, you'd already be back in chains and we wouldn't know."

My stomach sank at the description. As much as I wanted to deny the point, I couldn't. There had been five men in my place. More men in that other car. I really was only free because Alphabet and Lunchbox came back in after me.

"I hate this," I said, rubbing a hand over my face. All at once, the aches that I'd been ignoring crept through me. The bruises on my chest. The pulled muscles. The strain in my neck and in my back.

"I'm sure you do," Bones said in an even voice. The pale gray eyes didn't offer a lot of comfort or even platitudes. It was a directness I could respect. "Like I said, you have my word. We will take care of this."

That sounded fantastic... *in theory*. But I didn't know these men. "Why?" Were they do-gooders? Did they parachute into bad situations and save people? "Just because Lunchbox and Alphabet said they would help me?"

"Not only because of that. No. I explained it already. You need time to think about it and make your peace. You also need a shower and food. Voodoo got you some clothes." He pointed to the bag on the dresser that I hadn't noticed before. "There's some hygiene products in there too, the basics. We'll get more once we're back at base."

Base? What base? Were they military? That might make more sense and it seemed to fit these men. Bones was definitely as tall as the other two and the silk dress shirt and well-tailored slacks did nothing to disguise the thick nature of his muscles. The pair of rings he wore on his right hand —one on the index and the other on his ring finger—were squared and thick. Tiger's eye decorated one, but I couldn't see the stone in the other.

The man appeared urbane and well groomed, but that was all surface. He would fit right in on Wall Street. Unless you looked closer, and I wasn't sure I would see it if we were in a more normal situation. He dressed the part, he spoke in a cool educated voice that held no trace of an accent.

Everything about him was a distraction. Camouflage. Hiding in plain sight. There was a much deeper, darker pool beneath all the gloss. Recognizing that didn't make any of this easier.

"I'll shower, not sure I can eat."

The thought of food made me want to throw up. But I needed to scrub. I wasn't sure I'd ever be clean again. Pushing the blankets back, I slid out of the bed. I was still mostly dressed, so that definitely helped.

"Then I have to call my sister. That's nonnegotiable."

"When you're finished, come out to the kitchen. Just step out and come down the hall." With those words, he let himself out and left me alone. He didn't address my need to call Am or check on her.

Irritation rifled through me. I stared at the door for a long moment, then looked at the bag, then turned to the curtain. They were only in charge as long as I agreed they were.

I hadn't agreed to anything.

At the window, I drew back the blackout curtain to see —a wall instead of a window. Who bricked up windows and put a curtain over it anyway?

A brief search turned up no other exit from the room except for the door to the bathroom—which only went into the ensuite—and the door to the hall.

Aggravated didn't begin to cover it. With no other option, I dug into the bag. There were jeans, socks, panties, bras, and shirts. There were also a couple of hoodies. It was basic, but everything was in the right size.

I didn't look too closely at that. The second bag had a pair of shoes in it. They looked like running shoes. Nothing fancy, but again functional.

Also, I wasn't going to complain. The bag with the shoes also had another bag of toiletries. He'd even remembered a blow dryer, and clips to pull my hair back if I wanted.

The thoughtfulness sanded away some of my irritation. The shower heated swiftly and the water hit the perfect temp and water pressure. The combination made me linger, but I wanted to feel clean so I scrubbed every inch of me. Twice.

By the time I shut off the water, I'd turned a rosy shade of pink everywhere. Toweling off briskly added another layer of flush to my skin. I had to remove the tags off the clothes before I put them on. Normally, I'd wash them before I wore them, but right now—yeah, I'd just make do.

Once I was dressed, I combed my hair, put in a little leave-in conditioner, then debated using the blow dryer. My stomach cramped even as it released a gurgle. Was I hungry? Nervous? Or ill?

Maybe all three. I skipped finishing my hair to head out of the bedroom in search of my newly designated captors. At the door, I hesitated. I didn't want to think of them as captors. That was kind of insulting considering they'd been party to liberating me.

But they were also insisting on *protecting* me and Bones hadn't answered about calling Am or going back. He also dismissed me going to law enforcement. Or at least it *felt* that way.

Maybe I'd misread him.

Maybe.

Once I opened the door, the smell of bacon and eggs twined with coffee floated down the hall to greet me. My growling stomach grew louder. Arms folded, I headed down the hall.

Quiet male voices carried but they weren't saying much. A couple of syllables then quiet, then a couple more. Maybe no one here was a morning person.

The padding of happy paws penetrated the bubble of my bad mood. Goblin came trotting out to meet me and I crouched to greet him. "Hey there," I said, as he rubbed up against me. As soon as I started scratching him under his chin, he leaned right into the caress. "How are you, buddy?"

If only dogs could answer.

"He's better now that he found someone else to try and con bacon out of," Alphabet said from where he waited in the doorway to the kitchen. He looked a little rumpled and his eyes were bloodshot.

The lack of sleep had been on me. I'd crashed in the back of their SUV, but I had no idea if he or Lunchbox got any sleep.

"Well, he could deserve a slice or two."

Goblin wagged his tail as I rose and he moved with me as I continued down the hall.

"He thinks he deserves a whole pound of it." Alphabet's tone was exceptionally dry.

"It's good to know what you're worth." It was why we charged the rates we did for my time. I was worth it. That thought didn't really have time to make purchase before I found myself under the steady gaze of the other three men present.

Bones sat at the corner table, a mug of coffee in front of him and a plate of food that included a stack of pancakes. The man next to him was Voodoo. I'd seen him briefly on the bus. He had a sleepy look about him and his hair was longer, more tousled than the others. I swore I got a shiver when he looked me over.

Shoving that inappropriate reaction aside, I turned to where Lunchbox stood at the stove. Dressed in a pair of khakis alone, he was shirtless and had a dish towel over his shoulder.

"What'll be, Gracie?" he asked as he grinned at me. "Pancakes? French toast? I've got eggs, bacon, some grilled onions and peppers. The assholes ate all of the fried potatoes, but I can make you some hash browns."

Normally, I'd go for a protein shake and some fruit maybe. "Coffee?"

"We have that too," Lunchbox said, motioning to the pot. "But you barely ate anything yesterday, you need more today. So, tell me what you want. Omelet? Quiche? Quiche could take a few, but doable." He paused to consider the kitchen. "Might be able to throw together a decent breakfast burrito too. Do we have..."

He backed up to the fridge and pulled the door open.

"Yes, we have salsa! Excellent. We also have some fruit, if you'd like a salad. Granola and yogurt. Whatever you like, we definitely need to add some protein."

I swore my brain was not processing as fast as he was speaking. My stomach interrupted my musings with a gurgle. "Um... eggs and toast? Maybe a strip of bacon? No potatoes. The fruit would be nice too."

"On it, get the girl some coffee, Alphabet," Lunchbox said, then waved me to the table. "Have a seat. We'll get you all fed, then we can debrief."

"I can get my own or help—"

"Nah," Alphabet said, the corners of his mouth tilting up into a smile. He gave me a gentle nudge to the table. "Lunchbox is always in charge at mess times. Go sit. Let him feed you. He'll feel better."

I didn't want to go sit with the two men I barely knew. Goblin leaned into my leg and I glanced down at his happy expression. It looked like he was grinning.

Cooperation might buy me some favors and then get me a phone. The longer I stood here smelling the food, the hungrier I was getting. Finally, I headed over to the table. The weight of their gazes pressed in on me as I took a seat, but when I glanced up, they weren't paying any attention to me.

Taking a deep breath, I tried to get my rioting brain back under control. No one needed me paranoid. Alphabet was there with my coffee and not even a full minute later, Lunchbox put a full plate in front of me. The extra bacon and eggs wasn't lost on me.

"Eat," he said and gave my shoulder a light bump. "Don't worry about the rest of the guys. They can wait until you're done."

I didn't want to wait until I was done. I wanted to talk now, but no one said anything and the way Alphabet looked at me as he took the chair next to mine said they probably wouldn't until I ate.

Fine.

I'd eat.

TEN

BONES

Grace Black was a problem. The delicate, fragile looking woman with her doll-like features was likely used to getting her way. Doubtlessly, she charmed and coaxed her way through life and achieved what she wanted with a smile and a wink.

The fact Lunchbox nudged her to eat and no one said anything *while* she ate seemed to displease her. Despite those objections, which she didn't voice, she dug into the food. The first couple of bites were tentative. The next few were a little steadier.

Alphabet waited for her to begin eating before he tucked into his own plate. When my breakfast was done, I rose to wash the plate. Voodoo had eaten earlier, and currently he sat there studying Grace.

Instead of joining us, Lunchbox leaned against the counter. He had his arms folded and like Voodoo, he studied Grace as well. When I walked past him and broke his sight line he frowned at me.

I shook my head as we locked gazes. Not a good idea.

He raised his shoulders. What did I want from him?

I just stared. I wanted him to think. The woman was a client. That was all.

With a snort, he nodded back to the table where she attempted to stealthily slip bacon to Goblin. The only one unaware that we were all watching her *was* her.

After bumping a fist to Lunchbox's shoulder, I took the time at the sink to wash up. I'd washed the earlier dishes as well. Lunchbox cooked, one of us cleaned.

"Do you want any more?" Alphabet asked as he pushed his chair back. The scrape told me he was done with his breakfast too.

"No," she said. "I couldn't eat more. It was very good, Lunchbox. Thank you."

"You're welcome." He moved to begin cleanup at the stove and Alphabet eased his way over to the sink. The slow pace betrayed his discomfort. His leg was still bothering him. Lunchbox said it was hurting the day before.

We were going to lock down here at least one more day before we put him back on the road. No one spoke while we finished cleaning, then I carried the coffee pot back to the table so everyone could refill their cups.

Unsurprisingly, Lunchbox and Alphabet took the chairs on either side of Grace. They were already invested. Successful jobs required a certain amount of dispassionate commitment.

"Ms. Black," I said, opening the conversation. "We need to ask you a few questions, but before we do that—in the interests of covering all our bases—can you fill us in on the details of how you came to be aboard that rig?"

"Yes," she said, not playing any games. I appreciated the directness. "I can tell you what I know. First, however, I want answers to *my* requests beginning with a phone so I can call my sister."

"You'll need to wait a little longer," Voodoo said before I could respond. "I will get you a burner you can use. If you are being tracked, which the pair of five-man teams who attempted to reacquire you suggests, then we don't want to leave a digital trail for them to follow."

She paled at the suggestion.

Alphabet blew out a breath, his expression turning grim. "He's not wrong. Our phones are encoded and linked. If we used one of them, we'd need to dump them all and start over. Right now, we can't do that."

All rational explanations. We couldn't do it because we didn't have Alphabet's gear here. For her part, Grace worried at her lower lip.

"That means my sister is in danger."

"Highly probable," I told her and ignored Lunchbox's sharp frown. I didn't see any use in mincing our words. "That means the sooner we have actionable intel, the sooner we can make some decisions."

"But what if they get her while we wait for another phone?" Those words cost her, the hell in her eyes made that clear.

Time to rip this particular blinder off. "I would propose if she has been targeted the same as you or in order to get to you—then she's already been taken. Calling won't help her and will only endanger you."

The soft blue of her eyes went wet with unshed tears as she put a hand over her mouth. I wasn't telling her anything she wanted to hear. As unfortunate as that might be, she needed to understand that anyone sending trained teams after her weren't going to stop.

We didn't have time to softball this.

The expected tears didn't fall. We were given a front row seat to her wrestling her emotions back under some control. The struggle played out on her face as she finally dropped her hands to wrap around her coffee cup.

"I hate that you could be right." Temper blazed in those eyes as she raised them to meet my gaze once more. "I hate that maybe she was already gone before I was."

"Explain," I told her. It wasn't quite an order, but the time for coddling was later.

A sigh deflated her and she dropped her gaze to her coffee cup. "Amorette, she's my sister, and I had plans for a weekend away. She's an attorney, and a crusader. She's— the best." Grace licked her lips, gathering her composure. It was a fascinating process to watch. "We were going to meet at a place we rented at the Outer Banks and just have a girls weekend. She never showed up..."

With each sentence, Grace gained strength until she recited her hours from the drive to arriving to calling her sister and each call going unanswered and unreturned.

Amorette Black was likely gone before Grace left Manhattan, but I kept that assessment to myself. Her time in the Outer Banks probably only delayed her own acquisition.

When she reached the part about driving to her sister's place and then being grabbed it made me reassess. Maybe Grace wasn't the target. But who targeted an attorney *and* then took the model sister?

Alphabet's expression went stony when she described where she woke up.

"They knew you specifically?" Voodoo asked, shifting forward in his seat. "By name?"

The question stymied her for a moment, then she lifted her shoulders. "They kept saying 'you,' like they meant me.

I assumed they must have known me. Not trying to be arrogant, but I have a very well-known face. So, they might very well have meant *me* but not known my name."

"But your sister is your identical twin?" Voodoo continued and I could see where he was going. Grace's sudden hard swallow said she did as well.

"You think they took her thinking she was me?"

"We're not thinking anything," I resumed the line of questioning. "There are a number of theories we can speculate on, but I'd rather hold on all of those until we have all the information. No sense in wasting time or emotional energy on a worry that might not be one."

The way her teeth scraped over her lower lip nagged at me. It was such a sign of open vulnerability.

"I guess," she said with a sigh, then rubbed a hand against her face. "Anyway, the man who was in charge I guess—I never got his name—had the suit whipped for trying to hurt me."

No matter how hard she worked to divorce herself, the tone didn't quite ring true. Kidnapped. Waking up in a strange place. Shackled. Women being raped around her. Then being raped herself.

She didn't describe it that way, but whether she went along with the plan or not to prevent injury didn't make it anything but forced consent.

"In the morning, there were shouts and fighting. I don't know who the people were that came in, but there was also gunfire. I think I just froze, in the hallway. The man tried to make me go with him, but I couldn't move."

Now she folded her arms and rubbed her hands against her biceps as though trying to chase away a chill. I didn't doubt the memories she detailed were unpleasant.

"You were going into shock," Alphabet told her. While there was a rough sympathy in his eyes, he didn't try to comfort her. "It's normal in live fire. Especially if you're not used to it."

"He gave up and left me there."

"Fucking coward," Lunchbox muttered. I didn't disagree, but leaving her there put her on that rig. If he'd gotten her out, she might not be sitting here.

After, she described hitting her head and then waking up in the truck.

"I have no idea how long I was on there. I don't even really know what day it is. I was going to look at my place and then those guys came in and I froze again."

"You didn't freeze for long," Lunchbox said. "You were fighting."

"I guess," she said. "So...now you know what I know. Does that tell you where Amorette is? Or how we can get to her?"

"No," I answered. "It gives us a place to start. We need another day for Alphabet to rest and you should too. You're still shocky."

"I am not," she argued, a frown tightening her brow.

"You are," Voodoo slid right into the fray without batting an eyelash. He liked to smooth things over. "Your breathing is shallow. You're pale. Your eyes are glassy. You have zoned out twice during the debrief. Being in shock isn't an insult or a weakness. It is, however, something we can't ignore."

"He's right," Alphabet said, frowning as he studied her. "We need you whole and that means looking after yourself."

"But if we spend another day here, that's another day before we can even try to call Am." She clasped onto the razor thin thread connecting her to hope where her sister was concerned.

I was under no such illusions. Yes, we would verify everything, but based on what she told us, her sister was most likely abducted and was fuck knew where at the moment, or she was dead.

I kept the latter to myself.

"Gracie," Lunchbox put a hand over hers where she white-knuckled the coffee cup. "You resting doesn't mean we stop working. We need supplies and gear. We need to make arrangements to move to another location. Voodoo will need time to get you a burner and we can also reach out to contacts and start a line of inquiry."

Not a bad plan. One of those contacts would obviously be Doc. He was the one who called us in the first place.

"And I do what? Just sleep? Stare at the walls?"

"You rest, you regain your strength and tomorrow, we will get on the road." I rose. "If you want to argue and refuse to sleep, then we could be here another day or longer. The last thing that will help your sister is if you collapse or freeze up because you haven't dealt with the shock."

Cold? Maybe. But she seemed to respond to the facts.

Grace stared at me. A dozen arguments sparked and then died in her eyes without her saying a word. The impasse lasted another minute, then she jerked her hands from Lunchbox and shoved the chair back.

While she didn't run, she did stride down the hall to the room she'd slept in the night before. The soft click of the door echoed far louder than if she'd slammed it.

"That was a bastard thing to do," Alphabet said, glaring at me.

"It was necessary," I reminded him. "She's not the only

one who needs rest. Get some rack time. I'm going to make some calls."

None of them argued, not even the compromised pair. Voodoo had played his part, but he didn't look any happier about it. Making the girl miserable wasn't the goal.

Keeping her alive was.

She didn't have to like it. She just had to live.

CHAPTER

ELEVEN

GRACE

I couldn't hide in the room all day. No matter what the plans were. The only reason I'd come back in here at all was to keep from crying in front of them. I wanted to scream that every minute could be a minute Am was in danger.

She'd never give up on me.

I was never going to give up on her.

The inescapable problem came in the facts as Bones and Voodoo laid them out. Calling Am's place to see if she answered might only betray our location without proper precautions. While he didn't make it sound like an impossible task, it just wasn't something they were willing to do —*right now.*

Apparently, it was something we could do later, when we left this place. I slung myself down onto the bed. A place we weren't leaving because they had *decided* I needed to rest.

I scrubbed at the tears leaking from the corners of my eyes. Crying only made me blotchy, turned my nose red, and had my eyes swelling. It was a terrible look. It was also like admitting defeat.

Yes, I cried. I cried when *Maman* died. I cried when our old ginger cat passed away. I cried the first time a photographer screamed at me for eating in the middle of a long shoot because I was already too fat.

He was a dick, but the point was I did cry. I just hated crying. I hated the feeling of loss. I didn't want to associate it with Am in any way. It felt too much like betrayal. So did staying here to *rest* when we could be looking for her.

At some point, I must have fallen asleep because I snapped awake when a hand touched my ankle. Adrenaline spiked in my system and I jerked away, barely swallowing a scream as Lunchbox raised both of his hands to show me his palms.

Oh.

Not a stranger.

My breath came in fast, shallow pants.

"You with me?" Lunchbox asked in a calm, rational voice and I stared at him. Was I?

Yes. I closed my eyes and tried to take a deeper breath before I sat up and met his gaze. "Yes," I said aloud. "You startled me."

"So I gathered." He lowered his hands, his grim expression arresting me. "You were talking in your sleep."

I was? I pushed a hand through my hair. It was still damp since I hadn't used the blow dryer. My hair could take forever to dry.

"Sorry if it bothered you." I had no idea what time it was.

Lunchbox canted his head. "Never said it bothered me, Gracie. Just heard you through the door when I came to check on you. I knocked, but you were muttering."

That could be embarrassing. I fumbled for something to say, but what could I say? I wiped a hand over my mouth, checking to make sure I hadn't drooled.

"Do you know what time it is?" The lack of a clock or any structure wore at me. There weren't even any windows in here.

"It's a little after two," he said, then added a belated, "in the afternoon."

"Oh." I glanced at the bed and then back at him. "I didn't mean to fall asleep."

"You needed the rest." Everything about him was careful, contained, and gentle. Like he was handling someone volatile. "I'm glad you got some sleep. Are you hungry?"

I debated the internal question, but then shook my head. "Not really. I ate a lot at breakfast."

"Not really," he said. "I don't think you ate a combined six hundred calories."

"That's a lot when you're inactive." Not that it mattered right now.

His skeptical look was almost humorous. "Right. You could probably handle something light and it would be good for your system."

"Water, maybe." I ran my tongue over my lower lip. There wasn't a lot of moisture in my mouth.

"I'll grab you a glass," Lunchbox offered. He didn't wait for a response, just detoured into the bathroom. The water running echoed out briefly before he returned with a glass. It was a medium sized tumbler and he'd filled it three-quarters.

A part of me wanted to ask if it was filtered. The rest of me just didn't care. There were far more problems than whether the water was filtered or had lemon or lime with it. His fingers brushed mine as he handed it to me.

"It's not super cold," he warned. "But cold enough."

"Thanks," I managed, though it came out croakier. My eyes were still sore and apparently my throat wasn't much better. I drank about half of it in one gulp, thirstier than I realized.

Lunchbox folded his arms as he stared down at me. His fierce expression gave me pause.

"Something wrong?" Maybe that was a stupid inquiry right now. I had a lot of questions, and what few answers they'd been willing to share were ones I didn't like.

"You're upset," he told me. "You were crying."

I shrugged. "Stress relief." I downed the rest of the water, then scooted off the bed. If we were going to keep talking, I didn't want to be craning my neck to look up at him.

The room felt too small with him in here. I hadn't noticed that with Bones earlier. But when I woke up, he'd been seated in the chair and not looming over the bed. Empty glass in hand, I headed to the bathroom.

"Gracie..." Lunchbox trailed off as I closed the door. Leaning against it for a moment, I stared at the bathroom. Pushing off of it, I put the glass aside before I took the time to empty my bladder.

After I washed my hands and splashed some water on my face, I gave myself a once over. I didn't have any cosmetics to hide the pallor or the reddening around my eyes. For a brief moment, I could picture Am leaning against the bathroom door making faces at me via the mirror.

"You're beautiful just as you are."

I snorted. "You're just saying that because you look better than me right now."

Am rolled her eyes. "We look exactly alike. So if I look better then so do you."

"Maybe." But I'd hidden a grin. "You're still my favorite sister."

That earned me another set of rolled eyes before she gave me a playful shove.

The memory faded and took with it my smile. Shaking off the melancholy wouldn't be easy. Focus on how to persuade these guys to let me call Amorette sooner rather than later.

Had I merely traded one set of captors for another?

It wasn't a thought I was comfortable with, particularly after how nice they'd been.

The skeptical part of me wanted to turn that whole thought process over. Were they only nice to make sure I stayed compliant? Then, they weren't the people who pulled us out of that truck. Or brought a doctor to look after us.

No, they're the guys those guys called to see everyone to safety.

Everyone except me, which was also not fair. They had taken me home. It wasn't their fault *more* strange men broke in like they'd been waiting for me to arrive. Looking at every single person with suspicion could drive me insane.

My mouth went dry all over again. I refilled the glass with water and drained it once more before leaving the bathroom. Lunchbox remained where I'd left him.

"I'm sorry that our taking you home didn't work out," he said. "I'm not sorry that we were there to prevent whatever those assholes were there for."

"I don't recall asking you for an apology." I folded my arms as I studied him. He'd found a shirt, but the cotton clung to his chest, illustrating his musculature. The deep blue color of it though did pull my attention to the tattoo on his arm. I'd seen it earlier, but I hadn't really studied it.

"No," he said slowly. "You didn't. You're upset."

"My sister is missing. I was kidnapped. Then kidnapped from the kidnappers. Then freed by a third group and just when I thought I'd be home, I'm not." I unfolded my arms and spread them wider. "I don't know what to do with this. The one thing I really want right now, none of you are willing to let me do."

"You want to call your sister."

It wasn't a question. At my nod, he raked a hand through his hair. But it was too neatly cut to do more than ruffle it before it settled right back into place.

"Soon as we relocate," he promised. "If Voodoo doesn't get you a phone, I will. You have my word."

It wasn't exactly what I wanted to hear. "What if..." I didn't want to even finish the thought.

"Well, let's assess it this way," Lunchbox said, his gaze steady. "If she is or was also a target, chances are, she ended up in a similar place as you."

That made me sick to think about it. Am would not do well. She would never stop fighting.

"Stay with me," he ordered in a gentle tone. "The people who took you *wanted* you. They wanted you alive and in one piece. Right?"

That was true. The man in charge wanted me far more specifically, but it hadn't been abuse he rained down on me.

"The five-man team at your place *also* wanted you alive and whole. They were going out of their way to *not* hurt you. Because it probably would have been a lot faster for them to take you if they hadn't cared about your condition."

"I'm not sure that's as comforting as you might think it is." Because it meant if they'd taken Am, she could be suffering right now.

"I'm not trying to be comforting at all." Direct, no softening the words or his tone. I appreciated that. "I'm laying this out. If they have no reason to kill her and every reason to keep her alive, it gives us time to find her and rescue her."

Time for her to suffer. I folded my arms again, needing self-soothing. "Why are you helping me?"

"Because that's what we do." He said that like it was the most natural thing in the world. "For now, all you can do is take care of yourself. We'll find her."

"I want to believe you," I said. "I really do."

"But you don't know us well enough to trust our word." Again, it wasn't a question.

"Let's be honest—*Lunchbox*—would you believe me if I gave you my word about something important? Like, would you believe me if I said I'll help you find Alphabet?"

He canted his head to the side, his sober expression deadly serious. "I don't know," he said, finally.

For some reason, that answer, *helped*. Because understanding seemed to kindle in his eyes. "So, you see my position?"

"I do. I can't change your mind with a word, only with actions. Right now, we can't do anything more than make sure you continue to feel better. That means you need to eat and hydrate."

"I'm not really hungry," I admitted.

"Then you don't have to eat very much. I think you should try to eat *something*."

Since the other option was stay in here and stare at the walls, I nodded. "I can try."

"That wasn't so hard, was it?" He opened the door for me and I snorted.

"Don't push your luck."

"Alas, Gracie," he said, putting a hand over his heart. "I live to push my luck."

The corners of my mouth twitched. I almost wanted to laugh at the very dry, and very droll way he delivered that sentence.

Once we were in the kitchen again, the only other person present was Voodoo. He wasn't in the kitchen but in the living room, sprawled back on a sofa with one arm tucked beneath his head.

I thought he was asleep, but his eyes flicked open to track me. Bones and Alphabet were absent and, to my disappointment, so was Goblin.

"Making food for Grace," Lunchbox said. "You want anything, Voodoo?"

"Sure," he said, but the weight of his stare stayed solidly on me and I tried very much not to notice it. Of the four men, he was the only one I hadn't had a conversation with beyond the few words at breakfast.

Frankly, he seemed almost as stone cold as Bones. So I'd rather skip deepening the experience.

"Have a seat," Lunchbox said, pointing to the table. "Did you actually want some coffee? We have juice now. There's a couple of cans of soda." He opened the fridge. "We've got some energy waters—weird. Also regular water with some of those extra hydrating packets you can flavor them with."

"If fruit juice is orange juice, that would be great." There was something endearing about his puzzlement over the drinks.

"OJ coming up." After he set the glass in front of me, he

gripped the back of a chair and gave me a hard look. "Tough question time—are you a breakfast in the afternoon or evening kind of person? Or do your meals need to match the time of day?"

The intensity in his eyes suggested he was dead serious about the question. "It's five o'clock somewhere in the world. Which means it's also morning somewhere."

"That's not an answer." The twitch of his lips betrayed his smile.

"Well, then I guess you'll have to just trust it and surprise me."

Straightening, he nodded. "Game on, Gracie. Game on."

TWELVE

VOODOO

It was before dawn when I opened the door to the bedroom where Grace Black slept. Whereas Bones stayed in with her the night before, we'd let her rest peacefully, though I had checked on her twice. Nightmares and disturbed sleep were normal for this kind of stress. Both times I looked in, however, she'd been sound asleep.

She was, even now, curled over on her side and sleeping. She looked even tinier than when she was awake. The thick, silky look of her black hair added to the pixie effect. Alphabet was right to call her a pixie. A low light was on in the bathroom. She'd left it on when she went to sleep and I'd not disturbed it or her. Comfort and self-soothing came in a wild variety of methods and choices. No one would judge her for it.

The dim glow from the open bathroom door highlighted the soft curves of her face. Paler than in her many photographs and ad campaigns, the real woman seemed no less insubstantial than her images. That fragility generated such a demand for her. The far more interesting part of her was that core of steel inside of her.

It was an excellent quality for her to possess. She was going to need it in order to survive. I didn't cross the room nor did I touch her. I just said her name, "Grace." Then repeated it. Her eyes snapped open when I said it the second time.

The sudden flush, coupled with too wide eyes, and the shallow breaths betrayed her fear response. Completely normal. Unless she wanted to discuss it, I wasn't going to draw attention to it.

"We're moving out this morning," I said, keeping my voice low. "Just dress, stuff anything you want to take into the bag and we'll take it with us."

She sat up, the tousle of her hair giving her a wind-blown look as she blinked at me. "Coffee?"

"On the road," I promised her. "The sooner you get ready, the sooner we're gone."

After blowing out a long breath, she shoved the blankets off and rose. Dressed in a t-shirt that hit her mid-thigh, she headed for the bathroom. I stepped out and closed the door.

Everything else was ready, as soon as she emerged, we'd go straight to the car in the garage. Then out that way. I'd planned for an extra fifteen minutes if she required it, she was ready in five.

I was impressed.

Taking the bag from her hand, I pointed her along the hall in the opposite direction from the kitchen. She had on a pair of running shoes, leggings, a fresh t-shirt, and a hoodie. Her dark hair was pulled back into a ponytail and her cheeks were pink from being scrubbed.

She looked sixteen and I felt like a dirty old man checking her out.

"Ready?"

With one hand over her mouth to smother the yawn that tried to escape, she gave me a half-nod then said, "Yes."

"Good."

Promptness was a good quality. So was speed. Waking her up and making her move immediately also distracted her from asking questions. Parked in the garage was my Jeep Grand Cherokee.

It had specialized upgrades and armor to make it more bullet resistant. At the passenger door, I opened it to let her climb in. Standing right next to her drove home just how much shorter than all of us she was. The contrast was unsettling particularly when she had to put a foot up onto the running board and grip the side to climb into the vehicle.

Once she was inside, I closed the door then opened the door to the back seat and dropped her bag in there with mine. In no time, I was in the driver's seat and backing out of the garage into the deep dark of pre-dawn. The sunrise was at least another hour off.

We'd be well on our way by then. The air was a little damp and chilly, so I turned the air to warm. It didn't need to be hot, but she didn't need to get a chill either. I half-expected the questions to start once we were on the road, but Grace just sat with her arms folded and her head turned to stare out the window.

The detente lasted until I pulled off at the first drive-thru coffee place. I put in my order for a large, black coffee, no sweetener and then glanced at her.

"Flat white, oat milk if they have it please and the largest size it comes in."

I passed on the message before I added a couple of the breakfast wraps and sandwiches. I wasn't sure which she'd prefer and we weren't going to be stopping for a while. I had a theory to test.

After accepting the drinks and passing hers over, followed by the bag with the food, I paid for it with cash and then we were pulling out again. The darkness began to withdraw as morning slid her gray fingers in to peel back the night.

In addition to the rays of the sun beginning to brighten the sky, the weight of her stare rested on me. She was debating whatever she wanted to ask. I pegged the speedometer at eighty and followed the interstate west through Pennsylvania. We'd be in Ohio soon, and I might turn south then.

We'd see.

I slid a glance her way as I knocked back more of my coffee. It was scalding hot, dark, and bitter. Pretty much exactly what I needed.

She wasn't looking at me anymore but at her cup. I gave her five more minutes. Ten at the outside.

She lasted fifteen.

Impressive.

"Voodoo?" The way she framed my name it was almost a question in and of itself. Not just trying to get my attention but should she use those specific syllables to address me?

"Right here," I answered. Keeping my voice even and unperturbed made it more conversational.

"I should call you Voodoo, right? Or do you have another name?"

"I do," I told her. "But Voodoo is fine. Been Voodoo for years now. Pretty much used to it." Liked it too. Liked the air of mystery it seemed to give me. Even more, how unsettled it would make others.

"Right." She didn't fully understand, but she was attempting to. I'd give her points for the effort. "Where are we going?"

"We told you the plan yesterday." I was splitting hairs and being vague on purpose. With my attention divided between the road ahead and the road behind, I didn't make a big deal out of the answer.

"No, Lunchbox said we were going to move back to wherever your base is. I wasn't sure if that was your actual home or a fort or something. Though, I don't think you're active duty military anymore."

None of that was a question, but she was very observant.

"You didn't tell me anything." It was a light, if effective verbal slap and it landed.

"You were briefed," I reminded her, more than a little curious to see what she would do.

"Where are Alphabet, Lunchbox, and Bones?"

"Ah, you want to know why you're with me and not with one of them?" When you don't necessarily want to answer a question, just reframe the premise and redirect the other person's attention. If that failed, just change the subject entirely.

"Yes," she said. "You don't like me and I imagine you don't want me around. So why am I with you and not them?"

"You imagine I don't want you around?" I didn't have to feign surprise or curiosity. It was right there. "When did I say I didn't like you?"

Instead of answering immediately, she bit her lower lip and frowned. I stole another glance at her. Was she steeling herself or trying to back track? There were a lot of ways she could play this.

"I don't have to work that hard to imagine your disinterest," she said, doubling down on her initial statement. "You haven't spoken to me directly all that much except to inform me of how wrong something could go when you supported everyone else not letting me call my sister."

"I also told you I'd get you a phone." If we were going to examine the details, we should be accurate.

"Yes," she admitted. "You did." It seemed almost a concession. "But I didn't realize we wouldn't all be together." Not the whole truth there, but we were getting warmer. "You just... You seemed like the last one I would be traveling with."

I almost smiled. Almost. "Don't worry, Grace," I said. "I'll reunite you with the guys soon enough. Since you asked, we're clearing up our tracks. You left Manhattan with two men and a dog. You're now traveling in a totally different vehicle, different man, no dog. If people are looking for you, it's better to make it as difficult as possible to get an easy bead on you."

It was also better to clear the way if they were tracking her otherwise to let them make an attempt in the open *before* we moved her to a more secure location. If we'd had more time, I would have seen about getting a device to scan her. Without some idea of whether they'd been waiting for her at her place or tracked her there, we had to work with the idea it could be either.

The safe house had a Faraday Cage in it, which was why she was in that room specifically. It was also why she couldn't use any of our phones there either.

"Security," she said with a sigh so profoundly exhausted it tugged at me. "I get it."

"You don't have to like it," I told her. While there wasn't

much else we could do right now, it was important that she understood we weren't making any decisions lightly."

"Thank you for that," she retorted. "I wasn't sure if I was allowed or not." The bite underscoring those words did make me smile. It was better when she snapped back. I liked the fiercer side of her.

"If you'd like, I'll make you a list of all the correct etiquette so you know how to behave around us." I had my tongue firmly in cheek, but I kept my expression sober.

"You think you're funny," she challenged, nose wrinkled.

"Not really, no. I'm being perfectly serious. Especially if you didn't realize that you were free to like or dislike whatever decisions we make."

"What if I don't want to go along with any of your decisions?" The gauntlet landed with a bang between us. Much better.

"Perfectly reasonable response. You don't know us. You don't know you can trust us, though you are learning. You trust us on some levels, but not all of them. While you don't have to like it, you will be safer with us than without. As evidenced by the assault at your place."

I didn't want to keep drilling down on that last piece, but it was better she understood.

"That doesn't really answer my question, though. What if I just want to part ways? You drop me off at a police station, let me file a report and go home? I'm sure the FBI will help me." She didn't *sound* that certain though.

"Until we've completed a threat assessment that assures us you are not likely to be taken prisoner again, I'm afraid that letting you go is not in the cards right now."

"So, you guys are just my latest captors."

"In a manner of speaking, I suppose we are. I don't see

you as a prisoner, however. You are a client, we take protection seriously. The question you have to ask yourself is how hard do you want to make all of this?"

"In other words, I'm damned if I do and I'm damned if I don't?" More fire glazed those words, the burn sizzling where it grazed against me.

"I wouldn't put it that way, but I suppose if you want to frame it negatively, then yes, Firecracker, I suppose you are."

She scowled at me. "You're annoyingly blunt."

"But you like it," I countered. "Or you wouldn't keep trying to engage me."

Her mouth opened then closed twice without a single sound escaping. The muted shriek of outrage entertained me, but I didn't grin until she looked away to stare out of the car again.

The silence filling the vehicle lay heavily with all the things she wasn't saying. Still, I had to appreciate the effort to think her arguments through and not just making them blindly. She was every bit as intelligent as Lunchbox claimed.

He and Alphabet were already compromised where she was concerned, however. Bones noticed it as well. It was why he gave me the task of handling her transport. I didn't mind using her as bait, and I could keep my head while talking to her.

Lunchbox about turned himself inside out to make sure she ate the night before. He even went so far as to try and get her to confess her favorite foods. It had been moderately entertaining, particularly when she gave him so little to work with.

Still...

I glanced over at her. Her shoulders were rigid and her face turned to the window, resolute in how she ignored me.

I could definitely see the appeal.

An hour later, I considered broaching a detente to see if she wanted a bathroom break. Then I caught the SUV closing the distance between us. It had been there on and off the last thirty minutes, but I'd taken an exit like I was going for gas. It followed me and while I didn't turn in, it had.

Now here it was, having caught us up again.

I guess we had our answer.

They could track *her*.

"Grace," I said, then put a hand on her leg. "We need to talk…"

CHAPTER

THIRTEEN

GRACE

The weight of Voodoo's hand on my leg snapped me back to the present. I hadn't even realized I was zoning out until he touched me.

Jerking my head around, I stared at him. "What?" My brain was a little fuzzy. It had taken every bit of effort to not just burst into tears earlier when he played word games with my questions.

"I need you to focus," he repeated his earlier statement. It was like I was on a dubbing delay and getting the words a half second behind when he was saying them. "We've picked up a tail."

I twisted in the seat to look behind us. We'd been on the interstate pretty much from the moment we left the coffee place. There was still food in the bag at my feet, but the last thing I wanted to do was eat.

There were two cars behind us. A white four door sedan and a dark SUV that looked eerily like the ones in Manhattan. My stomach bottomed out. Alphabet had thrown that liquid bomb onto the other one and set it on fire.

"Do we have to throw something on it to blow it up?" I

did not have the best aim. The one year I'd played softball, I'd done it with Am for fun. They'd eventually put me anywhere I didn't have to *throw* a ball. I could catch one, but throw it?

Nope.

"That is not my plan," Voodoo said, his tone calm and even which seemed utterly at odds with the idea of men following us. Well, following *me*. How were they still doing that? I didn't even know where we were.

"You have a plan?" The knowledge rasped like sand-paper through me. "You planned for someone to follow us?"

Alphabet and Lunchbox had done the same. They'd even called someone. Then just kept right on going. At no point had it been serious, at least until Alphabet threw that jar with the liquid bomb in it.

So maybe this was what they did?

"You know what, let's argue about that later." If he had a plan, he must have assumed that someone finding us was a possibility. "What do you need me to do?"

The last time, I'd just hidden in the back. Oh, and I'd helped hold the jar while Alphabet got resettled.

"Take even, slow breaths. I don't want you to start hyperventilating."

Almost at once, I tried to calm my breathing. I had started panting, almost stupidly so. "Breathe, right I can breathe."

"I'm glad to hear it." He wasn't looking at me. The calm draping him left me envious. Lunchbox and Alphabet had been the same way. At least then, they'd had each other *and* Goblin for backup.

"I'm not going to be great at backup," I warned him, stealing another look at the side mirror. The SUV was still back there, behind the white sedan. Neither vehicle seemed intent on overtaking us.

That was good, right?

"You don't have to be, firecracker." He reached over to flip down the glove compartment. There was a gun in a holster right there. There was also a taser. "Those are right here if needed. If you aren't comfortable with a gun, don't pull it out. You're more likely to hurt yourself. Use the taser instead and never point it at yourself."

The sense of falling held me captive even as ice seemed to slick over my body despite the fact I was burning up. "Taser," I repeated. "I've used one before. Does this fire or do you have to be up close?"

"Up close," Voodoo warned. "You shouldn't need it, but if you do, let them get right there and then you send a few thousand volts through them until they drool into the ground."

"Are you sure they're following us?" Because those cars hadn't fallen back or gotten any closer.

"Hmm-hmm." Voodoo glanced at me then flipped the glove compartment closed. "Sit back."

I was, but he didn't give me a chance to ask why before he suddenly depressed the gas and the Jeep rumbled with unexpected power. We pulled away from the white car, and I kept my gaze fixed on the side mirror as the distance between us grew wider and wider.

The SUV jerked out from behind the sedan and acceler-ated past it just as we reached a slight rise. I lost sight of them for a moment, but I didn't have long to wait before they appeared in the side mirror. We were still pulling away though.

A ripple of apprehension seemed to skate over my scalp. The roots of my hair all seemed to tingle and if I were a cat, it would probably be standing a little higher. The road curved and I lost sight of the SUV again. The thud of my heart was far too loud, and it struck my ribs with dizzying force.

Flicking a look toward the dashboard, I clenched my jaw. We were well past three digits on the speedometer. Any complaints I had died unspoken. I gripped the sides of the seat and said nothing. The last thing I wanted to do was distract him.

Even more terrifying—the SUV behind us was working to close the gap. Cold flash-fired through me again.

"Tell me something, Firecracker," Voodoo said as if we were just out for some casual Sunday drive and not driving at some reckless speeds. "What do you like to eat?"

"What?"

"Food. You have to have a favorite. Like I'm partial to caribou steak. Can't really get it in many places, but when I can—nothing like it. Pair that with a huckleberry slump, and, let's just say, there won't be much I wouldn't do for that combo."

What was a slump? "Um… I've never had caribou."

"No? What about bison?"

I shook my head. "Red meat's a luxury. I don't usually have it that often. Mostly steamed chicken, some fish—also steamed—and sushi. Love sushi. But I have to be careful on the calories."

The SUV seemed to be getting closer. Unnerving when you considered the warning on the mirror said that objects may be closer than they appear.

"Not sure I like the idea of red meat being a luxury. Steamed chicken sounds terrible." He actually cut a glance toward me which was more terrifying than the car approaching. Why was he taking his eyes off the road? "Is that a biological—you know health requirement? Like Gluten-free?"

Like gluten-free. A semi-hysterical laugh slipped out of me.

"Not exactly. Red meat can make you puffy. Cameras already add ten pounds. My job is to look my best for both video and still photography. There's also not a lot of time to fix outfits, so they have everything sized to specification and it's important to stay in that range. That means steamed foods, vegetables, controlled calories, low to no carbs with the occasional splurge."

My mouth was so dry.

"Huh, do me a favor…"

"Sure."

"When it's time to explain to Lunchbox that you only want your chicken or fish steamed, make sure I'm there. I want to see the look on his face."

That pulled my attention from the side mirror. "Why?"

"He likes to cook and *steaming* everything will be an insult to his culinary soul." His grin held not even an ounce of malice. His amusement translated with his chuckle. "That will be popcorn worthy."

A laugh escaped me before I could suppress it. "That seems mean."

"Mean would be saving the information until *after* he prepared you something gourmet. Just remember, the man loves chiles on everything." He shook his head. "Though I have to admit red chile in hot chocolate is way better than I ever expected it to be." He made a little hum of sound. "Brace."

Brace?

I barely processed the word when something hit us. The

other SUV was right there, on our tail. They'd not only closed the gap, they were right on top of us.

"Hold on, firecracker." He turned the wheel hard as he lifted the safety brake. The spin sent up a stream of smoke from his tires and the sound was jarring.

He turned into the swerve, until we were heading the other way and he crossed the green median to the other side. The vehicle jolted across the uneven ground, and then we bounced as he cleared the edge of the road and then we were racing back the other direction.

I twisted in the seat, heart racing, but I didn't let go of the "oh shit" handle. No way I was letting it go. There was no sign of the SUV.

It couldn't possibly be that easy.

Apparently, Voodoo felt the same way because we didn't stay on the highway. He took the next exit to—a state route that was just a number and not a name. The road itself was empty. As soon as we were off the road, he turned left and headed south.

"But let's get back to your favorites," Voodoo said. "You eat a lot of steamed food, meat, and vegetables. But when you get to splurge—even if it's just a one bite splurge, what do you *have* to have?"

Pulling my gaze from the mirror, I looked at him. "What?"

The words just weren't processing. It didn't help that I had no idea where we were and I kept feeling like any moment that SUV was going to pop up out of nowhere.

Maybe it would T-bone us. Or it would be blocking the road ahead.

They could even have flamethrowers.

"If you get to splurge, just—cheat all the diets and food requirements. What's the one food you go for?"

"Um," I said, swallowing a hard lump. "I guess it depends on where I am."

"Okay, let's say here—or where we were in Pennsylvania."

"Um... banana pudding. Maman used to make that for Am and me. I loved it. Am would always let me finish her extras cause Nilla wafers were the best." I'd almost forgotten that. "Don't get me wrong, I like chocolate too. But Nilla wafers and bananas are just—heavenly."

"Got it." He turned a hard right onto a road I hadn't even seen there and we were just following a road into the hills. "So, what if you were in New York?"

"I have a weakness for cannolis. But if I'm going to be in New York, it has to be cheesecake from Juniors. It's to die for, especially the raspberry one."

"Europe?"

"It depends on where... the patisseries in Belgium and France are just the worst. I love bread. I love bread in all its forms whether it's dinner rolls or baguettes or donuts. So, pastries are excellent." My stomach cramped as I could practically picture the smell of the fresh baked bread. "I used to love cornbread and beans when I was little too. Not the same there, obviously, but still good."

"What about England? Or Scotland?"

"Sticky toffee pudding." A nervous laugh escaped. "Italy it's the gelato and Switzerland it's the chocolate. I never try to splurge too much but I do like to enjoy it when I have the chance."

He took another turn, this one a left and we were heading down what looked like a driveway. Were we at their base?

"I haven't had sticky toffee pudding," he said, slowing when we passed the treelined drive and into a clearing with a house, a barn, and an empty paddock. The house didn't look like it had any functional windows.

So abandoned maybe?

He circled around the two buildings and then pulled straight into the barn. Despite being abandoned, it was relatively clean inside. Empty stalls lined either side of the aisle. The stall doors were all open and a ladder stretched up in the middle to the rafters.

"Get the taser," Voodoo said, flipping open the glove compartment. "Take that and out, I want you up the ladder, and then laying flat against the boards over the feed room. You can't see up there unless you're directly under it."

"What's happening?" I was already moving. He'd turned off the Jeep and joined me in climbing out. Circling to the back, he flipped open the hatch and slid off his jacket. Next, he pulled what might be a flak jacket on. Or bullet proof vest.

It was something. He also had a gun out of his shoulder holster. Then lifted a rifle that he slung over his back, the strap securing it crossways. The last was a shot gun.

"Go," he said. "Up there and think about what dessert you'd like to splurge on tonight. Because we're going to earn that splurge."

"They're still coming, aren't they?" My stomach was on the ground. Clearly, they were or why else would he be getting ready.

"Yep, they are, but you're going to be just fine. This is a hiccup, Firecracker. Up the ladder, lay down flat, keep the taser in your hand. If anyone comes up there, you push that into them and squeeze the trigger. Don't hesitate. Got it?"

I wanted to argue with him. I wanted to offer him something that wasn't me scrambling up to the loft to hide.

"Like I said, think about dessert. I like ice cream," he

told me. "Whatever we splurge on, I'll be sure to eat more than half so you don't have to feel guilty about it."

It was the most ridiculous thing to find comfort in, but I nodded. "Be careful?"

One corner of his mouth kicked up and his dark eyes seemed to sparkle. "This is going to be fun."

He winked and then lifted his chin at me, an order to go.

The sound of a car outside had me racing upward. I climbed the ladder, taser clenched in my sweaty palm. Once I was up there, I sprawled, stomach down and ignored the dust that poofed up.

The engine idled outside and then cut off abruptly. A moment later, a car door opened.

Then another.

And another.

Eyes closed, I pressed my cheek to the wood. How the hell had they followed us so closely?

We were off the road and out of sight it was like…

It was like they were tracking me.

"Send the girl out," a man called and I jerked my eyes open. "If you cooperate, we might even let you live."

Voodoo didn't say anything. In fact, it was totally silent below. The door in the front rattled open.

I forgot how to breathe.

FOURTEEN

GRACE

The creak of the door had me torn between staying exactly where I was and peeking at who was here. I wasn't sure what I was laying there listening for —what did I hope to hear? Voodoo said he would take care of it. He was also armed...

Something fell below, it sounded like a bag got dumped. There was just a thud, followed by the bounce of something else.

"Tobin," a man yelled from outside. "Is it clear?"

Whoever Tobin was didn't answer. I blew dust away from me as sweat began to trickle down my face. It wasn't hot out here but my shirt clung uncomfortably to me. My heart beat out a rhythm against the wood where I lay. I was surprised the sound didn't carry.

A gunshot split through the silence and I let out a scream before I could stop myself. Shoving my hand against my mouth, I tried to stuff the sound back inside.

Nothing moved below. At least nothing I could hear. Lifting my gaze to where the ladder peeked over the edge of the loft, I waited. If someone heard me, that was where they would come up—right?

"Get back here," a third man shouted. He wasn't the one who said to send me out or the other who called for Tobin.

Was this another five man team?

"There's only one of him," a fourth man said, his voice heavily accented. There was a definite Eastern European edge to his voice. Czech maybe? Hungarian? I wasn't sure. Not western Europe. Not quite Russian. Somewhere firmly in between.

"That's why Tobin is missing and now Karl. The car is here, the girl must be here. If we can eliminate him, do it. But our orders are specific." The third man was quite firm in his command.

"I don't see her in the car." Apparently the fourth man hadn't left. They were right below. "Check the tracker?"

"Won't work if we're this close. It will just show her within the area. It's better at a distance."

Tracker.

They were tracking *me*.

The idea made my skin crawl.

"Down the full length, check each stall and above." The third man sounded like he'd passed me and kept moving.

"You want to go up now?" the fourth man asked.

"I said check each stall." The third man was not happy. "The stalls first, then up. But keep scanning... above just in case he tries to surprise us."

"Who are these people?" The fourth man complained. He was also moving away from me. They were heading toward the Jeep and maybe passing it on their way to the other side of the barn.

Five men.

Tobin wasn't answering—maybe that was the thump I heard?

The gunshot from outside—the second guy?

Did that mean that Voodoo was out there while I was in here with these two?

Where was the fifth man?

"Clear," the fourth man said.

"Body," was the third man's response. "Tobin. Throat slit. He's dead."

I was glad I'd kept my hand over my mouth or I might have let out another cry. Voodoo had been in here. The man who came in went down without a sound. That was creepy and terrifying and utterly badass.

Badass only because Voodoo was on my side. A new set of captors or not, so far they hadn't tried to hurt me. I also didn't think someone planning to keep me prisoner would offer to let me use a gun.

"Karl is likely dead then as well." Give the fourth man a cookie. Nothing got past him.

"Take the ladder," the third man said. "I will cover you."

"What if they are right up there?" The fourth man made a disgusting sound to clear his throat before he spit. "You climb up the ladder. I'll cover you."

"Climb, or I will shoot you."

Silence followed the threat. I suppressed the urge to cough as a violent tickle assaulted the back of my throat. I needed to be still. Now was not the time to shout, cry, cough, or draw any attention to myself.

I could hold position in a pose for an hour if necessary. Wouldn't cough. I refused to cough. My eyes watered from the effort. Then the fourth man swore.

"I'm climbing."

I moved the taser up closer to me. The heavy steps

against the ladder seemed to vibrate. The feeling carried through the wood. It added another layer to the dread curling through me as my nose began to itch.

The desire to sneeze weighed heavily in my face. The watery film over my eyes made the world waver. I had a firm grip on the taser and I stared intently at the ladder.

"Hurry up," the third man said. "We don't have all day."

"You want to go faster," the fourth man snarled back. "Do it yourself." Then he added something under his breath, but there he was, head clearing the top of the ladder.

Only he wasn't looking at me at all.

On my knees I lunged forward and put the taser right against his arm. He snapped his head around and our gazes locked as I pressed the button.

His whole body convulsed. The shaking wracked him and his hand seemed locked on the ladder until I pulled the taser back. Then his eyes rolled back in his head and he fell backwards off the ladder.

A sneeze ripped out of me and I wanted to cry as the third man swore. He fired and a bullet slammed into one of the wooden cross beams overhead.

"I know you're up there," the third man called. "Come down, now."

Did he really think that would work? I rubbed a hand against my face, trying to get the dust away from my nose. The watery eyes didn't improve, but I continued to hug the loft floor. The scatter of straw up here seemed to suggest it had once been used for hay storage.

"Come down," the third man snarled. Then a soft thud sounded. "I know you're there." Only he didn't sound so certain this time.

His breathing grew harsher. More intense. Another couple of steps, then he hit something against the ladder.

"If you make me come up there—" He didn't finish the sentence, instead he let out a hard grunting. Then something slammed into the ladder. A gun went off.

One shot.

Two.

Three.

One of the bullets smashed into the beam overhead again, but I didn't see the other two. Lower grunting, then an agonized sound as bone snapped.

Bile surged up my throat. I'd heard a leg break before. It was not a sound you forgot. The echo of it lingering in the air before the pain hit.

"I'll take that." Voodoo's voice was like a gift. "Good night." Then another thump drifted up to me.

"All clear, Firecracker."

I poked my head over to see him standing over two downed men. One guy was flat on his back, his sightless gaze staring straight up at me.

That was the guy I tased.

He was dead.

The other was down, blood trickling down his face.

"You did good, now come on down. Let's get you back in the car and on our way."

"What about them?" Did I care about them? They wanted to capture me and kill Voodoo. These men were not my friends. "They said they were tracking me."

The cold reality of that sliced through me.

"It's going to be fine," Voodoo said. He had put away his guns and he was working zip-ties around the downed man's wrists and feet. "Trust me."

I was still at the top of the ladder. What I'd just told him had not remotely been a surprise.

"You knew." An ugly uncomfortable feeling unfolded inside of me.

"I suspected," he said, glancing up at me. "Now I know. So do you."

"Why didn't you tell me?" My chest hurt. "And how are they tracking me?"

"Because why would I scare you if it was nothing?" Voodoo straightened. "You coming down or do you need me to come up there and carry you down."

I blinked. "You'd do it, wouldn't you?"

"Yes," he said. "But I'd rather you came down on your own. We can't stay here too long."

"I'm not done arguing."

"I'll keep that in mind," he said. Heart still in my throat, I climbed down the ladder. An arm locked around my middle before I could step off and Voodoo lifted me clean over the body laying at the base.

He set me down and then gave me a visual once over. "All good?"

"I think so." I glanced at the dead man, but Voodoo stepped between us.

"Nothing for you to see there, Firecracker. Hang on to the taser and back in the car. I just want to pack up this guy and his gear."

"Pack him up?" Did that mean we were taking them with us?

"Getting him ready for transpo." He had a phone in his hand. "Car, go on. Eat some sugar from the bag and drink some water. I don't want you getting shocky again."

I didn't think I was going into shock, but I was definitely off kilter. Not looking at the corpse, I studied the third man. He had a tattoo on the back of his neck. I couldn't make out much of it. He also had tats on his hands.

At the Jeep, I opened the passenger door and glanced down the aisle to where Voodoo snapped pictures of the guys on the ground. That was—

Weird.

The whole thing had completely blown past any normal metric I might have been familiar with. Voodoo was still armed. The shotgun was under one arm and the rifle across his back. The handgun was back in its holster. He was still wearing the bullet proof vest.

He also didn't have a scratch on him that I could see. I didn't even think his hair was messed up. He stripped a bag off the third man and went through it, then he pulled out a tablet and a phone.

Using the man's face, he unlocked them. Then typed a few things before repeating the same process with the fourth man. He shoved all of the devices into a ruck I hadn't even noticed and then he was striding toward me.

After stowing his gear, he slid into the driver's seat and backed out of the garage. "Change of plans, Firecracker. We need to take you somewhere to see if we can find the tracker."

"It's inside of me." Where else would it be?

"Probably," Voodoo said. "But we're going to make sure we get it out. Not taking you to base if you can compromise it. The point of base is to be a safe place."

"What about the house in Pennsylvania?"

"It's just a safe house. It's set up like a faraday cage though, containing the signal while you were in it. We might be able to do that in a car, but I'd rather get the tag off you entirely."

"Me too," I admitted. I had my seatbelt on, the taser rested in my lap and I had my arms folded.

"Eat," he ordered, leaning over to snag the bag of pastries from near my feet. The warmth of the back of his hand brushed down my calf. It was almost too much stimulation. He set the bag in my lap.

Not that I felt much like eating, but I still pulled out one of the croissants. It wasn't warm anymore, but it smelled fine. I waited until I finished it and we were back on the highway to speak again. "Did you kill the other men?"

"Yes." No hesitation. No soft balling it. "They would have killed me and taken you given the chance."

"That's what it sounded like." I folded my arms again and rubbed at my biceps. I was so cold. "I killed that one guy."

"You didn't kill him," Voodoo said. "The taser is non-lethal."

"I shocked the shit out of him on the ladder."

Voodoo shrugged. "If he hadn't been trying to hurt you, he wouldn't have been on the ladder. You might have facilitated his leaving the ladder swiftly, but you didn't kill him."

"How can you say that?" Had he done something when I couldn't see what he was doing.

"Because how he landed killed him," Voodoo deadpanned.

"Then I did kill him—"

"No. You shocked him. He fell. He landed badly. How he landed killed him. It's not your fault he didn't know how to land it."

I gaped at him. "Are you serious?"

"Yes," Voodoo said, this time with a grin. "I'm very serious. You're just going to tear yourself up about this. You're a fighter. That's important."

After rubbing a hand over my face, I looked at my palm. There was still grit and dust on it from the loft. It was probably on my face too.

My nose burned. My eyes weren't happy. "I hate this."

"I get that," he said, then bumped my knee with his fist. "Eat some more and drink some water. I've got people meeting us two hours away. They'll find the tracker and we'll get it out."

Exhaustion draped me. I still hadn't called Am's place or checked to see if she was okay. This whole time, they kept telling me I had to wait. No wonder they found me so fast when I went home.

If I'd gone to Am, would I have been leading them right to her?

"It's going to be fine, Firecracker. We'll take care of this, then get you a phone and call your sister."

Somehow, that just wasn't the comfort it had been.

FIFTEEN

ALPHABET

An update came through just as I pulled into the garage. Bones and Voodoo were on my shit list. Lunchbox's too based on his reaction. We'd dropped the borrowed cars with a guy to clean them up before we went to the airport. The flight back was uneventful, particularly because we hadn't had Gracie with us.

No, Bones pulled rank and sent her with Voodoo. The fucker didn't even bother to tell us. He just left with her before dawn with only a two-line note for explanation.

Transporting the client. See you at house.

See us at the house. That was going to take him a day or two to drive her there. Longer if they ran into trouble. Bones only said they would be fine and we needed to head home.

"We should have tagged her," Lunchbox said as he opened the back door of my car. Goblin hopped down and circled around to wait for me.

"Not sure if you noticed," I said as I levered myself out of the car. "We were a little busy."

"I noticed." Lunchbox snagged my gear along with his

before he headed inside. I'd bitch, but my back was hurting and my leg hadn't shut the fuck up in two days. Pain sizzled along my quad and up to my hip where it joined the flash fire in my back.

Rather than leave me to limp alone, Goblin moved along with me. "I'm good, buddy," I assured him, not that the Staffy seemed to be buying what I was selling. Not getting underfoot, he twisted to check on me regularly as we made our way to the door that Lunchbox left open.

Unsurprisingly, our duffels were left in the mudroom. He was likely sweeping the house. I paused at the control panel. I checked base regularly when we were on the road. Multiple cameras, motion sensors, and alarms kept us in the loop. We brought no one here and did the majority of the work on the place ourselves.

Goblin stayed with me while I entered my code, then pulled up the log. Nothing had changed since my last check-in, but it was always better to be certain. Just because we were paranoid didn't mean everyone wasn't out to get us.

Work like we did earned enemies. We tried not to leave any behind us that weren't already six feet under, but we couldn't claim a perfect record. Hope for the best and plan for the worst.

The scanner showed movement on the second floor. Lunchbox was finishing his sweep. I waited for his all clear on my phone before I entered the code which would send the messages to Bones and Voodoo that we were tucked in securely.

"Come on, Gobs," I said to the dog watching me so closely. He rose to follow me inside as I headed for the kitchen. I wanted coffee. I kind of wanted food but with Lunchbox in the house, I'd leave the meal planning to him.

It was generally safer for all involved. I got the coffee loaded and the water refilled. Pausing at the fridge, I scanned the contents. We needed a restock run.

That was Voodoo's job.

Goblin settled in the middle of the kitchen while I moved around. As much as I wanted to sit, I needed to stretch. So, I'd take the light exercise while the coffee brewed. I pulled out one of the bigger dental treats for my buddy.

He watched me, not leaping up from his resting position until I clicked my tongue. Then he was up and in front of me, waiting patiently.

"Good boy," I told him before I handed it to him. He carried the treat over to eat it under the table while I flipped open the cupboard. Protein bars were still in stock, I grabbed a couple to shove in my pocket.

I'd take them to my office with me.

"I'm grabbing a shower," Lunchbox said over the intercom. It was easier to just broadcast if we needed to pass a message and we didn't know where the others were. "I'll take care of dinner after. See if you can figure out how far away they are?"

"They won't be here tonight," I informed him without touching any of the buttons. It wouldn't be a surprise to him either. When the coffee was ready, I poured half of the carafe into a tumbler, then carried it and the protein bars to my office with Goblin trailing behind me.

I shoved the barn door wide. Roughly ten by fifteen feet, my office was a comfortable rectangle. There was an emergency exit located in the middle. The room could also be shut down with one push, dropping shields over the windows and the door.

Once engaged, safe room mode could only be lifted

from the inside. The same with the emergency exit. It couldn't be opened from outside. Right now the windows overlooked a huge meadow with three board fencing visible in the distance.

A barn was set up on the property. It hadn't been renovated when we did the house. Instead, we kept it as it was. The plan was to remodel it later. For now, it worked to store some equipment and for target practice. Outside of Goblin, we didn't want animals here. We didn't keep a staff and we could be gone for weeks at a time.

"Take a break," I said to Goblin and he headed right over to the giant dog bed in the corner. It was big enough I could sprawl in it, and had before. Gobs and I had taken more than one nap right there.

Coffee on the desk, I brought my systems up from shutdown then let them run through their cleanup programs as they came up one at a time. I plugged my phone into a charger, then eased down into the chair. I could make myself more comfortable and just use my crutches, but I wasn't in the mood right now.

Once I was in my seat, I lifted my left leg and rested it on the bench meant for the purpose. The relief was almost immediate and I blew out a breath before I downed a swallow of coffee.

It could clean the pipes, it was so damn strong. Just what the doctor ordered. Another message popped on my phone as I began logging into my machines. Bones had detoured.

I frowned, then pulled it to me to read more firmly.

He detoured to backup Voodoo with Grace. I scrolled to check the other messages that had come in. They were circumspect, mostly delivered in code on the off chance someone hacked our system.

Voodoo had proven a theory that just planning takeout didn't mean we could skip on the bill. They would come looking for it.

She had a tracker.

A string of invectives fell as I pulled up the server that let me track the guys when they were out. These trackers were specific to our phones. Easier to never leave anyone behind if we knew where they were.

Same for Doc, but we kept that part to ourselves. He rarely left Braxton Harbor and his clinic. If he did, however, and needed us, we'd find him. It was why we'd gone the moment he called us about the trucks and the passengers.

Three offers were in the inbox. I ignored that for now as I zeroed in on Voodoo's phone. They'd have been on the road for hours, and they'd be nowhere near here. So where were they?

They weren't far from St. Louis, Missouri. What the hell was in St. Louis? We had a handful of connections there, including at least two certified physicians within The Network. Another swallow of coffee, as I tracked Voodoo's phone by tower pings.

It was stationary.

Clinic.

I ground my teeth but kept my eye on the prize. The clinic had a decent system, but they allowed you to log in from beyond the firewall to see what was going on.

It took me ten minutes to get in. I'd need to shore those up before I left, for now, I flipped through the camera angles.

Reception.

Waiting room.

Hall.

Doctor's office.

Exam rooms—only external cameras for each door.

I pulled up three windows to keep an eye on all of them while I checked the lot outside of the clinic. There was Voodoo's Jeep.

It looked fine, no signs of visible damage. I flicked a look back to the other three as an exam room door opened. The angle wasn't great, but I caught Voodoo's profile.

They were in exam room two.

Since I was already in part of their system, I went digging into the patient files. I didn't care about the others but I wanted to see who'd been checked in recently. The door was visible and the colored flag was set to red. That usually meant occupied.

Brittany Talbot. She did not look remotely like a Brittany. She was there for possible illness, flu or pneumonia. Smart, that meant he brought her in masked. Reduced the chances of her being identified.

The doctor was talking to one of the nurses, then he went down the hall and disappeared into his office. He wasn't there long before he returned to the exam room. The patient in there left. The patient in one didn't make an appearance.

A nurse didn't join the doctor in the room with Voodoo and Gracie. That would fly in the face of protocol. Not that I was worried about the physician getting frisky. Voodoo was *right* there.

Still, the other cameras showed the staff and patients trickling out. The doors locked. The clinic closed, and the whole time the door to exam room two stayed closed. Then it was just the doctor left and everything else was secure.

He opened the exam room door and Voodoo stepped out, his gaze tracked right to the camera. With care, I tapped a message to him using the red light. Instead of surprised, Voodoo just shook his head at me before he looked at the doctor again.

Then he held out a hand to the woman inside and I got my first good look at Gracie since Voodoo took off with her. She was pale. Paler than I liked to see. She also had a smudge on her cheek and she was dressed in an x-ray gown.

Oh, that was excellent. Probably trying to block any signal from the tracker. It had to be working, they were still in the clinic. If I had the right equipment, I could do a search for the signal and try to jam it.

The smell of burgers and peppers reached me a beat before Lunchbox did. He'd made his favorite. The man would put chilis on just about anything. It was fine, I didn't mind them on my burgers.

"Found her," Lunchbox said. "They getting her tracker out?"

"Not yet, I don't think. Probably waited for the clinic to empty."

"Makes sense." He pulled up a chair and settled at the corner of my desk. We both ate in silence as I tracked her to an actual x-ray room.

"That's helpful." If they had to find the thing.

"Can you get into the…"

"Machine?" Since I already had a window open to let myself into their equipment. I spared him a look. "Who are you talking to?"

"Just checking," Lunchbox said.

The screen generated an image and we both found the tracker almost immediately. It was in her back. Not somewhere easily accessible. Thankfully, they did a full set of scans to make sure she didn't have any others.

I bit into my burger while we waited. Scrolling the

images let me watch their backs. Unsurprising was when Bones arrived. Of course, he'd go there to spell Voodoo out. Even if they drove all night they were easily a little under twenty-four hours away.

They wouldn't drive all night. Not when they would want to make sure they'd flushed any possible tails and verify that her tracker was gone. Then they could bring her here.

Lunchbox's phone rang and he showed me the contact was Bones before he answered it by hitting speaker. "You've got both of us here."

"I figured," Bones said, his tone dry. "Find us a place to stay for the night. She's going to need rack time and Voodoo's been running point all day."

"Funny how that happens," Lunchbox said in a droll tone. "Particularly with both of us right there. We could have all been on the road with her and no one would be tired."

"Save your bitching for later," Bones said. "Just get us a secure bunk for the night. Once we're in the clear, we'll head to you."

"You planning to let her call her sister while out there?" I already knew the answer when I asked. At the same time, it was the one thing most vibrantly important to her. More delays would just upset her.

They didn't want *her* calling. Didn't mean I couldn't hunt.

"Save it for later," Bones said. "I'll check in when we're back on the road."

Then he was gone. It didn't take long for me to track down a decent place. It wasn't fancy, but it was available for online rental and you didn't need to have contact with anyone. After I booked it, I forwarded all the information to Bones.

It took about an hour, but Gracie emerged from the x-ray room with a definite look of discomfort on her face. They had a brief conversation, then they were leaving. I tracked them all the way to the car.

No one was watching that I could see. No one to deal with, so while they drove, I started up a new search window.

"I'll get us more coffee," Lunchbox said. "Then help with the search."

I nodded as I typed in Amorette Black's name.

Let's see what we could see.

SIXTEEN

GRACE

After the doctor applied the compression bandage and held it in place, he detailed the next few days to Bones and Voodoo. I still couldn't believe there had been a tracker inside of me. It had been just below my shoulder blades. I couldn't quite reach it with my hands, which would have made it impossible to remove on my own.

"You can shower," the doctor said, meeting my look. "The bandage is waterproof. Leave it in place for at least three days, five would be ideal. Then you can remove it." He passed over a sheet of paper. I had to wonder if his name was on it. So far, we hadn't said our names nor had he given us his. Maybe that was how they did things. "Things to keep an eye on, if you begin to run a fever or the area becomes hot to the touch, go to a doctor. Also... avoid any heavy lifting over the next four days or so."

That seemed pretty basic and straightforward.

"Thank you, Doctor," I said as I eased off the table. Voodoo had stayed with me for every piece of this. Weirdly, his presence helped when I had to lay face down and the doctor dug the tracker out.

I'd gotten to see it briefly, and it looked just like an air tag that I would put in my luggage, just smaller. The tiny looking flat pill was how they kept finding me. I'd be safe now, right?

"You're welcome," he said, his stern visage relaxing into an encouraging smile. "You be careful and listen to these reprobates. They might be surly, but they know their stuff." The older man with his salt and pepper hair made me think of sharing butterscotch candies and sitting around the diner playing checkers in the summer.

There'd been a lot of men like him when Am and I were growing up. They were everyone's uncles and grandparents. They would buy you a soda when you were short the money, and teach you how to thread bait properly on a hook. If you had a school project, you could more often than not find a volunteer and his friends to help you set it up.

Leaving that life had been the primary driver behind pursuing my career. Probably because life was a lot simpler then.

Simpler and boring.

"Thank you again," I said, turning to Voodoo who held up my hoodie. He helped me thread my arms into the sleeves, one after the other.

"See you around, Doc. We'll make sure the bill is covered." Voodoo shook his hand and then he opened the door to lead me out of the room. Bones waited for us near the nurse's desks. He straightened, phone in hand, before he gave me a once over.

"All good?"

"For now," Voodoo said. "We ready?"

"Green." Honestly, the short hand they spoke in was becoming almost normal. Some of it made sense. Then again, speaking in code meant the words might not mean what I thought at all.

Fifteen minutes later, I was in the backseat of Voodoo's Jeep with Bones in the passenger seat. They didn't say much. Probably wanted to wait until I wasn't paying attention in order to brief each other.

The spot where the doctor removed the tracker was numb. Awareness of the area was ever present in the back of my mind. It was probably going to hurt when the numbing agent wore off. The lidocaine had stung like a bitch going in. Fortunately, once he started the procedure it had gone swiftly.

The sun had gone down while we'd been inside. The headlights of other cars highlighted the profiles of the two silent men in the front. We continued west for an hour before Voodoo followed the instructions to leave the highway.

As tired as I was—and I was dead exhausted, no pretending otherwise—I didn't think we were anywhere near our destination. With that in mind, I didn't assume we were heading to where the others were or whatever their home base was.

Maybe I didn't want to go to their home base. Going there could mean I wouldn't be allowed to leave again. Voodoo didn't deny that I'd exchanged one set of captors for another. Not that this set had tried to beat me or rape me, so it could be worse.

I couldn't escape the fact that just because they hadn't *yet* didn't mean they *wouldn't* ever. No matter how nice they seemed. That seemed to be the big problem at the heart of the matter. I didn't *know* them, but what I had learned about them made me *want* to trust them.

Wrapping my arms around myself, I leaned my head against the seat and stared out into the darkness. The lights were coming fewer and farther in between. Wherever we were headed, it was away from the city.

"Hey, Firecracker," Voodoo said, raising his voice and it penetrated the haze around me.

"Are you talking to me?" Had I missed a question? Bones half-twisted in his seat to glance back at me. Of the four men, Bones seemed the least warm. The least personable. I wasn't sure if it was just the chill in the air around him or the long, studying looks.

He didn't say much, even in direct conversation. Yet, I couldn't escape the idea that he weighed each word before he said it aloud. Yet, he said very little of what he truly thought.

"Yes," Voodoo said, tugging my attention from Bones to him. He didn't glance over his shoulder, but somehow, I didn't think he missed much.

"Do you mind repeating it?" It was a confession that I hadn't been paying attention, but I couldn't really hide it.

"Are you hu—" He cut off abruptly, and his hands flexed on the steering wheel.

Apprehension sliced through me.

"Brace," Bones ordered. I reached up for the "oh shit" handle even as he did the same. Headlights suddenly flooded the interior of the car. The crunch of metal being slapped by metal ripped through the vehicle even as we jerked forward.

I half-expected another hit, but Voodoo was already accelerating. The lights weren't going away though. If anything, they seemed to be fighting to catch up with us.

The light made it impossible to see and I winced for Voodoo who kept his eyes narrowed on the road.

"Get ready," Voodoo said. "They're going to hit us again."

Even expecting it, the slam of car against car rattled through me. My teeth clacked together, pain shivered up my spine toward the numb area the doctor had carved into me. The snapping of my head forward and back just made everything hurt.

"This is going to need a steadier hand," Voodoo warned. I wasn't entirely sure *what* part of this required that, but I could guess it was either dealing with them hitting us.

The scream of metal shrieking against metal ripped through the car. My teeth scraped against my lower lip and there was the dull flavor of copper in my mouth.

"Agreed," Bones said, then glanced at me. "Stay down, Miss Black. As soon as we come to a full stop, down to the floor and stay there."

Right. Hit the floor. Stay there. *After* we stopped.

"Do I want to know how we're going to stop?" That came out a hell of a lot more pitiful than I intended. Still I licked my lips and tightened my grip as the car hit us again. We fish-tailed and I grimaced at the spin. Another slam and we were whipping around backwards.

The sound of a gun going off cracked through the sounds of tires squealing against the pavement and the metal buckling. I held on for dear life as we spun right off the side of the road.

Then we were plunging downward at a sharp angle. A scream erupted as we fell, then bounced as we hit something. The tires scrambling just added more adrenaline to pumping through my system. I half expected we were going to roll.

We teetered precariously before the Jeep slammed downward with another crunch and we stopped. There was lights above us on the road. Our headlights blazed out into the empty in front of us.

"Down," Bones ordered. With shaking hands, I unclipped the safety belt and then slid down to the floor. Every muscle in my body hurt and I was shaking all over again. He was already slipping out of the passenger side and vanished like so much smoke.

"Taser," Voodoo said, slipping a hand between the seats and wrapping my fingers around the device. "Stay down, I'll check the best side for you to get out if you need to."

I barely had time to process those words and then Voodoo disappeared after Bones. I hugged the floor, torn between straining to listen for what was happening outside the Jeep and not hearing it.

Gunfire exploded through the darkness. I put a hand over my head like it would stop a bullet if that hit the car and went through it to shoot me. Right. The vehicle shook.

The motion had my stomach bottoming out. Head lifted, I stared upward at the door. Voodoo was going to tell me what was safer to get out, but he was gone.

Did that mean there wasn't a safe path? Or was it just a case that he was distracted? The explosion of gunfire cracked on. One.

Two.

Three-four-five in rapid succession just added to the terror sliding through me. Guns. Running people off the road. Chaining men and women inside a truck. Being coerced or raped—

I didn't know what the hell had happened to sink me so deeply into all of this, but I desperately needed it to stop.

Glass splintered on the passenger side. Another bullet

plinked through it and then into the windshield. The spider web of cracks spread out like we were in some kind of disaster movie. The whole effect was made eerier still by the low-radiance blue lights that were on around the floors and doors.

Not enough to really see, but to give everything a blue cast. There was a masculine shout somewhere and my heart plummeted with it as the man fell. He sounded like he was falling and his cry followed him.

Something hit the side of the Jeep and it gave a little shudder.

I needed out of the car. *Right now*. The bullets hit the passenger side so they had to be firing from that direction. Driver's side would be safer. I scooted over to that door and flipped the lock to unlocked.

More gun shots ruptured the unsettling silence. Frankly, I wasn't sure what I wanted to hear more. Sucking in a deep breath, I pulled the handle to open the door and a light turned on over my head.

Bullets sprayed the back window then hit the seats over my head and more glass broke. Unwilling to stay in here now, I shoved out, staying as low as I could. The ground was uneven. Rocks dug into my knees and grass tickled my palms as I crawled away from the Jeep.

Shouts came from above. There were headlights slicing through the darkness up there. Shadows leapt upward, covering the light then vanishing again. Staying by the Jeep was a bad idea.

Going up would be a bad idea. What I needed was to get away from the Jeep. The battle in the barn had been more controlled. Even then, Voodoo disappeared, and he dealt with the men but I'd had a place to be.

In the dark, with two of them out there and the rest of

me hurting? No, I didn't want to stay still. Not rising, I moved on hands and knees to stay down and figure out where the earth fell away.

It didn't actually take that long before the surface seemed to be angling downward. I'd encountered more rocks, and pebbles. There was broken glass too. Twisting to sit, I slid down the side a ways. The lack of any light down here made it almost impossible to see. In theory, there was a road down here, right? The road going the other way?

I hesitated with each spot I slid, I didn't want to fall or go tumbling down the hill. A sound like a boot on a rock scuffed behind me and I crouched lower. I didn't think anyone could see me, but I couldn't see them either.

Glancing back the way I'd come—I thought—I searched the darkness for any sign of the men or Voodoo or Bones. But if they were there, I couldn't make them out. My pulse hammered faster and it was getting hard to take a deeper breath.

Another scrape of a shoe and I twisted to look the other way. Had I gotten turned around? What if I was moving closer to the car? No, the hill beneath me still angled down, so uphill would be where the car was. Downhill was safety.

Maybe.

Did I stay? Did I need to continue scooting?

Rocks went flying, skipping over each other and scattering. Then one of those pebbles hit me.

It didn't scatter so much as thunk.

Everything went quiet. Even the gunshots and shouts from above. The night was utterly, bafflingly silent.

Then an arm wrapped around me from behind and hauled me upward and backward. Maybe it was the guys?

That hope died with the smell of heavy onions, garlic, and what could only be cilantro.

The taser slid in my palm as I clawed at the arm around me. It released a little whine like it was charging. I couldn't get his arm off of me, but he was still holding me, so I tased his arm. His guttural shout was a reward as he convulsed around me.

Then we were both falling.

SEVENTEEN

GRACE

I was lucky I didn't bite my tongue, as it was, I bashed my elbow and narrowly avoided hitting my head as I slid. I scrambled to hang onto the taser, but my hands and arms weren't doing what I told them to do.

Bouncing over the roughness of the ground just made it harder as I tumbled. I wanted to try and catch myself. Casting up against a heavier chunk of rock, I stopped sliding. The surface was rough on my palms. The taser was gone and I fumbled in the dark for it.

My jaw still trembled and my teeth clacked together. It seemed to take me more than a minute to think about what I wanted to do, process it, and then get my body to do it. Even then, I couldn't get my legs under me. It was like I couldn't process the fight or flight colliding in my system.

A grunt came from the man in the dark. There wasn't enough light from the headlights above to see where the man was. I made it to my feet and a hand clasped my ankle.

"Goddammit," I swore, jerking my foot back and toppling at the same time. It was like something right out of a nightmare. The man was just there, gripping my leg again and dragging me. Pulling me toward him, I surmised.

I didn't want to go to him. I didn't want to go to anyone. I just wanted to get away. I started kicking with one foot for all I was worth. I couldn't seem to break his grip on the one leg, but the minute I made contact with his chest, and shoulder, I kicked harder.

His grunts punctuated swear words. "You fucking little cunt..."

The voice gave me another target, and I managed to land my foot against his cheek and jaw. His grip on my leg spasmed and I yanked it free. Crab walking backwards, I didn't get far.

The slap of his hand on my leg halted my progress. Dragging me toward him, he banged me against more rocks and sharp stones. A light burned into my retinas and left me seeing halos dancing in the air.

It also gave me an up close and personal look at the man holding onto me. Dark eyes, dark hair, a red angry mark on his cheek that looked like something my shoe had left. The rushing of footsteps rustled through the grass.

My assailant jerked his head to look past me. He struck me with an elbow and I went down sideways. My face exploded with pain and my eyes went blind with tears. I tried to cover myself from more blows, when something slammed into the man over me.

I barely got my head up to see him hit the ground. Then a fist landed into his face. Then another. The wet impact of flesh slamming into flesh filled the air around us. The light that had dazzled my eyes came from a high-powered flashlight laying on the ground a few feet away.

For all that it seemed I'd traveled farther in the dark, the Jeep was only two dozen feet away, maybe less. The man who'd been attacking me was down, and there was a distinct crack of bone to go with the wetter blows.

Something hot splashed against my face. Eventually, the rain of blows slowed as the man ceased any attempt to fight back. He wasn't moving at all. If anything, I didn't even hear him breathing.

The smell of hot copper stained the air to go with the metallic flavor in my mouth. I tried to look for the taser, but the world was cast in an array of shadows thanks to the blazing bright single light.

I needed to get out of here before whoever that was decided I was a prisoner too. Climbing to my feet was a challenge, particularly with how hard I was shaking. A shift of the light cut across the downed man's face.

Or what was left of his face. It was mostly a bloody, swollen mess and I jerked my gaze up from it immediately. The man turning to face me was—

Bones.

I sagged at the recognition which brought a certain amount of relief with it.

"Why are you out here?" His voice was so soft, I almost didn't hear it.

"Because bullets hit the car and I didn't want to get shot inside of it."

"So you decided to get shot outside of it?"

"No, I decided to run. I had my taser."

Shaking his head once, Bones grabbed my hand and tugged me with him. "Stay close."

Not like he gave me a choice. He moved at an angle, zig-zagging his way back to the car. Something moved in the dark ahead of us. Bones shifted his weight, releasing my hand before he lashed out at what turned out to be a man.

Three strikes and the man went down and didn't move again.

When he clasped my hand again, I dug my nails in to hang on. Then we were heading up the hill again. Two sharp, short whistles sent a shiver over my skin. He answered with one longer whistle.

"All clear," Voodoo said as he suddenly rose up out of the darkness. A second flashlight appeared in his hand and he used it to do a scan of the hill. "Did you decide to take a walk, Firecracker?"

"They shot the Jeep." Despite my effort to keep my voice calm, it still came out broken. "I didn't want to get shot."

"Seems fair," he said before turning the light back to the Jeep. His sigh was eloquent. "Probably a loss."

"Need to burn it," Bones said. "Grab our gear, throw their bodies in, and light it up."

"How do we get out of here?" If we burned the car, we were in the dark, in the middle of nowhere.

"We get creative," Voodoo said, before he glanced me over again. "Here." He passed me the flashlight. "I'll get the other one. Stay with Bones while I drag bodies."

"We could—" I broke off the offer, because he was already gone. It was eerie how they moved in the dark.

"Come on," Bones said. Without further elaboration, he set off up the hill and it took some effort to keep up with him. Each step we took higher earned more protests from my body. It wasn't just a hill anymore but a very steep incline that had me using my free hand to climb as well as Bones tugging me with him

At the top, I wanted to double over. Sweat slicked my face and my shirt stuck to me. There were two more men on the ground, both dead. A fifth one was dead in the front seat of their car. The headlights and grill were crunched from them ramming us.

"Stay here." Bones let me go and then moved over to one of the bodies. He shoved it with his foot and it went tumbling down the incline. The second body followed the first. When he opened the driver's side door and pulled the man inside out, I had to look somewhere else.

The headlights being on revealed far too much. Including the fact we were on the side of a road, at night, and so far, no one had driven by. How much longer could our luck hold out?

As if reading my mind, he tossed the last body down the hill.

"Son of a bitch, Bones," Voodoo called. "Some warning next time."

The man standing there, with his expression a slash of violence in the darkness stared down the hill as one corner of his mouth kicked a little higher. The smile was more unsettling than the cold expression.

"Move it," he said finally, seemingly trusting his voice to carry. "We're exposed up here."

With that, he turned back to the car and shut off the lights. He had a set of keys in his hand. That was something. I wrapped my arms around myself as I tried to see around the dazzled retinal burn left over from the headlights.

I could see a flashlight moving below. It wasn't hard to figure out what he was doing. The car doors opened, then closed. It took another ten minutes, but Voodoo appeared at the top of the hill with the pair of bags.

"Come on, Firecracker," Voodoo said as he opened the backdoor on the car we were acquiring. It was an older model Bronco. The interior didn't smell pleasant either. "Don't worry, we're getting rid of this soon."

Still, I climbed inside, but I didn't see Bones anywhere. Voodoo was in the front seat and he pulled out his phone. The whole front screen was cracked. What I could see of it was all spiderwebbed glass.

Not a good sign.

When Voodoo held something over his shoulder, I stared at it. "Your taser," he said and I accepted it. "Try not to drop it this time."

Surprise filtered through me. "I didn't mean to lose it that time. I dropped it when I tased the guy and we went down the hill."

Voodoo twisted in the driver's seat and gave me a firm look. "Did you hurt anything?"

"Probably," I answered. "Everything hurts. But we need to go, right?"

So far, everything had been about running. Staying ahead of the people trying to take me.

"Does this mean taking the tracker out didn't work?" Cause we left the doctor's office hours ago, right?

"Not necessarily," Voodoo said, but he didn't continue with anything resembling an explanation. Bones had also not gotten in the car. Where was he?

Just when I'd about given up on waiting for Bones, he suddenly opened the passenger side and slid inside. I got a brief look at his hands under the overhead light. One set of knuckles were raw and bloody. There was blood on his shirt too. Voodoo had blood on him as well.

"Let's go," Bones said.

Without comment, Voodoo started the Bronco and turned back onto the stretch of road we'd been driving along.

We'd barely gone a few hundred feet when something went up behind us in a plume of too bright fire. There was also the sound of shattering glass followed by an intense vibration.

"Did the Jeep just explode?"

"Yes," Voodoo said over his shoulder. "Gas tank was three quarters full. It's going to burn for a while."

Regret tangled in my gut. "I'm sorry about your car."

Voodoo shrugged. "It'll be fine, we can replace a car."

Bones' phone began to ring. He pulled it out of his pocket. It didn't look shattered like Voodoo's but it was definitely filthy. "That didn't take them long."

He didn't answer the phone, however, he just sent a message then lowered the phone again.

"You know," Voodoo said, almost conversationally. "Just cutting them out is going to make them more stubborn."

"I'm aware," Bones said. "By the time we get back, I'll have a better plan for them and for us."

For them?

Lunchbox and Alphabet.

"Did I get them into trouble?" My side hurt and so did my hand. Even my cheek ached. I just wanted a bottle of some painkillers, an ice pack, and a very long nap.

"No," Voodoo said easily.

"They got themselves into trouble," Bones said, as he switched screens on his phone. "We need a new contingency."

He didn't say anything else for quite a while. After another thirty minutes or so, he said, "Uranus, forty-two miles."

"Lake of the Ozarks?"

"Maybe."

They were talking in code again. Or maybe they meant

exactly what they said. I was almost too tired to care at the moment.

"Let's find a highway motel, get you two settled, then I'll go for supplies and a new car."

Voodoo didn't say anything, he did frown. Despite shooting a look at Bones, he didn't say anything at all. He didn't like the plan?

It took over an hour, but they found a cozy little hotel just outside of town and off the highway. The rooms all had external doors, so we could go straight inside. Bones left us in the car while he cleared the room Voodoo had rented.

How they managed to not look covered in blood impressed me.

As it was, Bones also unscrewed the light that was right outside the door to the room and then unscrewed the light on the door next to it. It created a deep shadowy relief against the building, almost masking the doors.

"We're clear," Voodoo said, sliding out of the car. He snagged the bags and then came around to open my door. It took me a moment to stand, as it was, I listed heavily. "Hey," Voodoo caught my arm when I would have just fallen back into the car. "Woah—"

The bags hit the ground suddenly as the world went sideways.

Then everything went dark.

CHAPTER

EIGHTEEN

VOODOO

Her face had gone positively ashen. That should have been my first warning, but with everything else, I hadn't focused on her color. Not under the flashlight or dashboard lights. It wasn't enough illumination. I let the bags fall as I caught her before her head could slam into the side of the car.

Sweeping her up, I balanced her against my chest. Bones melted back out of the darkness, his expression fierce as he gave her a hard look. "What happened?"

"No clue," I said, and left him to grab the go bags as I carried her inside. I needed to get her under light so I could get a good look at what was going on with her. The darkness kept us shielded and hopefully it was enough.

Inside, the lights were on in the bathroom and near the door. It was a large room with a wood floor, two oversized queen beds, and far more space that two people needed for an overnight. Right now, I just wanted to get a look at the firecracker.

She looked worse under the yellowy light if it were possible. The ashen color turned to something far more ill.

The bags hit the floor near the door before it closed. Bones strode across the room and grabbed some towels. Then he was spreading them on the bed.

"She's bleeding," he said and I laid her down carefully. The blood was coming from her back. It had soaked through the shirt and onto my arm. "The question is did she get hit or is this just her surgical site opening?"

"Fuck a blind duck," I muttered, then stripped off my jacket. I didn't care about the blood on me. "Grab a med kit out of the bags, then go and get rid of the car."

"That's usually your job," Bones reminded me, but he didn't waste time on retrieving the first aid box out of the bag. We didn't carry a lot with us, just enough to patch on the go. Medical could wait—most of the time.

The t-shirt she wore was definitely sticking to her and the only way to get it off would be to wrestle it up and over. Not ideal at the moment. I pulled the knife out of the sheath where it rested at the small of my back.

"You're not as good with her," I reminded him. He'd been downright cold with her and while I got it, she didn't, and frankly, she didn't deserve to suffer while we figured things out. "I'm also better at stitches."

I slit through the cotton. It offered almost no resistance to the sharp edge. She wore a tiny lace bra under the shirt. It was all white and didn't hide her nipples or anything else about her to be honest. For now, I pocketed the mental snapshot to admire later.

Moving Grace onto her side, I balanced her as I peeled the t-shirt away from her back. The blood was definitely escaping around the pressure bandage the Network doctor had pressed into place.

"No lifting," I muttered. She hadn't lifted so much as struggled. The tumble down the hill probably didn't help.

Then she chose to leave the Jeep. Considering the gunfire it took, I couldn't really blame her.

"We have what you need?" Bones returned from the bathroom with a wet wash cloth. As I held her in place, he wiped down the more visible blood, gradually revealing her skin. The bandage was soaked a deep red. We were going to have to change it out entirely.

"I think so," I said, then I rolled her onto her front, using pillows to balance her. I needed to make sure she didn't suffocate while I treated this. Once she was balanced, I used the remnants of her shirt to wipe down my hands. "Gimme a sec."

I washed my hands in the bathroom, then gathered up the rest of the towels before returning to where she was out. The breathing was deep and regular. Hopefully, that meant she'd stay out while I did this.

Flipping open the case, I pulled out a set of gloves. Located suture needles, then the thread, and antiseptic. We had a handful of medications including antibiotics. No lidocaine.

We needed to restock.

I set out a stack of fresh gauze, then another pressure seal. I needed to pull the original bandage off and check the rest. We had some skin glue, so I'd use that if I could, but I worried there was significant damage. Until I got a good look, I wouldn't know.

With everything ready, I pulled on the gloves. "You going?"

"You trying to get rid of me?" The words didn't seem to house any judgment.

I spared him a look. From his bloodied and raw knuckles to the blood on his shirt, he looked every inch the man who'd just waded through a group and killed two with his bare hands. Bones enjoyed a good fight, all of us did. But when he got angry, people died in brutal fashion.

At the moment, the flat look in his eyes told me everything I needed to know about his mood. Them coming after her with him right there just pissed him the fuck off. I couldn't say it hadn't made me angry—twice on my watch they'd gotten too damn close.

"Yes," I told him, not willing to play a game right now. "We need to debrief, but you'll handle it better if I doctor her up while you get rid of the car and make sure our tail is clear."

"How did they find her that fast?" The question had been bugging me since I picked up the people following.

"I think they've been on us since the clinic. I think they were biding their time and just fell in and followed. If they kept their distance, they could have hidden their approach." It was all I had. "We did a whole body scan with the x-rays. There was only the one device."

"With it out and them gone, then she should be in the clear." He didn't sound like he believed it anymore than I did at the moment. A muscle ticked in his jaw as I began to peel the tape back from the wound. I was using the damp cloth to keep wetting the edges so I could pull it away with doing more damage.

"That's a working theory," I said, then gave the little firecracker all of my attention. From her dark hair and delicate features to the lightness of her bones, she seemed almost insubstantial. After Lunchbox pointed out she was a model, I skimmed some of her advertising spots.

Whether she was dressed to the nines or in nothing but a thong, everything about Grace Black captivated. I thought she was even more beautiful without the cosmetics, gems, or fancy clothes.

The door closed softly and I spared a glance at it. Bones was on his way. Blowing out a breath, I focused on Grace to finish getting that bandage off. The bleeding bothered me, along with the fact she fainted. So far I hadn't found any other wounds, but I also wasn't seeing any blood from anywhere else.

It took me about thirty minutes to free the bandage without tearing her more, then to clean the wound. It had pulled wide. He had used steri-strips rather than stitches. As tempted as I was to sew her up, I checked the wound from top to bottom, flushed it out, then used fresh skin glue to close it before using what the doctor had.

He'd said something about reducing scarring. Probably a concern for Grace. I had more than a few of my own. Once I had the wound closed and resealed, I checked her pupils. They weren't reacting fully, but they were reacting.

"Okay, Firecracker, let's go over everything shall we?" I stripped off her shoes, then her socks. The jeans went next. It kind of killed me how slender she was. The fact I couldn't quite see her ribs didn't give me a lot of assurance about her diet.

There was a bruise around her ankle. One that looked like it had been made by a circle of some kind. A shackle? Possibly. There were bruises on her knees and legs. Most looked like something she could have gotten running into something.

Casual injuries, nothing to worry about. I went over her hips and abdomen. There were bruises on her hips—finger-shaped bruises. I just made a mental catalog of every mark on her. When I'd finally assured myself that she wasn't hiding any other injuries, I pulled out one of my t-shirts and slid it over her before I tucked her into the other bed so I could clean this one up.

Her pulse was steady, her breathing deeper, and her color looked better now that I got the bleeding stopped. Hopefully, she was just sleeping this off. I sacked up the towels that would have to leave with us. Not leaving a blood trail behind was the way to go.

I made the cheap hotel room coffee and killed a couple of protein bars. My phone screen was cracked and didn't want to respond to half of what I did. We'd need to replace it the following day.

As it was, I checked in with Lunchbox and Alphabet. They'd been watching at the clinic, so they knew about the tracker. The text took a little finagling to send through.

When Alphabet asked how she was doing, I glanced over at her peaceful expression. Then went with the truth.

ME:

She's asleep. It's been a hard day for her.

ALPHABET:

Let us know when you're on the road tomorrow. I'll keep an eye on your six.

I sent him back a thumbs up. We'd brief them on the ambush later. For now, I settled in at a table and cleaned one of my guns while the other sat on the table next to me. Bones might be a while, but I still wasn't sleeping until I heard from him or he was back.

When I finished cleaning the first gun and put it back together, I started on the second. I had it reassembled and pulled out the whetstone. With care, I went over my knives. I wanted all three sharp.

It was nearing ten when my phone buzzed.

BONES

Took longer than I planned to acquire new
wheels. Going to park on the lookout next
to the hotel. Get some sleep. I'll call you at
five.

That was all I needed to hear. I packed everything up,
got the gear ready to go. Double-checked the doors, then
eyed the beds. If I slept on the other one, it put her between
me and the window as well as the external door.

Any attack was more likely going to come at us from
that direction. I checked my watch, shut off all the lights
except a single one in the bathroom in case she woke up,
then I settled on the bed next to her.

I was on top of the covers. Gun on the nightstand and in
easy reach. One arm behind my head, I closed my eyes.
Sleep was a discipline as much as anything else.

Right now, I needed sleep.

When a hand touched my side, I flicked my eyes open
and glanced down at her. She'd moved for the first time
since I put her in the bed. She rolled onto her side and
pressed up against me.

If I were a good guy, I'd shift her back into her spot. If I
were a good guy, I wouldn't just enjoy the contact. While I
wasn't a bad guy, I wasn't opposed to her leaning on me.

A little sound escaped her and I shushed her. "Shhh,
sleep Firecracker. You're safe."

I wasn't sure if she believed me or she wasn't ready to
wake up yet, but she went back to sleep. When her
breathing deepened and relaxed, I closed my eyes again.

Dawn would be here soon enough.

CHAPTER

NINETEEN

GRACE

The world was hazy when my eyes opened again. Hazy, dark, and unfamiliar. It took two blinks before I jerked my eyes wide open. Where was I?

I tried to sit up, but a sharp pain in my back had me gasping for air. It was like someone had slammed a knife into the middle of my back or I'd swallowed something too hot and it scalded down my back as it went through my esophagus.

"Easy, Firecracker," a sleepy voice wrapped around me, and vibrated beneath my ear. "You're safe."

A hand brushed over my hip, just a light caress and it was more unsettling than comforting. I scowled into the darkness and pushed upward again. I didn't want to be lying down or lying with *someone*.

The man had chained me to a pallet at the foot of his bed. This was me *in* a bed with—

My stomach bottomed out, but I managed to get myself up partially by wedging my hand against the bed. The man I'd been using as a pillow shifted beneath me.

165

"You need to be up?" All traces of drowsy left his voice. The fight to get up vanished as he sat us both up.

Pain raked right between my shoulder blades. It was so intense, I thought I would throw up. As it was, I hissed out a breath as words abandoned me totally.

"Breathe," Voodoo said, the order penetrating the fog around my brain. "You tore open the wound where the doc took out the tracker."

"That's bad," I managed to push the words out around the bubble of pain trapped in my throat.

"It could have been worse," he said, in a voice filled with gentle kindness that seemed grounded in practicality. "The blood loss wasn't ideal, but I got it cleaned out, the bleeding stopped, and resealed it."

"That must be why it hurts like hell." I hated complaining, but I was still sitting right there with his arm around me. Beads of sweat popped all over my face even as I shivered.

"How much pain are you in?" He moved behind me, then lifted me like I weighed nothing and shifted me to the edge of the bed as he rose. "Watch your eyes."

I barely managed to close my eyes before the light came on. It seemed almost red from behind my eyelids. When I squinted them open, I found Voodoo crouched in front of me. The intensity in his dark eyes added another shiver to my trembling. I folded my arms trying to ward off the cold.

"It feels like someone is stabbing me," I said. "Not that anyone ever has, but if it feels like there's something ripping into me from my back and hitting so deep, I can almost taste it when I breathe. But I don't want to breathe at the same time cause it makes it hurt more."

"Well, that's about what being stabbed feels like,"

Voodoo said. "Usually *after* the blade comes out. Let me take a look, cause you're flushed and shaking."

I raised a hand to check it and it was definitely trembling. Then I looked down at my bare legs and the t-shirt I hadn't been wearing before. It was far too large.

"I changed you." He was all business as he rose and he grabbed something from his bag—a little travel toiletries bag maybe. He set it on the bed. "Need me to help you with that or can you lift it up?"

There was vulnerable and then there was on display. Nothing in his manner suggested lust or demand. It was a body. Everyone had one and plenty had seen me in far less.

Not usually in a hotel room—I guessed that was where we were—or when alone with a new captor.

"I don't know," I admitted. Those words were loathsome. "Do I need to take it all the way off?"

"It would be easier," he said. "Here, roll onto your stomach and I'll lift it in the back, then if we need to take it off, we can revisit."

That seemed fair—reasonable even.

"Okay," I said, around another hard breath and he helped me as I tried to turn. Pain seemed to sizzle along my nerves and it was hard to do anything that *didn't* pull against my upper back.

Far more breathless than I wanted to admit, I pressed my face against the duvet of the bed. At least it smelled clean.

"Touching you now," Voodoo warned. The glide of his warm fingers against my skin sent another shudder through me. The air was suddenly chillier against my skin and I swore I was sweating. "Yeah, okay. That's not pretty."

"I'll have you know, that my ass is insured for close to a

quarter of a million dollars. I think it's a little more than pretty."

"Quarter of a million, huh?" He placed the flat of his palm right over the center of the knife digging into my back. I was really missing that lidocaine shot. Or any shot really. "I think they weren't going for full value there, Firecracker. But give me a minute and I'll do a squeeze test. Maybe it's a little jigglier than it looks."

I laughed and it turned into a gasp. Oh fuck, that hurt.

"Sorry, Firecracker, I think it's infected despite what I did. The rest of it is just how raw it is."

"Do we have anything I can take? I promise, I'm not usually a wuss about pain, but this is bad."

"You're not a wuss at all. Stay here."

The bed moved as he rose and I turned my head to track him. He didn't go far, though he disappeared into the bathroom briefly. The sound of running water gave me some idea of what he was doing.

When he came back, he had a washcloth in his hand, with care he placed it on my back. It was too cold and not remotely cold enough at the same time. Then he went back to the toiletries kit.

I rubbed my cheek against the cover as he flipped the folded kit open. It was for first aid. Oh, that made more sense. He pulled out small vials and checked each one.

"Drugs?"

"Nothing that hardcore," he said as almost an apology. "We don't tend to travel with the heavy duty stuff and I'd rather have an actual physician handle the dosing."

That made sense.

"So what are those?" Talking didn't help with the ache or the cold, but it was distracting me some.

"Antibiotics," he answered. "If that's infected, the best

thing to do is hit you with some broad spectrum, then give you some acetaminophen for the pain. Do you know if you're allergic to anything?"

"Not that I know of," I said. "I was lucky as a kid. Didn't get sick that much." We lost so much family to illness. It seemed almost cruel that they got so sick they ended up dying, while I was so healthy. "So I don't think so."

"Right—I have one epi-pen, so let's go for not allergic. I'm going with this one—it's a cephalosporin. I'm going with a half-dose, make sure you don't have a reaction then we'll do the rest."

He was already drawing up the medicine with a kind of competency that helped me to relax. I wasn't a huge fan of needles, but I wasn't scared of them either.

When he had it ready, he glanced at me. "Probably better to do the injection in the soft tissue near your ass." He was almost apologetic.

"Be careful, it's very expensive. I wouldn't want to void the warranty or anything." It was a weak joke, but he offered up a quick smile to humor me.

"Do you mind if I do the squeeze test before the shot?" Just the barest hint of teasing underscored the words.

I snorted. "Better than doing it after—but thank you for asking."

He winked, then ran a hand over my hip to my ass then gave one cheek a solid squeeze. Heat raced through me to combat the cold and it felt ridiculously good. Particularly because I watched his eyes the whole time. His expression was an open book of surprised enjoyment.

Then he was cleaning a spot just below the curve of my ass with an alcohol swab.

"Little prick," he warned and then jabbed me.

"That's what he said," I muttered. The shot stung, but it

didn't hurt as much as I expected. It was done soon enough and he got rid of the supplies, then returned to the bed.

"Firecracker, if a man tells you he has a little prick. Believe him. Cause that ass deserves the best."

I laughed again, the pain so sharp that it bloomed through my back like I'd set it on fire.

"Yeah, I saw that."

"Not trying to hide it," I told him around a series of shallow breaths.

He crouched again, then stroked the hair back from my face with care. "Tell me what I can do…"

A part of me just wanted to go to sleep and wake up at home with all of this as a distant memory from a half-forgotten nightmare. The rest of me was too well aware that the ship had long since sailed.

"I need to pee," I admitted.

"You up for walking, once I get you on your feet, or do you want me to carry you in there?" Somehow, he managed to make the offer sound perfect and it didn't make me self conscious at all.

"I'd like to try and walk." I didn't like not being able to move or breathe or do anything.

"You got it." He rose and then I went from being on my stomach to my feet with such smoothness, I barely noticed the transition. He didn't let me go immediately. "Good?"

I nodded slowly. "I think so."

At my word, he released me but didn't back off. It was weird, the men were all tall but more often I dealt with them while they were sitting. He seemed huge standing right next to me. Even bigger than when I was lying on the bed.

When he offered me his arm, I didn't bother with pride, I just gripped his forearm so I could take a step. It was like

I'd suddenly become weaker than a kitten. Still, he paced me all the way to the bathroom.

The lights were on already and it was a reasonable sized, standard hotel room bathroom. "Leave the door cracked," he said. "I'll be right out here if you need help."

"Thank you," I said, taking slower, even breaths to make pushing the words out not sound like an effort.

The corners of his mouth twitched, but I couldn't evade the way he stared at me. It was like he could see right through to my bones and assessed every part of me.

In the bathroom, the cold tile on my bare feet was magnificent. The chill made the sweat seem much more intense even as another set of shivers went through me. Yeah, I felt so off and staring at myself in the mirror was like staring at a stranger.

My hair was a mess. Strands of it clung to my face, the rest of it disheveled. I looked like I'd been through the wringer. If Am saw me right now, she'd make me go to a hospital.

Then again, I'd be more than happy to go cause that would mean she was right here.

"Firecracker?" Voodoo called.

"Yeah, I'm going to pee. Sorry." It took more effort than I cared to admit to tug down the panties and pee. When I finished, I gritted my teeth so I could wipe. Reaching of any kind was just painful, period.

After I flushed, I washed my hands, then my face. Then I used my fingers to try and straighten the mess of my hair. Then I ran out of every ounce of energy.

"Voodoo?"

He pushed the door inward before I even finished saying his name. He held my gaze in the mirror. "How we doing?"

"Terrible," I admitted. "I want to shower but I don't think I can."

"I can help you." The lack of any leering in the offer actually had me considering it. "Or you can rest for a few more hours and we can try then. Whatever you need, Firecracker."

What did I need?

CHAPTER

TWENTY

GRACE

What I needed was Amorette. What I needed was to have met with her for our girl's weekend where we would both be safe and sound at the rental by the beach. What I needed was...

A sigh escaped me as I turned to face him. "Do you have a real name?"

"Voodoo not real enough for you?" The barest hint of humor slid into his eyes and his voice. One corner of his mouth kicked upwards, an invitation to play.

"Sorry, not judging, just—curious." I glanced at his hands. There were no rings. No tan line where a ring might have been. No jewelry of any kind—well correction, he had a silver chain that stretched under his shirt, but that was it.

"Nothing wrong with curiosity, Firecracker."

Weariness washed through me. I felt scummy inside and out. "Were you serious about helping me with the shower?"

"Yes," he said without hesitation or flirtation. "Are you comfortable with me doing that?"

Was I? "It's a body," I told him, with a wave down at myself. "Being nude has never bothered me."

"Good to know. If you're going to shower, let me grab you some water and a couple of pain relievers. Best to get them into your system. Go ahead and have a seat," he waved me toward the closed toilet.

The idea of getting the skin crawling sensation off of me was worth some discomfort. The seat was cold and sent a jolt through my system. At least it was distracting from the pain between my shoulder blades even if it couldn't touch the worry or the pain in my heart.

Voodoo didn't keep me waiting. He walked back into the bathroom with some clothes in one hand, a water bottle, and a pill bottle. He set them all on the counter next to the sink before he handed me a protein bar. "Eat that, drink the water, then take the meds."

It was flavorless, tasteless, and had the consistency of cardboard. Arguing about it wasn't really worth it. Methodically, I chewed each bite and then washed it down with the water. While I worked my way through it, Voodoo turned on the shower.

"How hot do you like it?"

"Scalding," I admitted. "But that's not good for my hair and I'm assuming the wound on my back." The doctor had done his best to minimize scarring. He wasn't a plastic surgeon though. Now, Voodoo had to reseal it. Was I going to have a scar there?

Maybe I could get a tattoo over it. I could hide it, disguise it—something. What I couldn't paper over was my sister. If she were here right now, she would probably give me hell for being melodramatic.

I would so love to hear her teasing me right now. Just anything...

"Firecracker?" Voodoo snared my attention with the quiet emphasis on my nickname. I blinked to look up at him. He'd stripped off his shirt and had the belt on his pants was open. There was a gun visible on his hip and a knife in a sheath as well.

The broadness of his shoulders seemed to increase without his clothes. The light brown of his skin extended to his chest and across his abdomen. It was a deep, unbroken tan. Or maybe it was his skin tone.

At six foot plus, he seemed to fill the whole bathroom. Somehow his shirt had blunted his attractiveness, fuck knew how, because he was beautiful, cut, and toned everywhere. Well, there were some scars and a tattoo but I forced my eyes upward. Ogling him was hardly polite. The faint smile on his lips deepened.

"You can look if it helps," he said, then motioned to my shirt. "Can you get out of that?"

"Yes, sorry." I rose slowly, my legs weren't the steadiest. The whole world seemed to be weighing on me. I tugged the shirt off slowly, pulling my arms in and then trying to tug it up and over without stretching my arms.

Voodoo didn't say anything as I tugged it over my head. I was panting a little when I was free of it. He removed his gun and set it up on a high shelf next to the shower right on the extra towels stored up there.

His knife was gone, but I didn't see where it went. His jeans went next and the cut muscle he had on his chest extended down his thighs. Apparently, he went commando too or he'd taken his briefs with the jeans. His dick was right there and impressive, considering he wasn't hard at the moment.

I tried to reach behind me for the bra clip and winced. "Okay, maybe I need a little help with this."

Twirling his finger, he indicated I should turn. Facing the mirror, I couldn't miss the way he studied me as he undid the bra. Then he hooked his fingers into the sides of my panties and tugged them down where he waited until I stepped out of them.

The heat rolling off him chased away the chill. Voodoo rose, panties in hand and he set them on the shirt I'd taken off. I dropped my bra on it while meeting his gaze in the mirror. He was over a full head taller than me. I was hardly blocking my own view of him.

"Still with me?" His voice might have held some humor, but his nearly black eyes were intense and sober.

"Yes," I said, then turned to look up at him. There was something unnerving about staring at him in a mirror. "Are you married?"

He raised his eyebrows. "Not wearing a ring, Firecracker."

"That doesn't mean anything. Lots of married guys don't bother. I know more than a few married women who don't either."

"Ah," he said, then gave me a gentle nudge toward the shower. "You're starting to shiver."

I was? I glanced at my hand when I braced it against the tile wall before I stepped over the edge of the tub and into the shower. The bottom of the tub was toasty where the warm water had heated it up and the water splashing against me was so damn welcome.

Showering before had helped. That shower felt like a million years ago. And all I wanted to do was scrub away any reminders of the past few days. Turning my face into the water, I let it stream over me and soak down my hair.

If only I could wash away the memories with the same

ease. The throb between my shoulders beat away sullenly like an angry bruise.

I listed a little, leaning to the side as the water kept beating on my face. Light hands rested on my hips and kept me upright. The contact reminded me that there was a naked man in the shower with me and I'd asked him for help.

Stepping back, I brushed against him but he didn't retreat. "I'm not married," he said, answering the earlier question. "Not dating currently. Haven't in about seven or eight months. Last woman I went out with was a waitress at a country club. We saw each other for about two weeks, had a good time and then I had to move on."

Huh. I glanced around the shower and then reached for the pumps of shampoo, conditioner, and body wash fixed to the wall. I kind of hated when hotels did that, but I also understood the whys behind it.

"Did you miss her?" When I raised my hands to my hair, however, I couldn't quite reach my hair. The intensity of the pain between my shoulders had me dropping my arms immediately. Frustration welled up and tears burned in my eyes.

I rinsed off my hands and then scrubbed them against my face. Even raising my hands that high made that wound throb. I hated this. I hated every damn minute of it.

"Not so much," he answered in an easy tone as he slid his hands into my hair. The unexpected contact jolted me. Then he worked his fingers against my scalp. "To be fair, I wasn't much more than a distraction for her too. Sex can be calisthenic. The release of endorphins helps with stress and it can definitely relax a person."

A weak laugh escaped me. "Not all sex."

"No," he said, agreeably. "Usually, only the sex where

you enjoy pleasing your partner and they enjoy pleasing you. When it's just about getting your rocks off—well, I can do that just as well with my hand as a pretty girl's cunt."

God I appreciated the bluntness. It helped to chase away the tears. With the lightest of touches to my shoulders, he turned me to face him.

"Keep your eyes closed, Firecracker, we need to rinse your hair." I wanted to protest not being able to see him but I never lost contact with him. When he nudged me backwards and into the spray, I put a hand on his chest and took a deep breath in case the water against my bandage hurt.

He finger combed through my mass of hair as he rinsed it. The contact with him helped, particularly when my nipples went tight as tingles spread out from where his fingers glided over my scalp.

"There we go." He guided me forward and I used a hand to wipe the excess water away from my face. Voodoo watched me with hooded eyes as he leaned toward me, his arms extended as he pumped out the conditioner.

Then he set those magical hands in my hair again, combing the conditioner through it and alternating with massaging my scalp and my neck. Every touch had weight to it, but not too much.

Drinking in the contact, I let my eyes fall closed.

"Stay with me," he murmured.

"Not going anywhere." That was a promise. "At least not yet." I would have to eventually. "What you're doing feels really good."

"I'm glad," he said, his voice low and almost melodic. "I can make you feel even better if you want."

That offer had me opening my eyes once more. He ran his tongue over his lower lip and I swore my insides clenched. It was both intimate and open.

"To be perfectly clear," I answered in a rough voice. "We're discussing sex still, right?"

"Yes," he answered, his smile growing.

It was the absolute sobriety in his eyes though that held me captive. He wasn't getting himself off by staring at my body. In fact, we were close enough to be in contact everywhere but I only had one hand on his chest and he had his hands in my hair.

"We are definitely discussing sex. I can eat you out, let you fuck my fingers if that will get you off or I can sit down and keep you on my lap while I fuck up into you. We have a few options we can explore."

Heat scored through me at the offer. It was decadent, direct, and desired. Voodoo was a good looking guy. He wasn't model perfect or movie star styled. If anything, he was grounded and so very real. From his strong jaw, to his dark hair and eyes, and light brown skin—he was everything I wasn't.

The dick that had been impressive before thumped against his belly now. It was red and engorged.

"The offer is there," he continued as he nudged me back toward the water still keeping his contact light. "You can take it or not. There is no demand."

"You're not interested?" The question escaped me before I could quite think through the implications of it. His chest was flush to mine this time as he rinsed my hair. I couldn't see him, but I could feel him everywhere.

"Firecracker, if I wasn't interested and if I hadn't seen similar interest in your eyes, I wouldn't have offered."

Another shiver went through me. My nipples tightened even more painfully. The brush against his skin was electric, but it was the light dusting of hair that tickled and felt so good.

"All of that said, I know where you were and what likely happened. So this is not on me demanding anything from you. When we fuck, Firecracker, it will only be when it is one hundred percent mutual."

Another shudder went through me. This time when he nudged me forward, he did so with his hand palming my ass. The heat and ease in the contact, crumbled whatever feeble resistance I'd been considering.

"I really want to fuck you," I admitted, lifting my gaze to his. "I want to feel you fuck me—I want to wipe away everything else and never think about it again."

"Then use me, Firecracker," he murmured as he tilted his head downward. I pushed up on my toes. Before our mouths connected, he lifted me like I weighed nothing, his arm an iron band around my waist.

I barely had time to process the feeling of grinding against him then his mouth was on mine. The world just kind of slowed as he teased my lips apart. At the first sign of them parting, he thrust his tongue against mine. It was equal parts gentle coaxing and wild demand.

The weight of his cock pressing against my stomach had me lifting my thighs to his hips. Despite how tightly we were both hanging on, he didn't shift our positions or break off the kiss.

The way he teased my tongue, then sucked at it to pull it toward his mouth, made everything inside of me go hot and soft. I forgot how to breathe without him, lifting his head in between sensuous explorations. Each time our lips collided, the kiss changed.

His beard was so soft where it teased against my face. I wanted to thrust my hands into his hair. I wanted to dig my nails into his shoulders. The desire to touch him competed with the need to avoid more pain.

"Tell me," he said, his lips mere millimeters from mine. "How do you want me?"

My brain short-circuited briefly. How did I want him? Licking the taste of him off my lips, I forced my eyes open. This near, there was no hiding our expressions. Heat licked through his dark eyes now. A kind of black fire that seemed to be held in check by the man currently cradling me to his chest.

What would it be like if he cracked and unleashed all of that heat? My pussy clenched so hard, I shuddered. The ripples of desire eddied out from my core.

"I want to feel you inside of me... everywhere. I want to feel hot pleasure, I want to come so hard I forget my back hurts. Then I want to do it again." I wanted to blast through every memory of the past few days and overwrite them until the only hands I imagined on me belonged to him.

His eyebrows raised and his lips lifted into a deeper smile. "Firecracker, have I mentioned how much I like your style?"

TWENTY-ONE

GRACE

As he had with the kiss earlier, Voodoo didn't wait for me to answer. After turning off the water, he carried me right out of the shower. He only paused to grab a couple of towels *and* his gun. The sudden pound of my heart seemed inordinately loud.

I'd never been in the arms of a man holding a gun. Not even for a shoot. In no way should it be as erotic as this felt. My skin was hot all over, the water and Voodoo having erased any sense of chill from my flesh. In the main hotel room again, it hit me that I barely knew this man and I already trusted him.

At least with my body.

The thoughts evaporated as he set me down carefully on the bed. I was going to get the whole thing wet, but all he did was spread out a towel on the cover and then another on the pillow he moved. Another shiver went through me at the assessing look in his eyes.

"I want one promise out of you, Firecracker before we go a step further."

Disappointment crashed through me. The clenching in

my pussy and the raw need flooding my veins wasn't interested in negotiating anything. I wanted a quick and dirty fuck. Or a slow and dirty fuck. I just wanted to *fuck* him and feel *only* him.

At this angle, I was eye to cock and I had to lick my lips. It was so tempting to just lean forward and suck his tip between my teeth. Would his skin be salty? Or more savory? Would the hairs at the base tease me? Or get caught in my teeth? A litany of ridiculous thoughts cascaded through me and then I had to wonder if his cock could reach the back of my throat.

I didn't doubt he could, I'd swallowed my share of cocks before. Voodoo's was damn sight larger than anything I'd touched in the last couple of years. Maybe even the last four years.

The question I should be asking was could I handle him at that size. My jaw wasn't exactly large. Sucking in a breath, I gripped the bed rather than reach for his dick. He wasn't touching without permission, I wouldn't either. Skimming my gaze along him, I found him waiting patiently.

Oh. Shit. I'd forgotten to answer.

"I'm listening," I said in a low, needy voice that barely resembled mine. The man had barely touched me and all I could think about was how it would feel when he thrust all of him into me.

I wanted to know what that was like...

"If you want to stop at any point, I don't care if my dick is in you balls deep, you say something. I will stop."

The words registered slowly as did the tense way he spoke, like he was still keeping himself firmly under control. His voice had gone deeper, huskier.

"I mean it," he said in a tone that demanded obedience.

"You will tell me. If you get scared, or uneasy, or I'm hurting you... you will tell me to stop. Do you understand?"

A part of me wanted to fire back that I wasn't a child, and that I'd heard him the first time. Another part of me wanted to push him. He didn't get to tell me what I could or couldn't do. The rest of me? It just wanted him and if agreeing to something I didn't think I'd need?

"Yes, I understand."

He cupped my face in his huge hands. Everything about this man was so damn big. "Good girl," he murmured before he brushed his lips over mine. It was a there and gone again kiss. Then another. And another. "Such a good girl for me, Firecracker."

I wanted more, but even when I tried to chase his lips, he withdrew.

"Soon, Firecracker. Now, I want you to lay back, carefully, I'll help."

Why would I need help? Yet as he eased me backwards, lowering me with agonizing tenderness, I raised my arms intending to grip his shoulders and help but the pinch hit as my elbows rose above my sternum.

"Fuck," I swore at the hot slice of pain.

"I'm working on it," Voodoo said, amused. "You good?"

"No," I admitted. "I hate that I can't raise my hands without feeling that slice and then it reminds me that they put a tag in me that we had to cut out."

I was lying against the bed now, all my damp hair on the pillow and my back against the towel.

"Then don't raise your arms," he cautioned. "If you want to touch something on me, let me come to you."

With the lightest of fingers, he traced a line from my shoulder to my hip.

"For now, though, I want you to lie here and take everything I'm going to do until you come or say stop." Sensual promise kissed every single word. While his gaze remained on me, he stroked his finger over my hip bone then across to the naked mound of my pussy.

Laser was expensive, hurt like hell at times, and left my skin smooth and unblemished. It also avoided the ingrown hairs after a wax. He drew a slow circle with his fingers.

"I like this," he said. "Never seen a cunt so smooth and completely bare." He followed the line along my cunt, tracing the lips to find them equally smooth. For some reason, his fascination and admiration swelled more pride inside of me.

"Laser," I explained as he slipped a finger up to draw a pattern around my clit. It was the epitome of the tease. It offered next to no friction, but it made me want to lift my hips and grind against him.

"Sounds painful," he murmured, then he slipped those fingers down to my entrance and teased at it with one finger while his thumb stroked my clit. "I forgot to ask one more question..."

"Hmm?" I was pretty focused on his hand and the way he caressed me. The petting sanded away the jitters and shudders that kept trying to rear their head. The feel of him pressing into me with his fingers was delightfully provocative.

"Do you want me to wear a condom?"

Like a record scratch, I hurtled back to Earth and jerked my gaze up to his. He increased the pressure on my clit, the strokes sending out waves to the rest of me. I couldn't quite lose myself in it, even if there was a hitch in my breath.

A dozen different thoughts collided in my head. None of which I allowed to escape. They were all things I didn't want between us.

"Probably wise..." I admitted. "After—" I waved a hand, I really didn't want to discuss this now. "They did tests and gave me some shots but I never went back to the doctor to find out the results."

"If they were bad," he said slowly. "Doc would have reached out to us. He knew we were taking you home. He would have wanted to warn you."

"Maybe," I said. "But I think it would be better..." All at once, the moment seemed to deflate. "The last thing I want to do is hurt you."

Voodoo grinned. "Firecracker, you're not going to hurt me. I can suit up to keep you comfortable though. So remind me again what you need to do if anything bothers you or causes you pain?"

"Say stop?" It came out more of a question than a statement. The smoldering look in his eyes was still there and the curve to his beautiful mouth beckoned for me to kiss him again.

Voodoo winked, then stroked his hands down my thighs. Laying this way, I was right at the edge, I half expected him to nudge me farther onto the bed. But that might actually hurt. The whirl of thoughts were falling like a storm.

I hated to admit it, but I might not—

One moment my thighs were straight, the next they were apart. A moment after that, he had my thighs over his shoulders and then he open-mouth kissed my pussy like he had my mouth in the shower. The strokes of his tongue were in no way hesitant. He licked me from entrance to clit, like I was his favorite treat.

The vibration when he sucked my clit into his mouth detonated a quake of sensation in my system. Pleasure blurred all the lines and I fisted the covers to hold on because he was relentless. An orgasm hit unexpectedly and I jerked upright, stiffening even as I came.

Pain filtered through the pleasure and I fell back again, then beat my hands against the covers. It was too much. Too good. The thing about Voodoo was he didn't stop with just one, another orgasm was right there. He swirled his tongue and then scraped his teeth ever so gently over my clit.

"Fuck," I said on a gasp as I fought to suck in a breath. My whole world had narrowed down the place where his mouth connected to my pussy. Long ropes of pleasure dragged through me until they tightened inexorably. With every caress of his tongue, he vibrated those ropes that seemed to rock me every time he struck them just right.

Instead of leaving my pussy, he would go for longer licks and deeper strokes as he tongue fucked me. When he added his fingers, I stretched my hand down. My back ached, but I could barely feel it. When I sank my hand into his hair, I arched upward.

I floated on a dark ocean of completeness. The pleasure was going to drown me and I didn't have it in me to fight. That he dragged a third orgasm out of me that had me sobbing. His beard glistened when he lifted his head to look up at me.

The tears fell out of my eyes as I shook from the release. Pinned in place by his gaze, I held a hand out to him. I didn't have words at the moment. I barely had thoughts.

All the dark ones had collapsed under the weight of his touch. They didn't belong here anyway.

"Are you in pain?" The ragged note in his voice reminded me of the firm grip on his own reactions he'd demonstrated.

"No," I answered, floundering for my verbal skills. "That—that was amazing. I want—I want more."

His grin was intense and blinding.

The smile transformed him from handsome to sexy as fuck and beautiful. Straightening my legs, he rose from where he'd been kneeling. Oh, right. He'd been on the floor. The thickness of his cock jutted right out and it was already suited up.

When had he…?

You know what, I didn't care.

"You sure, Firecracker?"

"Fuck me, soldier," I whispered, desperate to feel him inside of me. "Make me think only of you."

With one hard thrust, he pushed into me. The stretch of accommodating him burned in all the best ways. His thrust forced all the air out of my lungs and my mouth opened in a soundless oh.

There was a smug look of pleasure on Voodoo's face and he had every reason to be smug. I could feel nothing that wasn't him.

"Hard and fast?" How did he keep that laser focus and rigid control when I was desperately trying to not fall apart? "Or slow and deep?"

I clenched around him, the flutters of my inner muscles fighting to grip him even as he filled me so full. "Hard and fast."

Those were the last two words I managed because he took me at my word. Drawing back almost to the tip, he grinned down at me before he rocked back in. Every thrust lifted my hips, but he had my legs braced and I didn't drag on the bed.

Not that I cared. Everything narrowed down to where

we connected. The slap of his balls hitting my ass added to the symphony of the bed's squeaking, and underscored the raggedness of my breaths and the roughness of his own.

A vein seemed to throb in his forehead. The veins on his arms popped out. The image of that leash flitted through my mind, too swiftly there and gone to hold onto.

"So fucking good for me, Firecracker," he said. "So fucking good. You're taking my whole cock, and it feels so fucking good inside of you. That's it, squeeze me tighter."

He let out a grunt as if it was taking him real effort to keep pumping into me, not that it slowed him in the slightest. When he stroked my clit, I came like a rocket. I didn't pretend to hold back my reaction, some part of me heard my own scream as I tried to drag him closer, but this position and his grip kept me completely in his control.

"Keep taking me, Firecracker. That's it. Keep coming and let me fuck you so deep, you feel me for days."

Days.

Oh fuck.

The next time I came, he let out his own shout, but I was already slipping away. The drowning pleasure dragged me down and I tumbled even as his lips brushed against my face.

Warm, safe, and so damn full.

I wanted to open my eyes, and made one last attempt, then he was lifting me off the bed and onto the other. Sleep pulled me under. I resurfaced when he slid into the bed on the other side of me. When he curled me to him, I rubbed my cheek against his chest.

His phone buzzed and he must have answered it because his voice was a soothing rumble. The conversation faded like everything else.

The next day would be here soon enough, now? Now, I was one long sensual ache and I savored it as I passed the fuck out.

TWENTY-TWO

BONES

Dumping the other car and acquiring a new one hadn't taken all night, but I was loathe to return to the hotel directly. A part of me half-expected the bastards who'd come after her on the road to be tracking their own vehicles. It would make sense.

People who peddled in flesh tended to be greedy bastards. They didn't want to let go of their pets or their people. Clearly, they wanted Grace Black in their hands. The repeated attempts to reacquire her made that abundantly clear.

The fact someone had not only tried to take her from us once, but now twice, suggested they weren't planning to stop anytime soon. Worse, I wasn't sure whether they wanted her back as a possession or if they wanted to kill her ala, if they couldn't have her, no one could.

Maybe it was both.

Voodoo and I had been dealing with the attackers in the car efficiently until she got out of the downed Jeep. Considering they'd been taking shots at it, her escape from the interior seemed rational. Smart. It was an acceptable choice.

What wasn't acceptable was the man who then attacked her. She'd defended herself, while the taser helped her escape, it hadn't let her get far. The man had struck her—repeatedly.

My intention had been to get him away from her, restrain him, then question him. Then he landed a blow with his elbow and she went down. The fact she'd put her arms up to shield herself had snapped what was left of my reason.

The world narrowed to the target in front of me and the fact he was too damn close to her. Any sudden move on his part could end her. The man was nearly twice her size. For all the spirit she showed, she was not physically a match for the man.

Slamming my fist into his face rather than using a weapon to disable swiftly, I'd ended him with a series of swift blows. The blood spraying from his face offered me a reward in the moment. I could have stopped.

My brain recognized the moment I could have stopped.

I chose not to. They wanted to take her? They wanted to *hurt* her? Then they deserved no mercy and I showed none. Blood from the assault decorated her face, highlighting how ashen she was. The fact she'd just had a small procedure to remove the tracker probably didn't help.

The best thing for her was to go with Voodoo while I dealt with the bodies. I loaded them all into our downed vehicle and set it up to burn. I stripped them for any identification, including their phones.

Nothing they were carrying revealed their identities or their employers. Even the phones appeared to be burners. I'd shut them all down and sacked them up. Alphabet could check them and verify for us. After collecting their finger-prints, I headed up to the car where Voodoo and Grace waited.

She looked even worse in the backseat, her eyes too wide and her pupils too large. Not wanting to see fear on her face, I kept my gaze forward. Her collapsing when we arrived at the hotel only added to my aggravation.

Voodoo usually would have handled the car and the resupply. He preferred it. But I didn't doubt he'd seen the need for me to go and it was better for her if I absented myself and got my temper back in check.

I took my time setting up their vehicle for a trap and spent half my night waiting for the other side to make a move. They never did.

Bastards.

After dumping the car in a junkyard to be smashed, I acquired another and spent the rest of the night across from the hotel, dozing fitfully and keeping an eye on them.

The earlier anger was absent, I had the bones of a plan ready to go and I'd checked in with Alphabet—who was still awake and at his computer rather than resting. Lunchbox said he'd take care of it, but I told them it might be another full day before we made it back there.

"If necessary," I told Lunchbox. "You two may have to come out and meet us."

"I'd prefer that," Lunchbox said, his tone even. "I'd rather just head out and meet you guys now. We could fly to a local airport, pick you up, and get her completely off the grid."

"Tempting." Not a hard admission to make. "But we need to make sure we've scrubbed all their attempts to recapture her."

"You planning to put her through another x-ray?" It was a fair question.

"Not immediately, no." I'd skipped the part about her passing out. She'd had enough to deal with and her passing out wasn't a life threatening injury. "If we end up with another encounter, we'll revisit that strategy. In the meanwhile, get the safe room ready to go. If we have to, we can keep her there."

Lunchbox grunted. It was a noncommittal response, but he didn't like it. "I'll do the full check and make sure we get supplies laid in. But I don't think she's going to go for being on that much lockdown."

"She does it with us or she ends up in some truck chained to the wall or worse, and no one ever sees her again. She doesn't have to be happy about the accommodations." I didn't want her to be unhappy either, but living was far better than death.

Or worse.

"You keep telling yourself that." Then Lunchbox hung up and I leaned my head back. We weren't in the field, he didn't have to wait for me to dismiss him. The hang-up though was another sign of his displeasure with me.

At dawn, I went for coffee and food, then headed over to the hotel proper. My temper was in check, I'd cleaned up, and Voodoo hadn't sent up any alarms after I called to make sure they were secure. If anything, he sounded like I'd woken him up.

If he was sleeping it must have meant she was better. I hadn't missed how badly she'd been bleeding earlier. Another reason I needed to get out of there. Probably a solid reason to stop thinking about her injuries.

Civilians did not belong on the field of battle. Whether

they should be there or not, they were most often reduced to rubble when the wars we fought ground them down.

Well, not on my damn watch.

At the door, I knocked once to let Voodoo know I was coming in. "Friendly," I said, then used the key to unlock the door. The last thing I expected to find back in the room was Grace, sprawled in the bed and in a deep sleep. Despite the fact she was under the covers, she was clearly naked.

Equally naked, and next to her, was Voodoo and he had a gun in hand and pointed right at me. He'd already aimed it away before I closed the door.

"Really?" I stared at him.

He shrugged as he set the gun down. He spared a glance at the woman sleeping next to him before he focused on me. "Coffee?"

"Yeah. Breakfast sandwiches too." I set the food and cups down on the desk. "All fresh."

"Good." He shoved the covers back and eased out. I didn't give a damn about his nudity, I did care that they'd clearly been intimate.

Fuck, this was going to create problems.

He disappeared into the bathroom with one of the cups of coffee. I scanned the room. There were towels spread on the other bed, one on a pillow. Her clothing was absent. The sound of the toilet flushing preceded his emergence from the bathroom.

Downing more of the coffee, he paused to set some clothes on the bed before he set the coffee cup down. Then he was dragging on his jeans. Not a word passed his lips until he was dressed.

I debated how bad things would become if I belted *him* right now. This was not the decision I anticipated him making. Lunchbox and Alphabet were already compromised by her.

"How soon do we need to be on the road?" That was what he opened with.

"That's it?" I studied him, unamused when he met my gaze evenly.

"The last time I checked, I don't clear with you who I have sex with. If that's somehow changed, understand that I still won't be doing it." Nothing ruffled him and as much as I wanted to punch him, I wouldn't.

"It's not about clearing with me who you have sex with, jackass." Like I fucking cared where he got his dick wet. "It's about the fact that Lunchbox and Alphabet are already invested. I sent her with you because *they* are compromised."

He shrugged then took another swallow of the coffee. "I can and will do my job."

Scrubbing a hand over my face, I tried to ignore the headache pulsing behind my eye. "That's not the point. She's a *client*."

"No," he said. "She isn't."

I snapped my head up but before I could say anything, a movement on the bed dragged my attention.

Grace was up on her elbow, her dark hair a cloud around her. It looked like she'd been fucked and fucked well. Her sleepy gaze evaporated when she looked over at us and then focused on me.

"Oh." One single syllable. It held—something that I couldn't define. She didn't sound embarrassed or upset, but she also didn't seem pleased either. "Hi." With a grimace, she pushed upward to sit and the tightness around her mouth had me straightening.

Voodoo didn't cross over to her, he just waited patiently

until she was sitting. The sheet was locked across her chest, her arms holding it in place as she tried to run her hand through her hair. Aborting the action before she'd barely started it, she let out a pained sigh.

"I'll help you," Voodoo offered. "If you want."

"Yes," she said after a minute, then took a deeper breath. "But I'd kill for the coffee."

The shift in her micro expressions suggested she didn't care for the word play but she didn't take it back either. Voodoo carried the coffee cup and the bag over to her.

"There's food too and before you bring up your diet, just eat what we have for now. We can look at calories and requirements later. You need to heal and healing requires protein and sustenance." After he set the coffee cup into her hand, he dropped a kiss on the top of her head. "You also need to take some more pain meds, but you need to eat to take those too."

Nose wrinkling, she looked even less pleased than she had before. "You don't need to sound smug about it."

He chuckled. "That's not what I'm smug about, Firecracker."

I half-expected her to blush, but she didn't. If anything, she just looked pleased. Then she took a sip of the coffee. "Thank you for this."

"Thank Bones," Voodoo told her as he moved her clothes over to her. "Eat, drink, then we'll do meds, and I'll check your wound before we get you dressed. We need to get on the road."

You'd have thought we did this every single day. The byplay between them was fascinating to watch. His awareness of her was on full display, but he wasn't hovering.

At the same time, she didn't seem to like being told what to do but she muted her own objections. The shift in the dynamic made me wonder if we should expect more trouble when she was feeling better.

"Thank you, Bones," she said, meeting my gaze briefly. The dark, sad eyes were framed by impossible lashes.

"You're welcome." It came gruffer than I intended. Voodoo shook his head at me and I fought the urge to glare. "You know what, you two eat and gear up. I'm going to make sure the car has gas and supplies. I'll be back in an hour. Be ready to go."

Not looking at either of them, I headed out. The last thing I needed to do was start a fight with Voodoo or take my temper out on the client.

She didn't deserve it.

But Voodoo was on his own with the guys.

He made that bed, they could kick his ass out of it.

TWENTY-THREE

GRACE

The ride away from the hotel proceeded in a tense silence. Voodoo didn't hurry us out of the room after Bones left. If anything, he insisted I eat, drink the coffee, and then he checked my wound and the dressing before helping me to shower again.

This time around didn't turn to sex. Probably better, considering Bones was already waiting. Still, Voodoo was infinitely gentle and patient, particularly with washing my hair. Bed head looked a lot like I'd stuck a fork in a light socket and it blew me up.

He toweled us both dry, then helped comb my hair. Afterward, we got dressed. Despite all the sleep I'd gotten, I was exhausted all over again. But I felt clean, a real first after the past several days. So many of them had bled one into another that I wasn't even sure what day it was much less the date.

The sex and the showers seemed to give me my first real "distinction" in the monotony of the days. "Is it weird that the coffee tastes better?" Better than anything I'd had in a while.

There wasn't much of it left, but I finished my cup while he repacked our bags. He'd also sacked up the bloodied towels and stuff.

"I don't know," Voodoo said with a shrug. "But if you like it that much, we'll stop and grab you another cup."

I stared down at the takeout cup for a beat.

"Problem?" Voodoo asked.

"Just thinking that I should probably not overdo it with the caffeine." The diet I followed was a strict regimen. Too much caffeine could dehydrate me. That wasn't good for my system or my skin. The chances of a photo shoot in the next twenty-four to seventy-two hours was slim and none. "But I also think I really want more coffee."

He chuckled. "Then we'll get you coffee." The clothes I was wearing weren't mine, but they fit a little better than the stuff I'd been in previously. My back was still sore, and so were my thighs and my pussy. But I preferred the sore between my legs versus my back.

"Thank you," I said and he nodded before he grabbed both bags.

"You're welcome, Firecracker. Let's get going."

Bones waited for us in a dark SUV. He was behind the wheel and said nothing while Voodoo tossed our stuff into the back. Rather than sit up front with Bones' stony attitude, I climbed carefully into the back.

The seats were a lot more comfortable than our purloined car from the night before. A yawn cracked my jaw as I buckled in. "Thank you for the coffee and the food," I said to Bones.

He turned his head as if glancing over his shoulder at me. The sunglasses hid his eyes from me, so maybe he was just checking the other side of the car.

Voodoo climbed into the passenger seat and dragged

his seatbelt on. "We need to stop for more coffee. Fire-cracker liked what you picked up this morning. So let's hit there."

"You want more coffee?" Bones directed the question at me. The utter lack of inflection was unsettling. He'd been more animated when I woke up in the other house with him sitting in that chair.

"If you wouldn't mind," I said. "I am fine if you don't want to go there." Maybe he just wanted to get moving. The blood that had decorated his hands the night before was gone, but the bruises on the knuckles of his right hand were clear evidence that what I remembered had happened.

Instead of saying anything in response, he just drove. Twenty minutes later, he pulled into a little strip mall that had a dry cleaners, a place that offered physical therapy, another that sold insurance, a donut shop, and an empty storefront.

"Do you need more food?" Bones asked as Voodoo opened his door.

"If you want to save time on stopping later. The breakfast burrito was actually pretty good." And not at all greasy, so I didn't feel an ounce of guilt for eating it.

"I got it," Voodoo said, then he closed the door leaving me and Bones alone. The silence dragged between us, stuffy and oppressive.

Maybe I should have gone inside with Voodoo. The realization of someone watching me crept over my skin, leaving chills in its wake. I glanced at Bones and he had his head turned, like he was splitting his attention between me and the shop.

Or maybe he was watching the shop behind us. He had backed into the slot instead of just pulling straight in. There was no reason he was watching me. I was just being paranoid.

I shifted, trying to not rub against the seat back. I was already uncomfortable. The pain reliever had helped, but the dull throb seemed to be there to stay.

"Is your back bothering you?" The question pulled my attention to Bones.

"Yes, but it'll be fine," I said, dismissing the discomfort. "I just need to get used to it for the moment. I'm sure the acetaminophen will kick in soon." The tracker was out of me and that was worth some pain.

"When did you take it?" Coolness framed the second question.

"Before we left the hotel, after I ate, but before we showered." My voice hitched a little when I said *we*, but I didn't let that slow me down. "Are you pissed at Voodoo?"

"Does that matter?" Answering a question with a question was kind of rude.

"I don't know." That was the truth. "I also don't know if you're mad at him or not." He seemed unhappy for certain.

"You don't need to worry about it."

"Unless I'm the reason you're angry," I countered. "Am I?"

Instead of just giving me some platitude and telling me no, not at all, he went curiously silent. The truth was always preferable to the lie, but the lack of response grated on me. I'd just opened my mouth to prod him when the passenger door opened to let Voodoo back into the car.

Wreathed in the scents of sugar, coffee, and grilled sausage, Voodoo twisted to pass me a huge takeout cup of coffee. He passed a second to Bones, then held onto the third himself.

"I picked up some pastries, breakfast burritos, and three

breakfast sandwiches." Voodoo held up the bag. "You good for now or do you want to have one?"

"The coffee is more than enough." I could probably eat more, but I had no idea how long we were going to be in the car. Safer to take my time. "Thank you."

"You got it."

Bones said nothing at all, he just drove. It wasn't long before the long, winding two lane roads began to widen. Eventually we were back on an interstate.

The coffee was long gone, though it had been fantastic. I finally asked for one of the breakfast burritos. I should have saved some of the coffee. Voodoo had water bottles though. That definitely helped.

Two hours of silence in the vehicle while the tension between the pair in front of me thickened to something I could touch kind of made me want to scream. Then Bones took an exit off the highway.

"Change of plans?" Voodoo asked abruptly.

"You could say that." Bones' response was less than helpful, but I sat forward a little to see where we were going. We left the interstate and then followed a series of signs to a small, local airport. I didn't even realize there was one out here, but the place was pretty small and most of the planes were two engines or props.

The idea that we were going to get on a plane settled into my system. My stomach bottomed out and my heart began to race. If we got on a plane, we could go anywhere.

Then again, they'd been in control since they showed up at the clinic so it wasn't like I could just run away. Bones cleared the main gate, then continued through the airport to the far side where a small plane waited with a couple of familiar faces.

Alphabet stood with Goblin seated right next to him.

Lunchbox, however, crossed to the SUV as soon as we stopped. He opened the back door and glanced in at me. "Hey Gracie, looking good."

"You're a sweet liar," I retorted. The absence of cosmetics or hair styling meant I looked rough and pale. But that was fine. Once I unbuckled the seat belt, Lunchbox was right there with a hand to help me get out. My ass was numb and my legs were a little sore.

"At least you think I'm sweet." Lunchbox winked. The droll comment made me laugh. "Go on and see Alphabet. We'll get the gear."

"Are we getting on that plane?" Cause it looked awfully small for all of us.

"Yes, we are. Don't worry, you and Goblin barely make one person between the two of you."

I snorted but headed for Alphabet, who grinned as soon as I met his gaze. Goblin's tail wagged swiftly, but he didn't leave Alphabet or try to jump up on me.

"Hey there," I greeted the puppy. I wanted to get down on my knees and give him a hug, but I wasn't sure my back would tolerate it.

Oh.

Alphabet had done a flattening motion twice when I first approached. He was telling Goblin to stay down. They knew about the tracker. That made sense. Of course they knew, Bones or Voodoo probably briefed them.

They'd probably know all about the sex soon too. Did I really care about that? When I was working, yes. I did my best to never sleep with clients or photographers. Other models were pretty much a no go too.

Relationships made everything messy.

"Hi, Alphabet," I said. "How are you and Goblin?"

"We're doing good. How are you, Pixie-girl? I brought

some of the better pain meds with us in case you were still hurting."

I blinked at him.

"Bones said you lost some blood after the car went down the ravine, and you got banged up." The whole time he spoke, he gave me a firm visual once over. "You look all right though."

"I am," I said, raising a hand. "Just... sore."

"Get the lady in the plane, Asshat," Lunchbox said as he strolled past us carrying my bag, Voodoo's, and a third I hadn't even known was in the back. It made sense, it was probably Bones'.

"We were talking," Alphabet countered, but then he offered me an arm. "Come on, Goblin is going to sit with you. Flying doesn't bother you does it?"

"Not usually," I said, putting my hand on the crook of his arm and then moving with him as he took a slow walk toward the plane. I appreciated the pace, particularly after sitting still for so long. I was definitely stiff.

"Define usually," Lunchbox said after he stored the bags in a little cargo hold then opened the side door on the plane. Holy shit, that thing was small.

"Well, usually the planes are a lot bigger." That really made me sound like a diva. "And have room for guys as big as you four."

"Size definitely matters, Gracie," Lunchbox said with easy humor. "But in this case, we have skill to go with it. You're going to be fine. Now, let me help you in..."

Trepidation firmly in place, I climbed inside and sat on a fold down seat in the back. As soon as I was in place, Lunchbox directed me to buckle in and then he passed me a headset. It was heavy, but it had a microphone on it.

A moment later, Goblin hopped in and he came directly

back to me and curled up at my feet. His golden color seemed a bright spot in the day. The pressure was definitely welcome. Somehow, the four men all climbed into the plane and I was right—it shrank with all of them in here.

Bones took the seat nearest mine and Alphabet took the other. Voodoo had to sit up front with Lunchbox, who proved he was the pilot. One by one they had on headsets.

"I've requested permission to take off," Lunchbox said over the comm. "We'll be taxiing in a minute. I also filed a flight plan. How you doing back there, Gracie?"

I gave him a thumbs up and he grinned.

A moment later, the radio crackled to life and the words of the controller were clear on my headset too. We had permission.

My heart suddenly leapt into my throat as Lunchbox drove us to the runway, the ride was only a little bumpy. Then we were in place and Lunchbox informed the tower that we would be taking off.

I wasn't even sure where the tower was. Maybe it was that shack I could see?

"Hang on," Lunchbox said and then we were accelerating. A hand grasped mine, and I gripped it tightly. My eyes were closed because I just didn't want to see if we decided to crash at the end of the runway.

Stupid idea, really. But once I imagined the worst that could happen it would replay in my head until we were past the possible worst of it.

Then we were airborne and I let out a shuddering breath. Finally, opening my eyes, I fully expected it to be Alphabet holding my hand, but it wasn't.

Bones hadn't let go either. I wasn't sure what to do with that, so I just kept holding on.

TWENTY-FOUR

GRACE

The flight lasted a couple of hours then we were descending. I had no idea where we'd flown. Wherever was two hours from where we'd been. I was pretty sure we'd crossed the Continental Divide though, and it seemed a lot closer than when we flew past it in a jumbo jet.

Landing was a lot bumpier than I cared for. While Bones had let go of my hand after a while earlier, he held it out to me when I was white knuckling my knees. I wasn't too proud to refuse the offer. I held on tight to him until we were taxiing through a new, tiny airport.

I was pretty sure I left my heart up in the air somewhere. Bones gave my hand a squeeze before he let it go once the plane stopped. Then the doors were opening and the guys climbed out. Goblin followed Alphabet when the man whistled.

On shaky legs, I pushed out of the seat after I unlatched the buckle. Voodoo waited for me at the door and he lifted me right out and onto my feet. I held onto Voodoo when he would have released me.

"Need a sec," I told him. The racing pulse and shallow breathing wasn't helping. He didn't move as I held onto his arm. The rubbery feeling in my legs didn't just go away.

"You good, Gracie?" Lunchbox frowned at me. "If you were sick you should have said something."

"She's not sick," Voodoo answered before I could. "Back off, and let her catch her breath. She just needed a minute."

The air around them charged as Lunchbox shifted his attention from me to Voodoo. All the things they weren't saying swirled around them and I forced myself to let go of Voodoo. The last thing I needed was to trigger a fight between all of them.

My gaze landed on Bones where he stood, sunglasses in place, and his face unreadable. "Lunchbox, get the gear and stow the plane. Alphabet, go get the car. Voodoo..."

"I'm fine right here," he said.

"Wasn't going to send you away," Bones responded in a dry as hell tone. "Give Miss Black a hand. She could probably use a slow walk before we put her in another vehicle."

"Actually," I said, blowing out a ragged breath. "That sounds good. I don't know why I'm off."

"It's fine," Voodoo said. "It happens more than you think. We'll just take it slow and easy so you can stretch your legs."

"Thank you," I murmured as I began to walk slowly. Yeah, I was definitely not steady on my feet. Bit by bit, I was taking deeper breaths and my feet were feeling more firmly connected.

Voodoo let me set the pace and I held his arm most of the way toward what looked like a warehouse. "We're not going all the way," he said as he shifted our direction. "Lunchbox is gonna park the plane, but Alphabet got the truck."

"Okay." I just let him take the lead. By the time we returned to where Bones waited with the biggest damn Ford truck I'd ever seen, right down to having four damn doors, I shook my head. We would definitely all fit.

"You good to get in?" Voodoo asked.

"Yeah, I think so." I was feeling better and whatever that wild tightness inside my skin feeling was had passed. Voodoo opened the door and then flat out picked me up again and set me on the step to climb into the truck. "You're getting way too much fun out of that. I'm short, not infirm."

At my scold, Voodoo chuckled. "Firecracker, you weigh next to nothing and right now, we want that cut on your back to heal. Any climbing requires grabbing onto something and holding on while you do it."

I met his gaze when he said "grabbing onto something" and heat flushed through me. I'd had to grab onto him more than once the night before. "Right, I keep trying to forget it's there."

"Once it's better, you can forget all about it. Now, in you go and scoot over to the middle."

Instead of following me in though, he shut the door then turned to Bones. The intensity between the pair seemed to magnify. While they didn't *look* like they were shouting, they definitely seemed like they were disagreeing.

"Hey, Pixie-girl," Alphabet said and I blinked at him. Goblin sat in the middle of the front seat next to him mouth open in a wide grin that made me want to smile back. "You're going to be fine. We have another drive, but once we're back at base, you're going to be secure and comfortable."

"You guys keep mentioning that." Well not really, but it had come up a couple of times. "Where is Base?" Was it a town? Some actual army facility?

"It's home," he said. "Once we're there, we'll get you settled, you can rest and you can heal."

"I need to call Amorette." The driving need to reach out to my sister had kept me going for the past however many days. "We're going to be somewhere you can get me a secure phone, right? Voodoo was going to and then we got ambushed twice."

In the grand scheme of things, the ambushes took precedence over everything else. But they'd all said we needed to be secure. If Base was secure, then I could call Amorette.

"We'll take care of it," Alphabet said, then the passenger door opened as the two back doors did. Bones slid into the passenger seat while Lunchbox climbed up to sit on one side of me and Voodoo on the other. "Keep your arms and legs inside the vehicle at all times, sit back, and relax, we'll be about seventy-five minutes to get to base.

Seventy-five minutes?

"You good?" Lunchbox asked. "I packed a cooler with sandwiches and wraps. I made a couple vegetarian in case you needed something lighter."

I opened my mouth briefly, then closed it again. "Actually, that sounds great, but I don't want to eat in the car. Do you have water though?"

"Water. Gatorade. Beer." Lunchbox reached down and flipped open a cooler.

"Water. Please."

He passed it to me after cracking it open with a twist. The area outside of the truck was just... raw and beautiful. It was wide open, there were areas of grassy fields and other areas where trees gathered together like they were gossiping.

Ahead of us though was a mountain.

Mountains. Plural.

I kept scanning the area around the truck as the ride lulled me. My eyes kept trying to drift closed, but I would force them back open. I needed to know where we were going.

The last thing I wanted was to be trapped somewhere I didn't know where we were. Base was secure, I reminded myself. Secure was good.

The drive up the mountain was long and winding, we didn't pass many places along the way but when we flattened out again, I was leaning forward to try to see more.

"Come here, Firecracker." Voodoo unsnapped my seatbelt and lifted me, then he set me in his lap. "Better view from here."

He wasn't lying, the view was incredible. What I didn't see any of were other houses, stores, or frankly *people*. I didn't even see other cars. What was up here?

"Dude, not safe," Lunchbox muttered.

"We're fine," Voodoo said, dismissing him.

Then we were coming around a curb and my breath caught in my throat. It was a huge valley spread out below, but the land rippled with hills and more as it led to another mountain and another.

"Welcome to the Crazy Mountains, Gracie," Lunchbox said and I swung my gaze back to the mountains again.

"Do I want to know why they are called that?"

"Maybe," Lunchbox said. "We'll tell you the story later." The valley disappeared around another curb, then the road kind of flattened out, leading us straight to somewhere.

So weird, we hadn't seen a single other car. Maybe it was some kind of military base. Didn't they take huge tracts up? That seemed reasonable.

It wasn't until they slowed that I realized there was a

huge gate in front of us. Alphabet hit a remote that was pinned to the sun visor. The gate opened smoothly and then we were passing through.

The drive to get to "Base" was another eight minutes, but we weren't racing up the road. A house appeared in the distance. It was a big sprawling rambler style with a fat porch, railings and an overhang. There were empty paddocks off to the side near a barn.

Everything was a cherry-colored red wood—maybe an oak. It was like the house itself had been constructed as a log mansion rather than a cabin. It was incredible. I didn't get long to gawk at it before we were pulling into the garage.

It was one of the larger ones I'd ever seen. There were four other vehicles, not counting the one we were in already, parked inside. A pair of motorcycles were parked at the front. A third one, maybe, but it was under a tarp. The sunlight vanished as the door closed behind us and left us in shadows. The overhead was a yellowy light.

"One sec," Alphabet said and he had his phone out. No one moved to exit as he checked something on his phone. The light above us brightened and there was a panel on the wall that went from all red to all green.

The doors opened at once. Bones and Lunchbox were out. Lunchbox circled around to help me down. Voodoo handed me over like some damn package.

I could laugh or I could cry about it, so I just decided to laugh. Once I was on my feet again, I stretched my legs and fought the urge to stretch my arms and back. At the moment, that would just cause pain. Alphabet was out and he and Goblin were at the backdoor.

Bones, Lunchbox, and Voodoo had all grabbed bags and

the cooler, then they were motioning me to follow Alphabet. It was two short steps up into the house.

The cherry wood extended to the interior floors. There were also fat, thick rugs in varying shades of browns, creams, and reds decorating the hall. I turned out from what had to be a mudroom to find a huge kitchen with a pair of double ovens, a massive farmhouse sink, and a bowl of fruit.

The bananas were beginning to go a little brown, so they were real. For some reason, the bowl of fruit struck me as odd. I couldn't quite figure that one out. Goblin trotted after Alphabet as he made his way through the kitchen to a sunken living room. The windows here stretched all the way up to the second floor ceiling. The space was massive.

The view was just incredible.

"Come on in and make yourself comfortable. Plenty of space. We'll get the gear distributed and I expect Lunchbox will want to start on dinner. But I can make you coffee if you want? Or more water?"

It took real effort to glance away from the view to turn and look at Alphabet. He stood near the steps that led back up to the kitchen, his expression assessing. Goblin had sat down right next to him.

Voodoo passed through and then headed up the stairs with two of the bags, followed by Bones with the third bag. Lunchbox was in the kitchen washing his hands.

"Yes, I do want to make dinner. I've got some ideas I've been wanting to try out." He flashed a grin at me. "You like chicken, right?"

"Um, yes."

"Fantastic, so we'll do some Chicken Piccata, maybe a little garlic butter pasta—fettuccine I think. Garlic bread.

Maybe some grilled broccoli or brussel sprouts. Have to see what looks good."

That was a lot of food. But he was already on the move hustling around the kitchen.

"I'm going to get a little work done," Alphabet said. "There are remotes there on the table for the tv if you want. We don't get local networks, but we have tons of movies and shows downloaded. Help yourself."

"I want to call my sister."

Alphabet paused and then he looked to the kitchen and when I followed his stare, I found Lunchbox watching us. His gaze shifted and a sound on the steps alerted me to Bones and Voodoo descending again.

"You said when we were secure, you'd get me a phone so I could call her. We're secure here, right?"

The longer it took them to answer, the uneasier I grew.

I shot a look at Voodoo. "You promised."

"I know, Firecracker. I did."

"But he can't keep the promise," Bones said. "None of us can. So, do what Alphabet said, get some rest. We need to debrief and then we can get to work."

Anger struck a match inside of me as Bones began to walk away. I seized the nearest thing, ignoring the twinge in my back, and flung it at him.

TWENTY-FIVE

LUNCHBOX

I wasn't sure what happened that made Bones change his mind for us to pick them up but I also didn't stare at it too hard. We'd arrived at the airport two hours earlier than rendezvous, specifically to make sure nothing was waiting for them when they arrived.

Instead of experiencing relief at their appearance, I found myself in a front row seat to a gathering storm. Gracie's pallor and tension translated to everyone else. Bones and Voodoo were in the middle of some disagreement—never a good sign.

What I couldn't pinpoint was what specifically upset Grace currently. She had every reason to be upset from the initial kidnapping to being held to being transported. I wasn't sure if they'd tried to rape her to break her or what. The type of people who trafficked in women would more often than not. Rape them into obedience, or at least to break them from fighting, then use drugs to keep them docile.

Her injuries had increased during her absence. That fit with what we knew of the second ambush. She moved slowly, soreness evident in every step, but she didn't complain. The relief reflected in her eyes and her posture when she first saw me, followed by Alphabet and Goblin was also not lost on me.

When I pinned Voodoo with a look, he ignored me. I wanted an explanation, but that would have to wait until debrief. For the moment, Gracie didn't need to suffer through a breakdown of current intelligence. Most of it wasn't pretty. That briefing needed to happen before we broached any discussions with her.

Her nerves were on display during the flight. They didn't vanish during the drive to the house. She relaxed some when Voodoo put her in his lap. The familiarity and the comfort set off alarm bells.

Yeah. I really wanted the debrief on what the fuck happened between when Voodoo took off with her and meeting us at the airport. Still, the wariness returned to Gracie when we pulled into the garage. All of us waited for Alphabet to do the electronic sweep and deactivate the main alarm.

A physical and visual sweep would follow. We split up the gear and carried it in. Grace moved carefully, like she was hurting.

Of course, she was still hurting. I could have slapped myself in the head. She'd taken more than a few blows and with the narrow exception of two nights in the safe house, how much sleep had she gotten since—

Fuck, we hadn't even really tracked how long she'd been held. It wasn't a point I wanted to bring up and interrogate her, but knowing would just be another piece of intelligence to add to the puzzle.

Relaxing would be good for all of us. She was here

where I could keep an eye on her. Base was also a hell of a lot more secure than anywhere on the road.

Food was next on the agenda. Food, rest, and once she was settled, the team could debrief and plan.

"You promised." The wounded note in her voice sliced. Alphabet's expression tightened. I had to imagine mine was as well, considering the fact we all knew she wanted to find out about her sister. It was why Alphabet had started investigating as well.

"I know, Firecracker. I did." Voodoo's voice carried all the elements of regret his expression seemed to deny.

"But he can't keep the promise," Bones said, in a chilly voice that wouldn't be persuaded or argued with. He was issuing an order. For team cohesion we made it work in the field. The same could not be said for in private, but we'd really never had a reason to test it. "None of us can. So, do what Alphabet said, get some rest. We need to debrief and then we can get to work."

Son of a bitch...

It was quite possibly the worst way to address the issue. The threat was right there in her posture as Bones turned away from her. I should have predicted the next actions she was going to take. Should have predicted and should have done what I could to prevent it.

It was just the remote, though in our case the remote was almost ten inches long, four inches across and controlled more than just the television. Gracie balanced the remote like it was a throwing star.

Strategically, the overhand shot shouldn't have worked. But the thud of the remote hitting Bones in the head seemed abnormally loud. I blew out a breath and headed forward. Bones was turning with a cold look at the same time Voodoo moved to intercept him.

I clocked Gracie reaching for something else. Flashes of her throwing everything at the attackers in her apartment danced across my mind's eye. She already had a lamp in hand when Alphabet laughed.

His amusement triggered Goblin's barking, but the dog was still parked right next to him.

"Gracie—" I said, but she was throwing the lamp. Shit. "Voodoo."

He caught the lamp narrowly, but it was more because of the awkwardness. Gracie was already going for the next item on the table. It was a coaster, but a marble one. I leapt the railing as Bones crossed toward her. He narrowly knocked the coaster aside before he reached her.

Fuck.

Without comment or explanation, he put his shoulder into her belly and rose with her over his shoulder. He locked her legs down with one arm and pivoted. In four strides, he was at the stairs. His quick ascent echoed in his rapid footsteps.

Funnily enough, I wasn't the only one who'd gone still as we tracked his passage through the house. Then a door slamming closed—and I didn't doubt locked—drifted down the stairs. Bones returned with an even less fucking happy to be here face than earlier.

"Is she—" Voodoo started.

"She's fine. I didn't do anything that would open that wound. I am not going to vouch for her own temper not doing it." He reached for the remote to pick it up and then the discarded coaster. Voodoo had put the lamp down. Instead of following suit with his items, Bones paused to stare at Alphabet.

"Her temper amuses you?" Irritation rifled the words despite Bones' cool voice.

"Yep," Alphabet said. "That temper means she's alive and you still don't know shit about women." With that, he turned to head into the kitchen. "We should do the debriefing sooner rather than later."

"Or we can wait to make sure she is fine, fed, and given an explanation that involves a little more nuance than *I said so*." I shook my head. "Then debrief. I think she's had enough emotional upset the past few days, don't you?"

"Depends on the debrief," Voodoo argued. "If we have significant facts to cover, then yes, by all means, let's make this easier on her. If you can do it in five minutes or less, just get it over with. Then we don't have to lock her away twice."

"We're two votes to do the debrief, one to take the time with Gracie," Alphabet said, then looked at Bones. "You voting, Captain, or are we just getting the debrief done."

Bones glanced at me. I sighed. The debate was not one he wanted to have at the moment. No, he'd rather address the Gracie situation. "Fine, I withdraw my suggestion. Get in here and start the debrief Alphabet, I'll start food."

Alphabet took a seat, the stiffness in his posture had improved, but he was still sore. Bones folded his arms as he leaned against a pillar separating the kitchen from the living room. Voodoo rested against the wood rail that also demarcated the two rooms.

"In short order," Alphabet said, leaning forward. "The men who were controlling the truck are ghosts. They don't exist, their fingerprints are in the system, but they trace to men with identities that don't exist or died thirty years ago. They were backstopped damn near perfectly. If it wasn't so frustrating, I'd be impressed."

Goblin moved to settle next to Alphabet, but he'd also relaxed his wariness. I trusted the canine and started pulling out the burgers I'd prepped for grilling before we went to the airport.

"That said, I moved onto a full background on Grace Black. She is exactly who she appears to be on all fronts. A very influential and in high demand model who has been working in the business for nearly seven years. It's an impressive career if you read the stats."

"And because she's the perfect tiny pixie instead of a six-foot Amazon." Not that I had a problem with either type. I liked women in general. I liked them tall. I liked them short. I like them flat and a little curvy. I liked *women*.

"Apparently, that's added to her professional mystique. She gets chosen for a lot of 'delicate' or 'exotic' pieces, particularly with the all-natural campaigns. Not seeing exotic in her five foot two inch frame, but I can definitely see delicate and hot." Alphabet shrugged. "She's got a gorgeous body and presence and it's in nearly every image of her I could find."

The sizzle of the burgers filled the kitchen. I kept one eye on them as I set up the condiments, the various toppings for the burgers like lettuce, tomato, onions, and cheese. There was also plenty of chilis in a bowl but Voodoo was the only other one who liked them.

More for us.

"I did a cursory search for Amorette Black, also using info gathered from Gracie's background. She's an attorney, works for a law firm, a real crusader type. They're identical twins, the resemblance is uncanny—"

"If they're identical, it would be more uncanny if they didn't look alike," Voodoo stated in a droll tone. I shook my head then paused to flip the burgers.

"Regardless, they look a lot alike, they seem to dress

totally different. Kind of makes sense—look that's not the biggest problem."

"She's already gone," Bones said without waiting for Alphabet or me to fill in the blanks. "If you'd found her, you would have led with that. You're laying out the breadcrumbs so we can begin tracking, but her sister wasn't in DC and you don't know where she is or you would have shared that too."

"You're so annoying when you do that," Alphabet grunted.

"So is taking the scenic route when you wanted a fast debrief."

The two glared at each other, then Alphabet raised his hands in surrender. If I hadn't been watching him, I might have missed the way Bones seemed to force himself to relax. Everything about this situation grated on him.

Why?

"Conceded. Amorette Black is missing. No one filed a missing person's, yet. Though there have been more than a few inquiries. I'm going to guess the people calling the cops are her clients. At least based on what I could work up about the cases she was on. The best I can tell from area surveillance, she's been gone somewhere between six and eight days."

"Fuck." Voodoo dropped his chin.

"What about the law firm she works for?" Bones asked. "Why haven't they reported her missing?"

"According to them, she dropped her resignation on her desk and walked out the door without saying goodbye to anyone. If we are a client and need to arrange continued legal representation..." I recited the party line we'd gotten from four separate law firm employees.

"She lives alone," Alphabet said. "She's very active in

her community, but the places she spends her time tend to value privacy and discretion over security cameras. Most of it is domestic violence, workplace harassment, and immigration support—primarily for women, and children. She had some cases through her firm where she did the work for the firm's pro bono credits. She also does a lot more on her own time and has for years."

"So what you're telling me is the twin is a devoted advocate for abuse victims, served as her firm's PR sacrifice, and was up for sainthood in her attempt to save people, and *no one* has reported her missing? Which means no one is looking, and the one person who *would* have noticed her absence just happened to be taken by a human trafficking ring?"

When Bones put it that way, you couldn't illustrate our problems more clearly.

"There are no coincidences," Voodoo said.

"No," I said, agreeing. "Come eat. What else do we need to cover before we can let her out?"

She also needed to eat.

"I think we're going to let Miss Black cool her heels for just a bit," Bones said, without the customary bite to his words. In fact, he sounded far more circumspect. "She wants to contact her sister, for now, if we deny it, we delay her confirmation of what she's afraid of."

"She has to know." Voodoo wasn't wrong. It was why she kept bringing it up and then digging back in when we found a way to delay her.

Today? She'd crossed the imaginary goalposts that had been set and when we failed to live up to our end of the bargain?

"She knows she's missing and she's terrified of it. The first thing she's going to want is to get the cops and the

Feds involved," Voodoo continued. Since it matched my assessment, I tried not to let his sudden insight and understanding annoy me.

They had just spent twenty-four hours together. Not that much more than what Alphabet and I managed before meeting back up with them.

"Then we need answers, because letting her go to the authorities isn't going to happen." The finality of the statement made it difficult to dispute.

"Eat." I repeated before sliding a plate in front of Alphabet. I set the toppings out on a platter and let them all build their own burgers.

Bones hadn't abandoned his post, where he leaned against the pillar. The distance in his gaze told me without words that he wouldn't be eating right now.

"You sure you want to keep her up there until we have actionable intel?" Cause I wasn't sure that was a good idea. Not after everything else.

"No," Bones said. "But we have a job that's been waiting on us. We can't do anything about her problems *yet*. We can't let her make it worse for her or for us. So she can stay up there for the time being. Get your food, we need to brief on the factories."

TWENTY-SIX

GRACE

Despite the speed at which Bones ascended the stairs and the firmness in his grip, he didn't just toss me down onto the floor or the bed. He set me down, made sure I was steady on my feet and then straightened.

They were all so damn tall and with no heels, I had to settle for craning my head back to look up at him. Curling my fingers into my palms, I relied on the bite of my nails to keep me from trying to slug him.

Particularly because I wasn't sure that I would be able to do an open palmed strike. The man staring down at me wasn't furious. If anything, he was positively glacial. The hardness in his eyes contrasted with the indifference his expression seemed to suggest.

"You need to calm down," he informed me in clipped tones. "There is a restroom, a bed, and a television. In due time, we'll find you books if you require those instead. For now, I suggest you take the time to rest. When you are prepared to be more rational, we can discuss what is next."

When I was prepared to be more...

I swore, I could feel the steam building up like I was about to turn into some cartoon character and blow my stack. Not that Bones seemed to notice, he pivoted and stalked out, closing the door behind him. The decisive slide of a lock with the clicking of tumblers echoed through the room.

Not quite believing it, I walked slowly over to the door to test it. I took careful steps, not trusting my shaky legs. The door handle turned, but the door itself didn't budge. The presence of a deadbolt on an interior door didn't bode well at all. They were prepared to lock people in?

What had I said to Voodoo? *"So you guys are just my latest captors?"*

His response?

"In a manner of speaking, I suppose we are. I don't see you as a prisoner, however. You are a client, we take protection seriously. The question you have to ask yourself is how hard do you want to make all of this?"

"Really fucking hard," I muttered. When I had *clients* I worked for them. Locking me in a room didn't suggest they were working for me at all.

I rubbed a hand against my breast bone and paced over to sit on the edge of the bed. My stomach was a little sore where his shoulder had dug into my abdomen

Bruises seemed to litter my skin and I ached everywhere. The sharpness of the pain between my shoulder blades seemed the loudest and demanded the most attention.

The utter silence in the room grated on me. The focus to get where we needed to be, while also surviving the trip to get here, had kept me going from the moment they loaded us onto that bus.

It had been bait and switch all the way. First, Am didn't

show up at the girls' weekend, but I got grabbed right next to her place *before* I got up there to see if she was home.

Then, waking up in that place with the guy who was ready to rape me. Only he got beaten and then I was handed off to another. I sucked it up, focused on doing what I needed to survive.

If that meant sucking some dick, I'd suck it. All I found was that I traded one nightmare for another. The assault on the warehouse we'd been at followed by the violence of those taking the place. My would-be keeper abandoned me when panic cemented my feet to the floor.

Running my fingers through my hair, I tested the still tender spot on the back of my skull. It was where I'd hit the wall. The last thing I remembered before I woke up in the truck. That was twice I'd been knocked out? Three times? I'd lost track.

With the exception of a brief discussion with the doctor at the clinic and a morning after pill, I hadn't worried about anything else. I'd be home soon, see my own doctors, and find my sister.

Amorette was the most important piece. Calling her, making sure she was all right. If she wasn't? I needed to know that too. Trusting them with the fact I spoke English was probably my first mistake. Goblin made me trust Alphabet, and by extension Lunchbox.

Dogs were amazing and good judges of characters. Or at least, I'd told myself that. Once we got to Manhattan and I was back in my place, the exhaustion hit. Not that I was given any time to decide on what to do. Men broke into my place and if not for Lunchbox and Alphabet, I'd have been right back...

Where? The people who put me in the truck? The people in the warehouse? Somewhere else? I'd definitely traded one set of captors for another, but I'd wanted to believe that the guys were really on my side. Why else keep taking out all the people who came after me?

The world swayed and I buried my face in my hands. Almost as soon as I reached up and bent, the pain in my upper back seemed to scream. Straightening, I stared at the mirror. In the low light of the bedroom, I looked like a pale ghost, a remnant abandoned here and separated from my twin forever. The idea of existing in that world shredded me.

"Giving up? That's not you." Amorette leaned in the door frame.

"Who said I was giving up?" I glanced at her in the mirror. I'd been standing in front of the full length mirror with a pair of dresses I was deciding on.

The look in her eyes didn't fool me. Yes, she was worried about me, but she still wanted me to call the cops. She perched on the edge of my bed. "You sounded pretty defeated when you came." And she was here to give me a pep talk.

"I sounded pissed when I came in." Discarding the dresses into the stack on the chair with the other leftovers, I backed up to sit next to her. "I was pissed. I went to that party because the client invited us. Eleanor was tied up with work and I didn't think I needed a chaperone or protection—it was all the girls on the shoot. There were easily a dozen of us."

I wasn't going to get over feeling stupid anytime soon. I'd always been so careful since starting this career. Question and clarify everything. Assume nothing.

"Grace," Amorette wrapped an arm around me and tucked her chin on my shoulder. "You weren't dumb."

The fact she answered the internal doubt first had me sniffly.

"You weren't," she stressed the last word. "You didn't go off with someone on your own. You had access to your own trans-

portation. You let others know where you were. When you saw something you said something."

The vehemence in each statement demanded I listen to her.

"Then you got yourself out of there. Your pride might be tweaked and you have every right to feel mistreated, but you did nothing wrong."

I blew out a breath, letting go of that fear. I pressed my head to hers as she wrapped her other arm around me. With our gazes locked in the mirror, I couldn't hide my relief. "Doesn't always feel that way."

"I know. That's why I'm here to remind you." She smiled and I gripped her forearm, holding it as I blinked back the tears. "I just wish you would file the police report. I know you said nothing might come of it. But something could. If nothing else, you document it. That's how criminals get away with things, the lack of a paper trail."

She was winding herself up, but damn if I didn't love that about her too. "I know, you said that when I came in. But I called Eleanor when I was on the subway. She's more pissed than either of us. Maybe I don't have a legal case but Eleanor won't leave them with legs."

"I do like her," Amorette said. "I wouldn't want her angry at me."

"So you've said," I teased her, then sighed. "Thanks, Am."

"Always. You good now?"

"Another minute?" Sometimes I forgot just how nice a hug was.

"All the time you need," she promised.

The memory left me with more tears as I stared at myself in a different mirror without my sister right there. If Am were here right now, she'd be raging. She'd tear a strip off the guys downstairs. She would so have my back every step of the way.

I would have hers too, no matter what those men down there thought.

"No." I'd done everything right. I'd believed the people my rescuers entrusted me to. I agreed to the conditions. I trusted their word on what was required. Only to find, what? Their word meant nothing? The discussion was over before it began.

Absolutely not. If they wouldn't listen to me, then I would just make some different decisions. Period. Pushing to my feet, I turned in a full circle, studying the room and what was in it. The study turned into a full search.

I went through the bathroom, the cupboards, and the walk-in closet. The latter had clothes in here that seemed to be around my size, along with matching shoes. The closet was relatively empty based on its size.

In the bathroom drawers, I found razors for shaving, nail clippers, a manicure kit, some clips for hair. Everything looked brand new and fresh out of a package. Other drawers had different types of toiletries, and supplies.

There was a brand new plunger in the corner by the toilet. Heavy wooden handle, not some cheap plastic thing. I took it, along with the metal nail file I'd acquired. I scored large in the closet corner—ironing board *and* iron. I took the iron with me, it could work as a makeshift hammer.

The bedroom itself had fewer useful items than the bathroom. That was fine. With the door locked, I went to the windows. A wall of windows looked out over the landscape. The wide open field that dipped over the rise. What I couldn't tell was whether that was where this part of the mountain ended or if there was more land.

The wide wall had six total windows, allowing for a mostly panoramic view. They could be opened from the bottom and there were some standard blocks in the window path to keep them from going up too high.

Sensors were in place along the edge of each window where it connected to the base. Wired to an alarm. That made sense. Second floor windows may not be as easy as first floor windows, but you could still climb up here.

Opening them could set off an alarm.

I backed up to look at the top of the windows—they also opened. But it wasn't a raise or lower. It was a tilt to let fresh air in. Those were usually harder to get in and out of, not a lot of room.

Sucking up the irritation, I dragged the armchair over to the corner on the far side of the windows and with some effort, tugged the night stand over. The dresser would be better, but it wouldn't budge and my back screamed when I tried it.

The night stand was a little taller. If it didn't work, I'd go for the ironing board. Climbing up, I scanned the edge of the window, everywhere I could see. Nothing looked obvious, so I used the plunger handle to push the lever to release the window and it took a couple of hard tries and then it let out a hiss of air as the lock gave.

I had to go grab a couple of hangers from the closet, but soon I was back and used two interlocked to hook into the open lip and then tug the window inward. The cooler air rushing in tasted sweet and clean. It was a rush as the accomplishment washed through me.

The burn between my shoulders wasn't getting better. Worth it to get the window open. I eyed it, then down, then up...

I was pretty sure I could get through that opening. I could just pull the window wider, at least it was hinged to open inwards instead of outwards. I shot a look at the door then back to the window.

I set the other items down and then wrapped one hand over the edge of the window, I swung over like it was gonna hang from it and gripped it with the other hand. It gave a millimeter more.

So I jerked on it, swinging my feet a little.

Come on. I didn't need it to give that much, just an inch. It gave me a millimeter, I needed another inch. Bobbing, I shook and the window let out an ominous creak.

The sudden drop as it bent inwards and startled me. I managed to land on the edge of the chair and then my knees without rocking the whole chair. I split my attention between the door and the window.

No alarm.

No running feet.

This was a good sign. With care, I got the ironing board out then used it to prop against the top of the chair and the dresser. It would get me up higher.

That was all I would need.

Not giving myself time to think about it, I climbed up, grabbed the edge and scooted with a shove upwards. Going out face first probably wasn't the best move, but I'd work with what I had and hope I could either reach the roof or a ledge once I was out there.

A single-story drop wouldn't kill me, right?

TWENTY-SEVEN

ALPHABET

My leg ached, I'd been pushing it a lot over the past few days. Lunchbox had suggested I sit out the flight and I'd ignored him. I didn't need to run to be backup. After the number of ambushes we'd faced already in securing Grace Black, I didn't want to leave anything to chance.

"We've been asked to accelerate on the next job," Bones said. The debrief with regard to Grace had been swift. Probably wise, considering the dark looks being exchanged between Bones and Voodoo. "The request was made when you two were taking Miss Black home. There didn't seem to be any reason to *not* agree."

I wasn't thrilled with Bones just hauling her upstairs and securing her for the moment. Understanding the necessity, considering she'd gotten so angry, didn't preclude understanding her position. We'd told her we would let her get in touch with her sister.

But we didn't know where the sister was. Not yet. I had feelers out, but there were so many different trafficking groups in the world. She could literally be held by any of them.

I'd sent a message to Doc about the crew running the truck they'd found Grace on. If the answers were out there, we would find them. Unfortunately, it was going to take time. We needed to find a way to explain it to Grace.

"That's a bad idea right now," Lunchbox said when Bones took a beat.

I didn't disagree with Lunchbox's assessment. The factory job required transport, infiltration, exfiltration, and then demolition. The kind of job we excelled at, truthfully, save for a couple of potential snags.

"It's on foreign soil," Lunchbox continued. "We have Grace here now. We can't keep her locked up while we're on a job for three to five days."

"That's a generous estimate," Voodoo said. "They aren't just moving this job up by a couple of weeks, we were supposed to have another two months. I've got feelers out there but I haven't really been prepping this job. That would mean on the fly changes and working in less than optimal conditions."

"We've done more with less." Despite his lack of inflection, I didn't think Bones was any happier with this scenario than we were. "That may be the only option open to us."

"Unless we just refund their money and tell them to fuck off," I suggested. "They've only done a deposit." We were still in the process of cleaning that deposit. "Moving the job up, changing the timetable—there are penalties they are going to incur because our risk versus reward is going to be skewed."

Could we do it? Absolutely. Did I want to right now?

No.

Goblin shifted to sit up and he put his head against my leg. I scratched him gently between the eyes. The action soothed some of the irritation scraping along the inside of my skin. Sitting through a debrief while Grace was left to stew in her room didn't appeal to me.

"That's an option," Bones said, finally, addressing my suggestion.

"But you don't like it." Lunchbox had set out the platters of burgers. I'd put one together but I wasn't feeling much like eating. Though I did slide Goblin a burger of his own. Lunchbox nudged my plate toward me. "You need to take something for that leg. So eat."

"Yeah, yeah." I waved him off. My phone gave a mild vibration. Maybe one of my searches had turned something up. I'd left the Beast running several programs—including some searches on Grace, her sister, and the people around them. You didn't just pick a model of Grace's caliber, or a lawyer like Amorette Black, out of catalog.

Most women sucked into human trafficking vanished into a deep, dark hole and never emerged. The targets were most often going to be women who were not going to be missed. Those with families, social ties, and professional connections generally had folks to make noise.

Grace Black had an international following. No way they could make her disappear without causing a stir. So, who from their lives was *involved* in their disappearances? Were they linked? Or was it something from one of their lives bleeding over onto the other's?

No coincidences was a solid theory. I wanted facts.

The alert on my phone, however, was not from the Beast's search programs. No, it was a motion detector. Probably elk or moose wandering through. It happened. Occasionally, we got bears.

We left them alone, they left us alone.

Tapping the alert, I blinked as the camera view loaded. It was always a few seconds of delay before it came into focus. The side of the house was visible. Part of the fence line. No animals were around.

Rabbits didn't usually trigger the motion sensors. It needed to be larger and more solid.

"No," Bones said with a sigh before he pinched the bridge of his nose. Everything about him radiated dislike and impatience. Whether it was for Grace, the situation, or something else entirely, was to be determined. "I don't. We cultivated our reputation for a reason. They passed all their background checks, right?"

When he flicked a look to me, I shrugged. "Yes. But I still have one more deep dive to do that I thought we had a couple of months on. I can switch some bots from their current project after we get the first info dump."

It was hardly an impossible task. I could repurpose some of the searches to work on them then go back to searching for the sister. Without finding answers, we couldn't give them to Grace.

"How fast do they want us to accelerate the op?" Voodoo moved to the table and started putting two burgers together.

"This weekend," Bones said.

I wasn't the only one who snapped a look up at him. "That's incredibly and suspiciously accelerated, did they give you a reason why?"

"Elections are coming up in the country. They want the factories shut down, completely, and *erased*, before voting opens."

The alert vibrated my phone again and I dropped my

gaze to the open screen that let me see the side of the house. Maybe the motion sensor was malfuncti—

"I'm not sure I want to do any job for anyone that changes mid-stream to emergency because they want something gone before an election. It feels…"

"Dirty," Voodoo supplied the word when Lunchbox drifted off. "I get not everywhere works like here, but when you want to bury something like it never happened—that suggests coverup and conspiracy. Do we want to be in bed with these people?"

"We don't have to be in bed with them to do the job," Bones reminded us. "No innocents are involved."

"Allegedly," I reminded him. "We don't have confirmation."

"They are drug processing," Bones continued.

"Again, allegedly."

"We don't have confirmation," he said before I could and I met the impatience in his gaze with a shrug. "We need confirmation before we agree to move on anything."

"Safer that way," Lunchbox said and there was no mistaking the ease in his tone as he blew out a breath. "Maybe they really need the rush, but we risk too many mistakes if we do. So—we tell them we'll amend the timetable, but we will decide when, and if that isn't suitable…" It was his turn to shrug.

"Then fuck them," Voodoo said. "We have plenty of other jobs. Not to mention, Firecracker is here. We can't just leave her locked up while we leave the country."

"I wasn't planning on leaving her locked up," Bones said with a sigh. "We will need a backup plan for her though. Especially now that she's here."

Here. At our place. Where we never brought anyone.

Lips pursed, I stared at the screen and found the source of the movement pissing off the motion sensor. "Probably a good plan, since she doesn't seem to have any intentions of staying in her room either."

"What?" Bones frowned. Voodoo abandoned the food he was building to move over to where I was staring at my phone. I had to zoom in, but there she was, wiggling that tiny body right out of the hopper window.

"Is she..." Lunchbox said slowly, staring down at the image. She was damn near out, moving slow and steady. Which was good, because she was looking for somewhere to grab onto.

"Yes, our *client*," I said, stressing the last word with all the irritation I felt, "is trying to climb, headfirst, out of a window on the second floor to escape."

The flat look in Bones' eyes didn't shift. The captain was a good man. He'd always been an excellent soldier. He looked after his team. Somehow, I didn't think he'd ever had to deal with someone like Grace.

She slid downward, but then twisted to catch the lip of the window before swinging her legs free. My gut didn't like the drop it experienced at her swing.

"Are we just watching her?" Voodoo demanded. "She could tear that damn wound open."

"If we interrupt now," Lunchbox mused, "she could slip and fall."

As if inspired by his comment, she did slip. I gritted my teeth as she caught herself with two tiny feet on the damn near invisible ledge formed by the house design. She was pressed right up to the building, flattened to it.

"We should go get her," I said. Because I wasn't really sure I could take watching her fumble this anymore. A single story fall could kill her if she landed wrong. Even if it didn't, those were injuries she didn't need to take.

"Fuck," Bones swore, then pushed away from the table. Voodoo was one step behind him as they headed outside. Lunchbox waited for me. The limp slowed me some, but the more I moved the easier it became. Goblin trotted along with us.

The wind picked up, swirling in from the northwest. It was mostly overcast at the moment, but the clouds were much darker in the west. Probably a storm rolling through. Bones and Voodoo were just below where she was.

"Maybe we should go up and open the windows from there?" I murmured. Getting her down would be tricky.

"Probably not the worst idea," Lunchbox said. "Definitely not the best." He bypassed the others and went for the drain gutter that ran down one of the corners. He climbed it like it was one of the old obstacles during boot.

She noticed us about the time he started up, and she twisted to look—then teetered some before flattening herself against the glass again. Good girl.

"Gracie," I called, buying Lunchbox some time. "Whatcha doing?"

"Getting some fresh air," she retorted in a salty tone that made me grin. "What are you doing?"

Bones opened his mouth, but I cut in before he could say whatever remark he had in mind. "Came out for a walk. Wanna go with me and Goblin?"

"Sure," she responded. "Just give me a minute to figure out how to make my way down."

Lunchbox was almost there, edging along the building in free climb like it was nothing.

"Hey, Gracie," he said, not trying to pitch his voice quieter. "Looking for a ride?"

"Not really," she said. "Thought I could do this on my own, but...it's a lot farther to the ground than I thought it was."

"Right." He glanced from her to the ground, then to me. Voodoo was already studying their location.

"Handoff," Voodoo called.

Agreed. It would be the easiest way to get her down without further injuring her.

"Gracie, I need you to listen to me. We're going to get you down, but to do that, you have to follow instructions to the letter. Are you good for that? Or do you need an alternative?"

"And how is your back after your wonder wiggle?" Voodoo added.

"It's sore, but all of me is sore."

I did not like that answer.

"Yes, I can follow instructions."

"All evidence to the contrary," Bones said.

"Tell you what, Bones," she snapped over her shoulder. "Why don't you take your emotional overreactions and shove them up your ass?"

It took discipline to *not* laugh aloud. Voodoo didn't even bother to disguise his amusement. "You tell him, Firecracker. Now, Lunchbox is going to take your hand, you're going to hold on tight to his hand with both of yours and then he's going to lower you. You will fall—but not far and I'm right here."

"Oh shit." The shudder in those two syllables translated clearly. "Can I go back in through the window?"

"Maybe you should have thought of that first," Bones suggested.

"Shut up," I said in the same voice as Lunchbox, and the captain scowled at me. Ignoring him for now, I added,

"Gracie, just let Lunchbox do the work. You relax. Don't tense up—and yes I know that sounds easier said than done. Just grip and let him do it. Trust us."

Silence greeted those last two words and I winced.

"You lied to me before."

"We didn't lie," I promised her. "The situation changed. Intelligence is still being gathered. We should have explained it better."

"We can work on that 'explanation' after we get you down," Bones tacked on. "If you're ready to cooperate."

"Bite. Me." The vehemence in those two words had Lunchbox chuckling.

"Take my hand, Gracie, I won't let you get hurt." It wasn't about falling, cause she would have to drop some, but we would make sure she landed fine.

Goblin had gone incredibly tense next to me. We were both laser focused on what was going on above.

She said something that I couldn't hear as she focused on Lunchbox but then she took his hand, he locked his around hers then she was covering his hand with her free one.

"Hang tight," he said, then he dangled her over the edge. He didn't take his time or go too slow. Speed was on our side in this maneuver. Then he let go and dropped, only to grip the ledge they'd been standing on with his free hand.

It took a lot of control and there would have been a definite jolt. But she was a lot closer to the ground and Voodoo was right below her.

"I got you," he promised her again.

"Okay," she agreed in a shaky voice. Lunchbox didn't let her rethink it because he dropped her the four feet to land in Voodoo's arms.

Then, Lunchbox dropped after Voodoo backed away, still holding her bridal style. Relief raced through me.

"So," Voodoo said, pivoting to head back to the door. "Lunchbox made burgers. Are you hungry?"

TWENTY-EIGHT

GRACE

Voodoo carried me into the house, not setting me on my feet until we were inside. Then he pointed me to the sink and hovered as I washed my hands. There were scrapes on my palms. After taking a moment to study them, Voodoo hummed under his breath.

"I don't think we'll need to bandage them. Do us a favor, though, Firecracker, heal before you get hurt again?"

"Funny," I deadpanned. "I'm totally laughing on the inside."

"I'm glad you find this entertaining," Bones responded in a cool tone. Clean dish towel in hand, I pivoted to face him while I dried my hands.

I thought of and discarded a dozen responses, then just looked at Voodoo. "Why can't I have a phone?"

He didn't answer immediately. The glances exchanged between the others wasn't lost on me, but I kept my attention on Voodoo. Did I think intimacy earned me any answers?

No.

Did I think I could leverage it?

Maybe.

"This is really simple, answer the question or just take me back to that airport and drop me off. I'll figure out where I'm going from there."

"That can't happen," Lunchbox said, arms folded. "Before you start throwing things... we have our reasons."

"I'm very happy for you," I said as I pivoted to face him. The fact he'd climbed right up there and gotten me down wasn't lost on me. All of them had saved me over the past few days. "What are your *reasons*? I think I have a right to know that much."

"Maybe." He didn't glance at Bones but it seemed present regardless.

"Firecracker," Voodoo slid an arm around me, but I sidestepped away, shrugging off the contact.

"Don't try to handle me," I ordered, maneuvering so I didn't have one of them behind me. "If you don't want to or are not *willing* to answer me, fine. It's a free country—most of the time. But if that is the case, then I'll just go. I'm not your problem."

"You're not a problem, Gracie," Alphabet said as he shifted his stance. There was a flicker of discomfort across his face, but he braced a hand on the back of a chair. When I opened my mouth to argue, he raised his free hand. "I know, we've lost some ground in the trust department. But Voodoo was putting together a burger for you. Lunchbox cooked it and his burgers are pretty much next level. Maybe come sit and eat?"

Did the burgers smell good? Absolutely. My stomach twisted at the allure, but we didn't have time for that right now.

"Then what?" I shifted my gaze from Alphabet to Voodoo to Lunchbox and then back. I skipped right past Bones. If I never spoke to him again, it might be too soon. "You delay again? Or you shove me in another room? Maybe I'll get chained to another wall somewhere?"

It would hardly be new in this current experience. The circular bruise around my ankle and around my wrist were both clearly visible, even if they were varying shades of green, blue, and black. As many body aches as I had and as sore as my back was, I really couldn't feel the others anymore.

"We haven't chained you to anything," Voodoo said firmly. Dislike licked every single syllable. "You have every right to be angry. I did tell you that we would take care of it and I haven't changed my mind."

"But?" Because that unspoken word hung heavily in the air.

"But the situation has changed," Lunchbox said, picking up the thread from Voodoo. "The burgers are still warm and it would probably help if you ate."

I was going to scream. They weren't *listening* to me. "I want to leave."

None of them moved. Unsurprising.

"Gracie..." Alphabet said before he limped closer to the table and dragged a chair out. "Come on, come sit. You're pissed and you're frustrated. You're probably tired and in pain. Sit down, eat the food, let us try to explain this to you."

Twisting slowly, I stared at him. Some distant part of my mine said play along, lull them into compliance, then just go when the opportunity presented itself.

But I *was* tired.

I was *frustrated.*

Yeah boy, you betcha, I was furious.

"I want to leave," I repeated then pivoted to face Voodoo and Lunchbox. Neither man said anything.

"The answer to leaving is no," Bones said, interjecting into the conversation. "Now *sit down* so that Alphabet will."

The snap of command made me jump, but Bones wasn't looking at me, he was staring at Alphabet, who had two hands now on the back of the chair he'd pulled out for me.

It killed me to follow that order, but Alphabet's white knuckles and tense expression had my feet moving before I processed the fullness of Bones' statement.

I dropped into the chair. "Happy?"

"Delirious." You could have etched wood with the sarcasm in his voice.

Alphabet moved to sit in the chair to my left. There was an untouched burger in front of him. The minute he sat, the other three shifted, with Voodoo taking the seat opposite and sliding one of the two burgers in front of him over. There were condiments and toppings present.

I didn't want any of them.

The fact Bones yanked out a chair opposite Alphabet and sat seemed to let some of the ballooning tension out. Lunchbox returned with beers, water, and juice. He eyed me briefly, then the drinks.

"The water is fine," I said, then because I could probably catch more flies with honey than vinegar, I added, "Thank you."

"You want ice? Or a glass?" It was a nice gesture.

"The bottle is fine. I'm really not that high maintenance."

"Could have fooled me," Bones muttered and then his chair jerked and Bones glared at Voodoo.

"Ignore him, he hasn't slept and he's being a dick."

Voodoo nodded to the burger. "Let me know if you want us to warm that up or add anything else to it."

As much as I didn't want to eat, I took a bite just to shut them up about the food. Lunchbox came back with a second bottle of water, then passed the drinks out before he took the chair next to me.

The rectangle shape of the table left plenty of room. I was kind of surprised anyone took *my* side. Unless it was just to make sure I couldn't get away.

All four men were silent while I chewed the first bite. Then I took a second. The burger was actually pretty good. It wasn't too hot, but it was still warm and it was juicy. It was just a little on the medium-rare side of medium, which was also good.

Alphabet let out a sigh before he took a bite of his own food. One by one, the others dug in and ate or added stuff to their burgers and then ate.

About halfway through mine, I nudged the plate aside and took a long drink of the water. My stomach had cramped when I smelled it, now I felt almost too full. Painfully full.

"You want something else?" Lunchbox asked and I shook my head.

"No, I haven't been eating that much." If at all really. "Except what you guys have given me. That's making my stomach hurt."

"Take it easy then," Voodoo suggested. "You probably need smaller meals more frequently."

"I can take care of that," Lunchbox said and I sighed.

"Please... just tell me what's going on. If you really are my new captors, I'd rather just know that and as more than just a passing conversation." I flicked a look at Voodoo. "If it's something else, I'd like to know that too."

A cool nose bumped at my arm and I glanced down to where Goblin stared up at me. As soon as I moved my arm, he tucked his head against my thigh. With care, I scratched him gently between the ears before stroking down his back. The short hair was almost downy and soft. Had someone given him a bath? Or had I just not noticed before?

The contact helped ease some of the internal shaking that seemed to worsen by every passing moment. It didn't do anything for the headache forming behind my right eye or the urge to cry. I fought both, because I really didn't want to add tears to the whole situation.

The silence elongated to the point I thought they were just not going to answer me at all. Glancing up from where I'd been staring at Goblin, I found Alphabet, Lunchbox, and Voodoo all staring at Bones.

The fourth man sighed, then cut a hand through the air. "Tell her."

A wave of dread hit me at the resignation in his response. Whatever it was, it was going to be bad. The other three were not in a rush to say anything, and I had to fight to keep my hand steady as I pet Goblin, rather than fisting his coat.

"I can't find your sister," Alphabet said, finally and I whipped my attention to him. "I started the search yesterday. I've found her records, verified her ID, you're right, you're identical. We put calls into her law firm, I also checked the status of her apartment's lease and her bank account."

There was invasive and then there was...

"You said you couldn't find *her*," I tried to speak around the bitter taste those words left on my tongue. "You found everything else?"

"Essentially. She's been gone for at least a week that I can account for."

"So her law firm has already filed a missing person's report? They're lawyers, they always know how to work with cops." That was Am in a nutshell even before she passed the bar. If an attorney from her firm went missing, she'd probably be the first one to call the cops.

"Alphabet called them," Lunchbox said. "So did I, two separate times, two separate reasons, they gave us the same answer."

I cut my gaze back and forth between Alphabet and Lunchbox.

"They indicated she no longer worked there, that she'd sent in her resignation rather abruptly. When I pressed, saying I was a client," Alphabet continued. "All they would say was that her departure from the firm was unexpected and they didn't have a forwarding address or contact info."

"That's bullshit." I whispered the words, but there was just no way.

"I didn't say it was true," Alphabet told me, leaning forward and folding his arms together on the table edge. "To be frank, they wouldn't just give out that kind of information to anyone. They didn't even ask for a number to have another attorney get back to us. The thing is… there's a party line and a united front. It's even in the firm's electronic records. Their human resources manager noted her abrupt resignation and added no rehire to her file."

I sat back against the chair abruptly. The bump jolted the cut in my back but I didn't care. "Why would they lie…?"

"That, Miss Black," Bones said in those arctic cool tones, "is what we will have to find out. However, based on *your* experiences and the resemblance to your sister, she is most likely with similar human traffickers."

My stomach bottomed out.

"Captain," Lunchbox said with a sigh. "She gets it."

"No," Bones said evenly, not once taking his cutting gaze off of me. "She doesn't." While that may not have been pointed at me, he never looked away. "You really don't. You think, first of all, that you have some say in what happens next. You don't. You think you can just leave when you want. You can't. You might even be considering how to smother me in my sleep so that you can seduce these three idiots into doing what you want..."

"Hey," Alphabet snapped and Goblin made a quiet noise of complaint. I forced my hand to open since I'd started digging my fingers in.

"The point, Miss Black. You can't. We *will* help you. We *will* continue the search. However, that will have to continue in the background. *If* we get actionable intel, we'll make our calls then."

Loss and anger vied for top position in the tempest surging through me. Fighting tears was growing almost impossibly difficult. "And I'm supposed to just agree to all of this?"

"There is no choice for you to agree or disagree. This is the situation."

"So, I am a prisoner?"

"Guest," Alphabet said with another dark look at Bones. "You're not a prisoner." He sighed and shook his head. "Gracie, there is a lot I would like to just explain to you. To help you to understand. Right now, I can't. Because we've already compromised you by bringing you here."

"To your house?" I swiped at the tears that tried to escape. "I didn't ask for this. I didn't want to come here."

"We know," Voodoo offered those two words with an element of apology. "That doesn't change the outcome. You're here. That means you have to stay here or with us. For *now...*" On the last word, he shot a glare at Bones then refocused on me. "If we tell you any more, we will make all of this worse."

A huff of disbelief escaped me. "You can't let me go because you decided to help me and bring me here. But you can't help right now because you have something else to do and... I can't leave because I've seen here. If that's true— then it's going to be true *when*"—I absolutely refused to say *if*—"we find Amorette." I swallowed around that lump in my throat. "What *then?*"

"Then we'll find out," Bones said. "Whether you like the answers or not, now you have them. Continuing to ask will not change them."

"You're such an asshole," I told him as I shoved my chair back. Fortunately, Goblin had already retreated as I stood. A prick of guilt hit me for not thinking of him.

"Where are you going?" Alphabet asked.

"No where," I said. "Apparently."

I left them at the table with their food, their drink, and their secrets. I took one of the bottles of water with me as I retraced Bones' earlier path to get back to "my" room.

The deadbolt was just a twist. I had to stretch to slide the bolt out of the lock at the top and the bottom. Did they think I was going to break it down or something?

Shoving the door open, I returned to the room with the open window letting in the breeze and my view of *nothing* but the horizon to remind of the current facts.

They had me.

They weren't going to let me go.

What about Amorette? Would they *really* look for her?

Somehow, I didn't think I'd ever know, cause they'd never let me leave to do anything about it.

Closing the door, I headed over to the big bed. I curled up on my side, tucking my head to the pillow. Gradually, I lost the war with my tears, but I didn't let my sobs out. The tears could go, but I wasn't going to sob until I found Amorette.

TWENTY-NINE

I hadn't meant to sleep, but I'd apparently passed out. When I woke, someone had put a blanket over me and there was a glass of water on the nightstand. There was also a bottle of—

Rubbing a hand against my face, I grimaced at the residual bruising still there. I kept forgetting that one guy hit me in the face. I should probably check the mirror and make sure it was healing.

Sitting up, I squinted at the bottle. It wasn't just hard to read because I was tired, I needed to turn on the light. Damn, I was foggy. It was like I couldn't quite catch my brain up to being awake. With care, I flicked on the light and then eyed the bottle again.

Pain relievers.

There was a second bottle on the nightstand, another bottle of pain relievers. A sticky note in front of them had neat handwriting.

Take two from the blue bottle and one from the yellow. It will help with the pain and the inflammation. We also need to check your back when you get up.

No signature on the note. I read the bottles. They looked like what they said they were, so I followed the instructions, then washed them down. All at once, I felt scummy.

I needed a shower.

I needed clean clothes.

I needed coffee.

Rising, I stretched slowly and tried to ignore the protests in every muscle. I'd been still for too long. The window I'd levered open had been closed and the curtains drawn. No wonder it was so dark.

With one hand, I pulled back the curtain to look outside. It was a grayish light. Dawn, I guessed. Letting it fall back into place, I went to the closet to investigate the clothes. I found a shirt and leggings, they were close enough to my size.

There were no underthings, but I found some in a drawer in the dresser. All sealed in packages—so new and not used. Nothing fancy, just sports bras and boy shorts in super soft material, or so the details claimed.

Showering took a little longer than I wanted to admit. The supplies were all basic, but I made do with the shampoo and conditioner. The hardest part was raising my arms. I did it gradually, using the hot water to warm my muscles up.

Sadly, I was fucking exhausted by the end of the shower, but I was clean and I felt *better*. The weariness sweeping through me was harder to ignore than I liked. Washing my hair hadn't been comfortable, but I'd gotten it done.

After toweling off, I studied myself in the mirror. Bruises littered my skin like I'd rolled in some dusty ink somewhere. There was a new one on my cheek. It was a bit swollen, but I hadn't even noticed that one with the rest.

I was one long ache. This was not something a hot shower could just wash away. The smudges below my eyes were dark and my eyes puffy. It gave me a hollow look that photographers hated.

If I had the right cosmetics, I could probably cover it all up. Right now, as much as my looks were my livelihood, I really couldn't give a damn about them. The bruises would heal, and it wasn't like I was going to be doing a photo shoot anytime soon.

I hung up one towel, and then eased the one off my hair with care. I found a wide-toothed comb and went to work easing it through the strands. I had some knots in places. Nothing to be done for those but tease them out. The heavy conditioner helped.

Combing it in the shower would have been better but I only had so much energy. When I was done, I planted my hands on the counter and leaned there. I could probably go collapse all over again.

Several long, deep breaths brought the harsh hammer of my heart back to something normal and let me straighten up. I was *exhausted*, but I didn't have time for it. I sat on the cold toilet lid to pull on the panties and the leggings. The bra was a tad harder but I made it work, one arm at a time.

The t-shirt wrapped like a soft hug around me. The clothes were a little on the big side. But they weren't falling down. I'd take it. Done, I rose and reached for the door to the bathroom.

Voodoo stood in the middle of the bedroom, arms folded and chin tucked. He cut a look up at me as I opened the door. "Good morning, Firecracker."

"Morning." I didn't really think "good" applied. "Can I help you?"

"I want to look at your back, if you don't mind."

I sighed. "I wish I'd known that before I put on the shirt."

"It was on the note," he said as a faint smile creased his lips. "Don't worry, I can help."

He'd already had an eyeful, as well as a handful, of my breasts so it wasn't just about getting me naked. I pushed the bathroom door back so it was wider before I withdrew back into the bathroom. I also flicked the lights back on.

Facing the mirror, I gave him my back. "How do you want me?"

"This counter would be nice," he murmured, reaching past me to tap the marble top. "It's the right height.

Heat scorched through my system like a match set against so much dry kindling. I cut my gaze up to meet his in the mirror. The darkness of his eyes could be unsettling. They looked black, but the brown was just so deep you couldn't see where the pupils ended. The colors just seemed to flow into the other.

"Are your eyes why they call you Voodoo?" The question probably sounded like it came out of nowhere. He raised his brows as he hooked his fingers under the edge of my t-shirt.

"Let me do the work," he said in a low voice that added another flash fire of heat to my system. He'd wanted to do all the work before and that had been... I shivered. His lips curved a little higher. No way he missed my reaction.

He lifted the shirt easily, gliding it up until he could tuck it over my shoulders. I braced my hands on the counter. My palms still had light scrapes on them and coolness felt good against the raw skin.

"Bra next."

"Yippee," I murmured, but he was already lifting the back away from my skin and then up until it was also tucked over the shirt. One of my breasts popped free, but the other was cold. The flush of chilly air had my nipples tightening.

It had nothing to do with the extremely tall, sexy man who had his hands on me. That was my story and I was sticking with it.

"Not seeing a lot of bleeding through on the gauze," Voodoo said, his tone still warm if settling into something a little more professional. "You good with me changing the bandage?"

"If I said no, would you stop?" I lifted my gaze to meet his in the mirror again.

"Yes." The lack of hesitation and the single syllable answer with no qualifiers eased some of my objections.

My stomach made a faint gurgling noise as it curled over itself. I was actually hungry, but I really wanted coffee.

"Then I'm fine with you checking it. I'd rather know it was healing." I licked my lips. "But can we do it quickly?"

"We can. Let me grab the kit." He retreated from the bathroom, but returned swiftly with the box that reminded me of one that stored someone's fishing tackle. It had a lot of trays and options inside. I studied the contents as he raised the trays and then pulled out what he needed.

Fresh gauze. A clear patch to put over the gauze. Skin glue. What looked like antiseptic or antibiotic ointment. Maybe both. Once he had it all laid out, he used the antiseptic—ah it was alcohol—to loosen the adhesive and peel the patch there off.

It didn't even sting.

The gauze came next. There was dried blood on it, but not a lot. He snapped on gloves before he explored the area around the wound. It was definitely sore and uncomfortable. I hissed twice when he applied some pressure.

"Not a lot of heat. The skin looks flushed, but it's not angry. The swelling has gone down and so far, it looks like the skin glue is holding. Your escapade out the window doesn't seem to have done any damage. Just gonna dab this up, and seal it back closed. We'll let it heal from here."

That was all good news. His movements were steady, quick, and efficient. The tenderness around the wound itself had me wincing, but he didn't touch it more than necessary. Once he had the tape in place, he pulled my bra back down slowly. His attention flicked back to me in the mirror.

"Can you get your breast or would you like me to take care of that too?" The deadpanned delivery robbed it of any sarcasm, but not the heat flashing in his eyes.

"You'd do it, too, wouldn't you?" Playing with fire?

"Yes," he said. "But only with your permission."

"I have a feeling if you touch my breast, we won't be leaving this bathroom any time soon." How did I feel about that? Regretful? Maybe a little. At the same time...

"You need to eat and I *do* have some self-control." He almost sounded chiding, but when I raised my hand and nudged my breast back under the fabric of the bra, he tracked the movement with an expression that had my pussy clenching around the emptiness. It was a reminder of how much he'd filled me and how much I'd like to do that again.

Fuck. I really would like a repeat of the experience. Maybe with a little more active participation my part.

"Maybe next time," I said, trying to make it sound far more noncommittal than I was.

"I'll hold you to that," he said, his faint smile still present. "Hell, I'll hold you anyway you want."

Damn, if those words didn't trigger a wild flutter in my

belly. The man was far too damn tempting by half. He settled my shirt back into place and stayed there for a beat longer before he moved to close the kit and clean up the trash.

"Hungry?" The casual question was nowhere near as relaxed or informal as he tried to sound.

"Starving," I admitted. "I'd also kill for coffee."

"Well, if something needs to die for it," he said in a droll tone. "I'll take care of it."

Arms folded, I followed him out of the bathroom and to the door. "Sucking up?"

He snorted. "Trust me, Firecracker, when I'm sucking on you for anything, you'll know all about it." The deliberate wink just added to the wildfire swirling in my system.

"Flirt."

The low chuckle he released was every bit as decadent as the sensual promise in his words. "You like it."

As much as I should dispute that charge, I couldn't. I did like it. These guys were frustrating as hell and this situation was kind of a nightmare. At the same time? I was attracted to Voodoo in a way I hadn't experienced in a long time.

A very long time.

"You didn't answer my earlier question," I said as he began to descend the steps ahead of me.

"Funny," he commented. "You're right. I didn't."

Probably didn't intend to answer it. To my surprise, we were not the only ones awake. Or maybe it shouldn't have startled me so much. The other three were in the kitchen.

The scents of bacon, toast, and coffee competed to tempt me to head right over and just start eating at the stove. I had some manners though.

"Good morning, Gracie," Lunchbox said as Goblin lifted

his head to look at me. "Have a seat. I'll grab your coffee for you. Five minutes until food. How do you like your eggs?"

"Over medium," I said slowly. "And thank you."

"You're welcome," he responded easily enough even as he crossed over to set the coffee in front of me. "Once we've eaten, we'll brief you on what's happening next."

I blinked at him slowly. Brief me?

Curiosity speared through me and I kind of wanted the answers now. Voodoo grabbed his own coffee then pulled out the chair next to me. Alphabet saluted me sleepily with his coffee and Bones just ignored all of us, his attention focused on the tablet in his hand.

"Okay," I said, after debating and discarding a half-dozen other responses.

That earned me looks from three of the four Musketeers in the room. The fourth one didn't look up from his reading at all.

Voodoo gave me a hard stare and I lifted my coffee cup. "What? He said you would brief me. I'm willing to wait a few minutes for that."

It was about the only concession I was willing to make right now.

Hopefully, they had better answers than the ones they offered me the day before.

THIRTY

GRACE

We were on their plane again. They had gear stowed in the back. The bags they'd offloaded from the car looked a great deal heavier than what we'd come back with, not that anyone told me what was in them.

"This bag," Voodoo had said, "has your gear in it." Fortunately, that duffel didn't look near as large or as heavy as the others.

"I have gear?" That was news to me.

"Yes," Bones said. "You can go over it later. We'll finish the brief in the air." The dismissive notes in his voice irked me. The fact he was the same man who'd held my hand when I panicked on the incoming flight baffled me. The two images clashed so much it made my head hurt.

"Ignore him," Alphabet suggested. "I intend to. Come on... I'll sit back here with you."

He motioned for me to climb in and then Goblin and Alphabet followed. I buckled myself into the seat as Alphabet slid the cross straps into place. Goblin settled right between us. The others filtered in. Bones moved to sit up front with Lunchbox and that let Voodoo sit near us.

"Here," Voodoo tugged the headset on over my ears and they helped to blunt out the sound of the engine. "Check, check." His voice crackled briefly but I could hear him easier. "Hang tight."

Alphabet had his own headset on, as did the guys up front. The chatter from Lunchbox included him talking to whomever ran the local tower. It wasn't that long before we were taking off.

Seriously, this tiny little plane seemed so insubstantial versus these guys. I wasn't sure how it stayed in the air with all of them on board. The weight of Goblin's head on my foot tugged my attention. He vibrated faintly against me. I could imagine him snoring.

The relaxed posture offered some comfort. The "briefing" at breakfast hadn't told me much.

"We're at cruising altitude," Lunchbox said. "We're going to be pushing it some. But we should reach our destination in five hours, and forty minutes. Weather looks good so far. I'm keeping an eye on a potential storm. I don't think it will be a problem."

"Voodoo, SITREP?" Bones sounded less distant and dismissive at the moment.

"Transport will be waiting for us. I've got a couple of contacts with the border patrol. I know the best spots to infiltrate and get across the border. We're looking at another four to six hours in overland transport. Makes for a messier exfil if that becomes a problem."

"Noted. Alphabet?"

The flow of information was almost like hearing too much and not enough. The words were English, but they might as well have been in a language I didn't speak for how much of the context I was missing.

"Remote access isn't going to work. I've spent the last twelve hours trying to get the bots to penetrate their network. They are set up too tight to let that happen. Not without a lot of on the ground massaging. Even then, all that might do is trigger an alert on their end. If they box the bots, they can feed us misinformation, and that's worse than no information."

"How much time will you need on-site?"

"To be determined." There was a note of apology in Alphabet's voice and he shot me a quick smile. "Some jobs are very much a hands-on thing and until I'm in front of it, I don't know what it is going to take."

"I guess I can see that," I said slowly, but I wasn't really sure I could because I really didn't know what they did—you know aside from blowing up cars, taking out bad guys, and killing people trying to kill us.

Alphabet's grin was a brief flash of humor. "Just ask me if there's something that you want me to go into detail on."

"Or not," Bones interrupted the warmth with a cold douse of water. "This is need to know, and she doesn't."

I rolled my eyes and folded my arms. "Trust me, I won't be asking you to explain anything Boney Boy."

Yes, you caught more flies with honey than with vinegar. I'd be more than happy to douse Bones in one hundred percent pure vinegar. Maybe add some ammonia to it too. I was pretty sure some combo of that created a gas that would probably make him sick.

Voodoo chuckled softly, making no attempt to mask his amusement. Nor did he react when Bones shifted to look back at us. Well, he looked at Voodoo. I was kind of glad he didn't look at *me* like that. Head back in the seat, I studied the byplay between all of them, or at least the visible byplay.

I didn't understand the full dynamic happening here and I was pretty sure that I needed to get some grasp on it.

"What does Boney Boy do for the mission?" The question earned me a lot of silent looks. Alphabet's lips twitched, but he managed to hold onto his expression. Voodoo didn't even try, his smirk was almost adorable.

Almost.

"Excuse me?" the man in question said in a chilly manner.

"No, I don't think I will. Lunchbox is flying us there. Voodoo is getting us equipment and routes. Alphabet is doing something with their electronics and computers. What are you doing besides being a judgmental prick?"

Yep. It was official, I was angry and Bones had volunteered to take the beating for my mood. Even when he gave me a withering look, I didn't retreat from my question or my statement.

"Currently, I'll be your babysitter. Pray that doesn't change too much."

I snorted. The threat just didn't land the way he thought it might. I'd been threatened with rape. I had been assaulted. I'd been dragged from one place to another. I'd fucked one man to keep him from beating me. I fucked a second 'cause I wanted to. At the moment, I was on this plane willingly because it was taking us *away* from the house in the middle of nowhere.

Even going somewhere near a border was *somewhere*. If I was somewhere I could escape, then that was worth it. As angry and dismissing as he wanted to be, I would not be intimidated by him or anyone else.

I'd made it this far. I could go the rest of the way with or without the help of the men on this plane. At least three of them seemed interested in taking my side. Or maybe I was drinking the Kool-Aid and they were just interested in keeping me from making trouble.

The idea that you caught more flies with honey and all that worked for them too. I was cooperating, wasn't I?

"Here," Alphabet was saying as he passed me a tablet. "I loaded it with some movies, shows, and books. I lifted some ideas from your Amazon wish list and the rest from some social media posts."

Honestly, I had no idea what I expected him to say but that was *not* it. "Stalker much?"

His grin was not remotely apologetic. "Sometimes, it's faster to just go and get the information I need rather than hope someone will tell me in time for me to do something about it."

When I took the tablet, he let it go. There was a password required to unlock it.

"It's your middle name."

"I take it you pulled my birth certificate? Or my Passport?" Yeah, that was *definitely* creepy.

He winked. "Just let me know if there's something else you'd rather I load on there. You won't have access to WiFi, so everything needs to be side loaded."

Clearly, I wasn't allowed to use it for anything else. Noted.

"That said, you don't need to be bored. These jobs can sometimes take longer than any of us like."

If I was busy, then they wouldn't need to be as worried about me. Right.

I stared at the screen for a long moment before I began to type in my middle name.

"What's your middle name, Firecracker?"

I glanced up at Voodoo and raised my eyebrows. "You didn't also look it up?"

"No, and apparently Alphabet isn't sharing either."

"You want a prize, do your own homework," Alphabet told him, then he winked at me. I wasn't sure what that wink meant and reading men had never been a struggle before. I wasn't sure it was a struggle now so much as I wasn't sure what their long term goals were or how it affected anything.

Degas.

My middle name was Degas and it was for one of my mother's favorite impressionist painters. I'd always been kind of fond of his work, though I suspected it had everything to do with Maman's stories about the work.

She'd been a French expat settled here. When our brother died at fifteen, we'd only been seven, but Maman's grief had been ours. We'd done everything we could to look after her, but I really didn't think she'd ever gotten over his loss.

As promised, the tablet had been loaded with some action movies, romantic comedies, and a couple of thrillers. In addition to the films, there were a couple of full series including *Gossip Girl*, *Wednesday*, and *Reacher*. All shows I'd been meaning to watch forever, but I just hadn't had the time.

The books were an eclectic mix of romantic suspense, comedies, and erotic thrillers. Yeah, I wasn't going to comment on those selections. While I absolutely read that genre, they were absolutely *not* on my wishlist.

I caught a movement out of the corner of my eye, and tilted my head to track Alphabet reaching down to stroke

Goblin's head. The dog had moved to rest his head against Alphabet's lap while Alphabet worked on the tiniest laptop I'd ever seen.

The longer he petted the dog, the more some of the tension seemed to leech out of his expression. Dog and man both seemed more at ease, though neither shifted from their position.

A light touch against my foot had me shifting my gaze to Voodoo. Ah, I was staring. I gave him a small shrug then winced. He put two fingers on my knee and that snagged my attention. A moment later, he reached over to adjust something on my headset. There was a chirp.

Then he touched his own before he said, "I saw that. Are you hurting again?"

"It's sore, but it hasn't stopped being sore. I keep forgetting it's there and then I do things like shrug. I'll live."

"I know you'll live." Oh, now he was scolding me. "What I want to make sure is you're not in pain. Pain is debilitating, Firecracker. You have enough on your plate, you don't need that too."

No one else reacted to his words and I flicked a glance around the plane before I looked back at him.

"Different channel," he answered my unasked question. Oh.

"Privacy?" With all of them present, that hadn't seemed like such an issue. Then again, he hadn't invited anyone inside to help me with my back.

"For the most part. You don't trust us at the moment."

No, I really didn't.

"While we may not be offering you a lot of reasons to trust us, I need you to know you can tell me when you're hurting or if there's more pain than there should be. We need to avoid infection primarily and frankly—I don't want you to suffer if you don't have to. To do that, however, I need you to tell me when it does hurt."

As much as I wanted to just dismiss his comments, I studied him instead. Was he being honest? Maybe.

This didn't seem like something where a lie would serve him better than the truth. They did want me to trust them —maybe. Voodoo had done pretty much everything he said, from arming me, to protecting me, to getting that tracker out of me—not once had he left me alone with the doctor I didn't know.

Then when I wanted sex, he'd given me that too, without demanding a single thing in return. Men didn't usually have to be leveraged into sex. The only thing he'd told me he would do and had failed to deliver on was the phone. Somehow, I didn't think it was his decision. At least not his final decision.

The problem with that was he'd also not contradicted Bones. If he really wanted to, could he? Or was Bones the one they all had to obey? If they did—then *why*?

Too many questions, not enough answers.

"I'll tell you," I said finally. "It hurt when I shrugged, but not so bad I couldn't take it. It does feel better today than it did yesterday."

"If that changes..."

Was I up for making him any promises? "If I need assistance," I said, splitting the difference. "I'll tell you."

His mouth tightened. Not the answer he wanted. I didn't have it in me to feel bad about his disappointment. Not now.

Movement to my right pulled my attention, and I found Alphabet studying me then Voodoo. There was a beep in my ear and while I could see their lips moving, I didn't hear whatever the conversation was.

Bones snapped his head back to glare at Voodoo as well.

That was interesting.

Had Voodoo just given me a way to put a wedge between all of them?

THIRTY-ONE

GRACE

Despite the length of the flight, I wasn't one hundred percent sure of the destination *except* that we had to be near Mexico when we landed. They discussed border crossings. If we were going to Canada, I couldn't imagine them flying in circles for *hours* just to throw me off. That would be ridiculous, as well as a waste of time.

"Remind me I want to do some shopping when we're done," Lunchbox mentioned as he taxied us toward some hangers. The place had what looked like a total of three, as well as a dodgy looking control tower, and a single dude in a pickup who drove over to meet us.

The only person who got out was Lunchbox. He took five minutes to sign some paperwork and hand over a yellow wrapped package that could easily be a stack of cash. The guy in the blue baseball cap saluted before he climbed back into his pickup and drove off.

Lunchbox opened the door. "We're parking it here. They'll see to refueling and doing an exterior check."

"You can trust these guys?" Bones asked, shooting a look back over his shoulder to Voodoo.

"Yes," he answered. "Network."

Networking usually brought contacts into play, so that made a certain amount of sense. That was an odd way to say it though.

"Good," Bones popped his exterior door and climbed out. A moment later the door on the other side of Alphabet opened.

Goblin leapt out first, then Alphabet followed, albeit more slowly. I unbuckled my seat belt, but didn't rush. Alphabet seemed almost as sore as I was and no one was giving him hell about hurrying. Probably a good thing.

Once Alphabet was clear, Voodoo glanced at me and I extended my hand to motion him to the door. "I'm right behind you," I offered.

"You got that?" He nodded to the tablet in my hand.

I curled my arm to hug the table to my chest. "I have it." I didn't think they would take it away and keep it, but I didn't want to lose the device since I'd just gotten it.

The corner of his mouth kicked up, but he didn't comment. He pushed out of his seat and stepped out. He waited for me to reach the exit and then offered me a hand. The narrow steps were easy to miss, but I appreciated the fact that Voodoo didn't just pick me up and put me on the ground.

"Thank you," I murmured. The air was warmer than I expected and the landscape seemed almost painfully flat and *beige*. Cloud cover kept the sun from blazing down but it hardly looked like a storm was in the offing. There wasn't even a smell of rain on the air.

The guys already had the bags out of the back of the plane. There was a dirty, beaten up van waiting for us that looked like it could have made the trip to Woodstock back in the sixties.

I was pretty sure it was older than all of us. It was also an eyesore orange where the paint hadn't chipped away. I looked from it to the guys and back.

"Don't worry," Bones said. "The seats are padded."

"Yeah," I muttered. "That was what I was worried about."

They were tossing their bags into the back of the bus. The door on the side slid open to reveal a couple of bench seats in the back, with two bucket seats in the front. I climbed in and headed to the bench seat in the back.

Goblin leapt up to follow me. There were no seatbelts visible, so I parked myself on the bench with my tablet still hugged to my chest. Goblin wagged his tail as he nudged my knee.

"Hey, boy," I greeted him and then he was leaping up onto the seat next to me. He'd settled, laying there with his tongue lolling by the time the guys climbed in. Alphabet eyed me and then Goblin before he chuckled and took a seat on the bench in front of me.

Lunchbox followed him inside and gave Goblin the same look Alphabet had. He dropped onto the bench next to Alphabet and stretched his legs out. Voodoo climbed into the driver's seat with Bones in the passenger seat.

"Please keep all arms, legs, and heads inside the vehicle," I muttered, "and remain seated please. The vehicle doors will close. Thank you."

Alphabet flashed me a grin as he chuckled.

"Everyone's a critic," Voodoo called, cutting a look at me via the rearview.

"You meant, everyone's a smart-ass."

"That works too." He winked.

The bus gave a little jolt and barked out a backfire as we rolled out. I scanned the area as we drove. I still didn't know where we were, but I could see where we were going. Not that there were signs betraying the location.

I shifted my attention back to the men packed inside the little VW bus ahead of me. If I thought it felt crowded on the plane, this was positively claustrophobic. Did they make choices like this on purpose?

My bladder began protesting about two hours into the drive. I hadn't listened to anything on the tablet or tried to read. I didn't feel like throwing up. Yet, there was some comfort in just holding onto it.

The guys had gone quiet, not chatting or even doing that much moving that I could see. I was pretty sure Alphabet had gone to sleep. Goblin definitely had, his snoring vibrated against my leg where he rested. It was soothing in a way. I made it another thirty minutes before I reached forward to touch Lunchbox on the shoulder.

He glanced back at me. "All good, Gracie?"

"I need to pee," I said, an apology right on the tip of my tongue. It had been hours since we'd been anywhere near a bathroom. I'd been circumspect in hydrating, but I'd also had to drink too.

"Got it." He leaned forward, almost going into a crouch that put him between the bucket seats in the front. Voodoo shot me a look via the rearview mirror and he nodded.

Hopefully, we were going to find a spot with a clean bathroom. I hated public bathrooms in general. The road we'd been on had absolutely nothing off of it for the past ninety minutes. No gas stations, grocery stores, or even homes.

We'd passed a dilapidated barn and an utterly trashed billboard. The only things out here were some dust devils and an occasional tumbleweed. The clouds had also begun to break up, adding more brightness to the overall day.

I missed my sunglasses.

"We're looking, Gracie," Lunchbox said as he slid back into the seat. He had his phone in his hand. "Shit for signal out here."

He tapped Alphabet and I winced. The man sat up like he'd just been waiting to be brought in. "What's up?"

"Need to find a place for Gracie to use the bathroom." Lunchbox showed him his phone. "No service."

"Right." Alphabet scrubbed a hand over his face. "Give me a few. We may have to stop if I have to set up the dish."

I grimaced. "If we have to stop, maybe we can find a bush I can step behind." While I would prefer a clean bathroom, I could make do if necessary.

That earned me a surprised look from Lunchbox. Ten minutes became fifteen, then we were at thirty when Alphabet said, "Find a spot to pull off."

"Not sure where you think I'm doing that?" Voodoo said. "We have a fat lot of nothing, more nothing, and oh look—*nothing*."

My bladder ached and I was squeezing my legs together. Now that I'd given any thought to the need to pee, it was making me crazy.

"Can we just pull off to the side?" We hadn't seen any traffic at all. "If you guys just go to the other side of the van and give me some privacy, I can just pee in the sand."

Or at least, I thought it was sand. It could just be dirt. Voodoo sent me another glance and I could have sworn there was an apology in his eyes.

Thankfully, he pulled onto the shoulder without any further nudging. The guys spilled out like they needed to secure the area. I just let them. Goblin hopped right out, found a tuft of weeds and cocked his leg.

Lucky bastard.

The doors behind me opened and Voodoo was there. He opened one of the bags and pulled out handwipes and toilet paper.

"Do I want to know why you already had that in a bag?"

His flash of a grin was all amusement. "I think you can figure it out."

Clearly.

"Also, leaving this side door open and the door up on the passenger side. It will give you some cover from the road. I doubt anyone is coming but..."

"Yeah," I said, sliding out the side door to meet him. "It would be our luck this is the moment someone showed up."

"Give me one more minute," Voodoo said and he did a circuit around the side of the van and then dropped to glance under it before he kicked at the ground with his boots. "Okay. We look good. No snakes or scorpions."

All of a sudden I didn't want to pee ever again. I stared at him.

"I'll keep watch from the back." Then he was gone. The others were on the far side of the van or in front of it. I set the toilet paper and the wipes just inside the van and pulled the pants and underwear down.

After a swift internal debate, I faced the van and angled my ass away so I could squat and pee. The relief was so profound, I could almost forget *where* we were. Finished, I used a bit of toilet paper to wipe before I pulled my pants up, then I used a wipe to clean my hands and wrapped the wipe around the toilet paper.

"All good?" Voodoo asked, he still had his back to me but he was at the edge of the door.

"As good as I can be." Though to be honest… "And I do feel better, so thank you."

We took advantage of the break to deal with the trash. The guys also took the time to take a leak and I made sure to keep my eyes to myself. It had definitely gotten a lot warmer, because I was sweating by the time we climbed back into the van.

The air conditioner was going to have to work overtime but since I was no longer about to piss my pants, I could afford to wait. The water was cold, and there were sandwiches. I ate one that was all cucumbers, cheese, and ham.

When the guys weren't looking, I split some of it with Goblin. His goofy wide grins after he finished up each bite were a definite improvement on the day. At some point, I must have fallen asleep, because I woke up to Lunchbox lifting me out of the seat.

"Shh," he said in a low tone. It was dark outside and a great deal cooler. "Just go back to sleep, Gracie. We'll get you inside. We can't do anything until tomorrow."

A thousand questions bounced around in my head, but I was exhausted. I felt even groggier than I'd been after the heat of the day.

"Please just tell me there's a real bathroom."

His soft huff of laughter was only forgivable because he said, "Yes, and it's clean too. Bones said they even have hot water."

Oh, that sounded heavenly. I smothered a yawn and rested my head against his shoulder as he carried me inside. I didn't really get a good look at where we were or the place we were going into.

The lights were low and there was a kind of buzzing hum from them. Then we were in a bedroom and the door to the bathroom was open. Lunchbox put me on my feet carefully and balanced me until I wasn't quite so shaky.

"Try not to wake yourself up," he said as he reached in and tugged a cord to turn on the light in the bathroom. "I'm going to grab your gear."

Right. My gear.

"My tablet?"

"I'll get it," he said then he was gone. I went in and used the toilet—so much better than the side of the road. When he came back, there was a small bag of toiletries so I could wash my hands and face. I did a quick, if sketchy, brush of my teeth and then stripped out of my pants to climb into the bed.

I didn't care about the rest of the stuff. The sheets smelled mostly clean and the pillows were soft. "Thanks, Lunchbox," I said around another yawn. He was still in the room, but eyes were already closing.

"Anytime, Gracie. I'm going to shower…"

I was pretty sure there were more words, but I just curled up and went to sleep. The next time I opened my eyes, there was light showing around the edges of the blinds. My back protested when I shifted. Everything protested really.

The door to the room was closed, though the door to the bathroom was open. There was a faint hint of soap and dampness in the air. Like someone had showered. The bathroom was still humid. Someone had showered…

I glanced at the bed and it wasn't that rumpled. I'd apparently curled up on my side and then not moved. After I peed, washed my hands and face and found a brush with my toiletries to ease any snarls from my hair, I studied the bedroom itself.

A queen-sized bed, a dresser, a place where a mirror

used to be. A corner wardrobe for a closet. A wing-backed chair that was angled toward the bed, though there were rumples of the covers at the foot there, like someone had been sitting there...

I glanced at the chair again then back to the bed. Sitting in the chair and resting their feet on the bed? Had someone slept in here with me in the chair? The place didn't feel like a hotel, that didn't mean anything but still.

Honestly, after all the rest, I found it hard to find *that* part objectionable. At least not right now. I dragged on my pants and opened the door. It was unlocked.

Well, that was already an improvement over where we'd been. So the question was, where were we now?

CHAPTER
THIRTY-TWO
GRACE

S ome ancient motor seemed to rattle to life as I stepped into the hall of what had to be a house. The layout, the flooring, everything... Definitely not a hotel. The whir of fans and the hum of electricity joined the faint vrooming sound that reminded me of those window units used in some dressing trailers, particularly when we were on set.

The air was cooler out here, but not by much. The bedroom was hardly too warm. Other than the knocks and pings from that cooling unit, it was quiet. I headed toward the brighter end of the hallway. The other direction seemed lost in shadows and since there was some light coming from my room, I had to assume any other doors were just shut.

Carpet muffled my steps, but it didn't feel all that thick. Thankfully, it did smell clean in here. As I rounded the corner, I spotted Goblin flopped on a love seat. He was flat on his back, head turned toward where Alphabet sat working at a dining table. Mouth half-open, Goblin let out a faint snore but his eyes were also open. At least it looked like they were.

The dog was adorable.

Shaking off the distraction, I glanced back at Alphabet, who lifted his chin in greeting. Then he tapped his headset. Oh, he was listening or talking to someone. Folding my arms, I crossed to his set up. There were three laptops, and a tablet, and a small circular device in the center that they were all plugged into, but I had no idea what it was.

I pointed to his empty coffee cup and Alphabet's whole expression went lighter. He picked up the cup and pressed it to my hands, then he pointed to a plate that was also there. The plate was paper but the double-walled and insulated mug had to have come with us.

Before I could take the plate, he touched a finger lightly to the back of my hand then motioned to the screen. A text field popped up.

1-cup coffee brewer in kitchen. 3 dif types of coffee pods. No cream. Prefer the dark roast. Some sugar if you want. No sugar for me. In fridge are sandwiches. Same as on drive. Will talk 2 U as soon as we get a break.

He gave me a hopeful smile that practically gleamed in his sparkling blue eyes. The messy blond hair, that made me think all he did to tame it was rake his fingers, gave him such a tousled and sexy air. It was distracting as hell.

I offered him a thumbs up. Despite the absolute silence, I swore I could hear his cheer when he raised his hands. When I raised the paper plate and glanced at him. He shook his head, then signed "thank you" in ASL.

The moment he finished, he frowned. Oops. Worried I didn't get it? I tried to hide my humor before I signed, "I understand."

His grin widened, it turned up his magnetism by a thousand watts. My stomach bottomed out at the pure delight reflected in his expression. He gave a little jerk and focused on the screen. "I'm still here, Bones. Don't get your tighty-whities in a knottey."

I inhaled my spit trying not to laugh. The fact Alphabet winked didn't do much to help me resist cackling. I could almost picture Boney Boy's bitchy expression. With a mission in mind, I headed into the kitchen. The windows in here overlooked some rather yellow and ordinary hilly plains beyond. I found everything for coffee waiting right there on the counter.

Another one of those round devices had the coffee maker plugged into it, along with a toaster, and what looked like a dual hot plate that was plugged in but not turned on. I hadn't seen any of this stuff in the van, but it could have been in their bags.

A sticky note on the ancient fridge said *Use only water in fridge except to shower. Even brush your teeth with this.*

Did I use their water to brush my teeth the night before? I had to have. Well, I hoped I had. The water hadn't killed me yet if I didn't.

I pulled out a couple of bottles from the fridge and started coffee for Alphabet before I made one for me. I also retrieved one of the sandwiches. The last thing I wanted this early was a sandwich. Though, frankly, I had no idea what time it was, so maybe it was afternoon.

By the time both cups were ready, I'd finished the sandwich and cleaned up my small amount of mess. The trash bag attached to the door handle on the fridge needed no explanation.

"Scanning, hold position," Alphabet said as I came back in. His computer screen showed a slowly, but steadily populating image of what looked like a parking lot with one side of a warehouse growing more and more visible. "Sixty more seconds."

He didn't wave me off, so I took a sip of the coffee while I watched the scanning lines add more and more detail.

"In ten seconds, switching to Lunchbox." Then he was counting it down. "...three, two, and you're clear Voodoo. Lunchbox is up, Bones, you're next."

The image on the screen rotated as more details were added. There were vehicles in the parking lot. The license plates weren't familiar. Mexico? Maybe, but I couldn't quite make out the detail. There were people visible from this angle.

People, which included men with guns. Goblin let out a low whine. I glanced over to where he was stretching his whole body out as he climbed down from the sofa. On the floor, Goblin sat and wagged his tail as he stared at me expectantly.

A light touch on my arm from Alphabet snagged my attention. He signed, "Can you let him out? He won't take long."

I gave him a thumbs up and then headed for the front door. I wanted an excuse to see more of where we were. Goblin didn't move immediately, but when I gripped the door handle, I caught Alphabet giving the dog a signal.

Goblin bounded up and toward me. "Come on, good boy," I said, then let us both outside. The air out here was definitely warmer than in the house. The sun shone down with an almost unrelenting glare.

I shielded my eyes as I descended the steps. Goblin was waiting for me, so I headed toward the grass so he could too. The coffee was almost too warm for the heat out here.

I couldn't see the road we'd used to get here, though

there was a dirt track. The house didn't really have a drive. The sound of the motor out here was louder than in the house. Probably a generator. Goblin trotted around, peeing in several spots. He didn't seem in a hurry, so I didn't rush him.

A barn was visible in the back. Since Goblin seemed to be wandering that way, I drifted along with him. The dirt was exceptionally dry and cracked in places. The earth looked almost gray where it was splitting. The grass was yellow tufts. I wasn't even sure it was fully grass.

There was a shadow cast by the bar, and I pushed one the door wider. It was hung on a rolling caster and squeaked, but the interior was out of the sun. The scents of sawdust and manure made my nose itch.

Okay, so the barn wasn't in use now, I didn't hear any animals. Didn't mean it hadn't been used before. Goblin barked once and I turned to find him between me and the house. He darted to me and then back.

"Are we done then?" I asked. Goblin barked again, tail wagging and I got it. "You're as bossy as the other guys."

At least he looked happier when I started following him. I'd finished my coffee by the time I let him back in the house. Alphabet was standing, but relief flickered over his expression at our arrival.

It also let me notice the fact he was wearing a shoulder holster with a gun tucked into it. The laptop in front of him had a completed image and there were numbers flowing up the front of it.

Lifting the headset off, he set it on the table. "Heard him barking."

"I wasn't moving fast enough," I said, and a faint smile flickered over his face. "He's very bossy."

"He can be." Affection colored the words. "I'm going to hit the head. Stay close?"

"Not really sure where else I can go—there's a whole lot of nothing out there." As much as I tried to not let it come out whiny or petulant, I couldn't help the complaint. Really, where did he think I was going to go?

"Yeah. I'll be right back." At least he didn't try to apologize. I stared at the computers, the screens were all on but they were all doing something. I couldn't see anything from the other guys, but I assumed they were on the headset or maybe they were already en route.

As tempting as it was to hit some of the keys and see what was going on, I left it alone. A toilet flushed deeper in the house. Goblin had moved to the hallway when Alphabet went that way and stayed there until he returned.

Alphabet and Goblin were always together. Definitely his dog. The slow shuffle of Alphabet's steps seemed more noticeable, and he was definitely limping.

"Did you get hurt?" It was probably none of my business. But I needed more of them on my side and he *had* saved my life at least twice that I could think of—so that was a good place to start.

He had his hands on his hips as he leaned back a little like he was stretching his back. "Just sat still for too long."

Right. None of my business.

I looked back at the screen. "If I ask what you guys are doing?"

"I'd have to tell you I can't tell you," he answered without playing any kind of games.

"Can't or won't?" Yes, I was pushing it.

"Currently? It's both. To be honest, Gracie, I don't think you want to know." The presumption scraped against me like I'd slipped down a gravelly hill.

"Can we make an agreement?" I focused on him and he straightened.

"Depends on the terms." Smart man, never agree without knowing what was all involved. Normally, I'd admire that.

At the moment, it just added to my irritation.

"I'll try not to presume what nefarious acts you and the others are up to in a foreign country, and you don't just presume how I feel or what I want. Sound good?" It came out so snippy. I was biting off each word like it was impossible to chew.

Even Goblin stared at me, ears down like I'd upset him.

Alphabet sighed. "Gracie—"

A whistle and a pop came from the laptop and a message flashed on the screen.

"Dammit," he swore and limped his way back to the chair. He pulled his headset on before he took a seat, but there was no missing the way he stretched his right leg to the side as he sat and then moved it under the desk. "I'm here," he said. "Gracie's awake."

He glanced at me and I waved him back to the computer as I carried my coffee mug into the kitchen. I washed it out with some water from a bottle, then carried a fresh water bottle out to leave for Alphabet before I retreated to my room.

It wasn't much, but I could sit in here and try to figure things out. My tablet was also there on the dresser, next to the bag they'd apparently set there for me. I hadn't noticed either earlier.

The next few hours passed with agonizing slowness. I tried not to listen to the partial conversation in the front room while I attempted reading. Periodic breaks let me check on Alphabet and I took Goblin out once more after I left Alphabet a sandwich.

The hours trickled by until I gave up trying to read and

turned on one of the series he'd downloaded. I honestly wasn't even sure I heard any of it. At some point, weariness hit me, and as it grew dark, I went to sleep again.

The next day, I woke to the guys arguing over breakfast. At least, it sounded like they were arguing until I made my way out there. Then the conversation broke off and the subject changed.

"Subtle," Lunchbox said with a dirty look at Bones and then Voodoo.

"Whatever. Let's eat. I want everything ready to go. We're moving today."

I frowned but headed over to make my own coffee.

"Hey," Voodoo said, touching my arm. "How are you doing?"

With a shrug, I pointed to the coffee. "I'm still here. You?"

"Same." He glanced to where Lunchbox and Bones were in deeper conversation.

"Where's Alphabet?" I just realized neither he nor Goblin were here.

"Still sleeping," Lunchbox said. "I'm going to make you some scrambled eggs real quick and some grilled ham. I'd do more but we don't have time. We should be home by this time day after tomorrow, so I promise you a much better meal."

"I take it we're all leaving tonight then?"

"Don't worry, Firecracker," Voodoo said. "Soon as we wrap up business, we'll be back to get you and Alphabet. You'll have a couple of hours warning."

They weren't kidding about getting ready to leave. As soon as the scrambled eggs and ham were ready, Lunchbox put them on a plate and nudged me to it.

"Sorry it's not more," he said. "We'll be back soon."

There was a banging deeper in the house, then Bones announced they were leaving. Right, don't let Alphabet sleep cause I couldn't be on my own. Voodoo and Lunchbox both glanced at me like I was going to say something but Bones was already out the door.

"I guess, good luck?" What else was I supposed to say?

"See you soon," Lunchbox flashed another quick smile and then they were gone.

As much as I didn't want eggs or ham, my stomach was pinching from skipping dinner the night before. I should have eaten but I didn't want to.

Eventually, Alphabet joined me and he invited me to play cards. "We've got a few hours before they get to work and there's nothing else I can do, so—wanna try a hand or three?"

"Depends on what you want to play? I'm pretty good at gin rummy and poker."

The corners of his mouth quirked. "My kind of girl." It didn't take him long to put together some fake *chips* in the form of quarters, dimes, nickels, and pennies. He sorted out enough change for us to be evenly staked.

While he did that, I made him coffee and got him another sandwich. Then he took Goblin out for a few while I took a shower and changed clothes. Once we were back in the little living room, he dealt out the cards.

"Ante up," he said with a glance at his watch. "Show me what you got, Gracie."

THIRTY-THREE

ALPHABET

For all that she attempted to hide her reactions, Gracie had been unhappy about the guys taking off to finish the mission. Course, she could be upset about being in a safe house in Mexico. It didn't have to be one or another, we'd hardly been living up to the expectations we'd been trying to set.

Fortunately, she turned out to be a damn good poker player. The woman had to have tells, I just needed to learn what they were. About an hour out from "go time," I suggested a walk then I'd set her to getting everything packed here that *wasn't* my set up.

Outside, she squinted against the sun. I'd slid sunglasses on but she didn't have any. "You want mine?" I offered immediately.

"No," she said, descending the steps ahead of both me and Goblin. "Thank you, though." Turning, she moved backwards while shielding her eyes with her hand. "You probably shouldn't be sun blind when you go back in."

Still… "I'll have Voodoo bring you back a pair. You can at least have them for the road."

Her faint, if fleeting, smile didn't quite dismiss the offer but said she didn't really believe me either. Who could blame her? My leg ached but that was just the way it went. The walk would be good for all of us.

The fresh air, the sunshine, and the movement were helpful when I was about to be glued to my seat for the next several hours. She didn't say anything, just walked parallel to me with her hands in her pockets of her jeans. It was odd how much tinier than all of us she was.

"Okay, bad question, but it's been kind of eating at me," I said to her as a warning. "Feel free to tell me to fuck off if it's none of my business."

Amusement appeared in her smile as she slanted a look toward me. "I can handle that."

"I assumed." I told her. Goblin moved on a zig-zagging pattern. He scouted ahead but kept moving back to stay within range of us. Twice he jogged ahead to pee then came right back. "Aren't you a little short to be a model?"

A snort of laughter escaped her. "That's been bugging you for a while?"

"Yes," I admitted, not terrifically proud of it. "Don't get me wrong, you're sexy as fuck and gorgeous. But you're just…"

"Short?" Pure mischief lived in her expression and it robbed me of my breath. It was the most relaxed I'd seen her since meeting her at Doc's clinic.

I spread my hands. "You are."

"This is true," she said, almost too agreeably. "I am short. If all I did was runways… that might be more of an issue. But I do photo spreads, commercials, and the occasional music video."

"Was it hard to get started since most models are a lot taller?"

She shrugged. "Not that I noticed. There's always someone else who is going to be something I'm not. Taller. Thinner. Blonder. Darker complexion. Lighter skinned. More toned. Less toned. Better curves."

I glanced over at the perfect peach shape of her ass. The jeans she was in did nothing to hide it. You had to see her from the side to appreciate the roundness and firmness of it. Straight on, it was missing. Just like her breasts...

"Do you know how many clients have suggested I get a boob job?" The dry comment jerked my gaze back up.

"Don't," I ordered immediately. "There's not a damn thing wrong with your breasts."

I didn't try to duck away from her knowing smirk. If anything, I met the dare in her eyes head-on.

"Yes, I notice because I'm a red-blooded male and you're very beautiful."

"I've also done some nude shoots." Yep, there was the sting and I almost welcomed it as she gave me a verbal slap.

"I may have found those images," I admitted, then raked a hand through my hair. "Probably makes me sound like a creeper, doesn't it?"

She shrugged. "If I didn't pose for them and you hacked them from my phone or something... Maybe. But I know my body, it doesn't bother me. I used to worry that it would bug Am..."

All at once, what good mood she'd found fled. The sadness in her slashed at me.

"She doesn't mind?" I asked even as we shifted our angle to head back to the house. We'd circled the barn and come back up the far side. No movement or changes to the landscape. The guys would have done their own scout while they were here, but since it was just me and Goblin on watch, I liked to see it for myself.

Part of the reason we'd set this as our staging area. We were a solid ninety minutes from anywhere. Even if they back traced us, by the time they would head here, we would all be long gone.

That was the plan.

Her long sigh almost made me regret asking the question. "No," she said after a long moment. "At first, she wasn't a fan. She doesn't want me to do it gratuitously." A new smirk appeared. "I promised her, I never do it for free." The last was said very tongue in cheek, and I felt more than saw the look she gave me.

"Waiting for me to ask, 'how much'?" I teased and her laughter was a real reward for the choice.

"Maybe." Then she sobered. "But the thing is, when it's for an ad campaign or the story they are trying to tell with the product, I get it... I'm the canvas. Sometimes, you want a blank canvas so what the customer sees is the product."

"Not sure I follow that," I said as we followed the house around to the porch. Goblin was roaming, but the day was already promising to be a very warm one. "No offense to the products, but not sure a car or cologne is going to make me look at your body any differently than as *your* body."

"Thank you," she said with a kind of gracious ease. "But... think about it this way. Is it the cologne or the car that got me naked?"

The minute she proffered that idea, my dick was suddenly a little too tightly tucked. Fuck.

"Your expression right now is all the evidence we need that," she said as she climbed the steps, "sex sells."

"I really can't argue with that." Didn't want to either. My phone was vibrating as we re-entered the air conditioned space. It felt a lot cooler and better on my overheated skin. The walk had also gotten the knots out of my back.

"Still can't tell me what we're doing here?" She had gone to get fresh water bottles and emptied one into Goblin's bowl before setting a fresh one on my desk.

"No," I answered. "We'll be done soon and I can put some more hours into looking for your sister."

"Sure," she said, saluting me with the water bottle. "At least until whatever comes up next."

That doubting note drew blood from my conscience as she headed down the hall.

"I'm going to repack my stuff. Should I add any of their stuff to their bags?"

I sighed. "They did it before they left."

"Right, so just you and me. I'll be back to help you then."

Then she disappeared down the hallway and Goblin walked over to flop at my feet on the wooden floor, panting. He stared up at me until I met his gaze, then he cut loose with a ripper of a fart.

"Everyone is a critic," I informed him, but he just wagged his tail. Then I looked back down the hall. Bones wanted to keep her clean. It made sense. She couldn't betray what she didn't know.

But we'd taken her home and we planned to keep her there. We didn't take just anyone there either. Granted, she didn't know where it was exactly *right now*, that could change the more trips we took.

Then what excuse did we use to keep from letting her go? Because we absolutely *should* let her go.

I just didn't want to.

Somehow, I was also pretty damn sure that Lunchbox and Voodoo were on my side in that argument.

Goblin farted again and I grimaced. "Goddamn, what are we feeding you?" I waved a hand in front of me and settled back at the table. The walk had definitely helped to ease the soreness and the stiffness.

That would have to do for now.

Right on schedule, I pulled my headset on and logged in. "Online," I answered the call with one flick of the key. "We ready to go?"

"Standby," Bones said. "We have more activity at El Mal Lugar." The name of the factory was a dead giveaway or maybe it was just an inside joke. "What did our intel say about their movements?"

"Not as much as we would have liked," I reminded him. "You wanted us in position sooner rather than later. As far as I can tell, they rotate between these three factories, but in a random-non-random pattern. El Mal Lugar was the prior alpha spot for distribution. Current spot should be El Lugar Agrietado."

"Yeah, El Mal Lugar is far busier than yesterday," Voodoo warned. "Like, I think they brought in a whole crew."

It took me a few minutes to bring up their location. I'd spent most of the day before hacking into the local security systems while we did our scans. Voodoo and Lunchbox had also attached splitters to their landlines which got me in behind the firewalls.

If anyone found the equipment, they could boot me out. But I'd already built a backdoor, so I didn't need that to be in. The CCTV coverage in this region was in no way thick or useful. So good for exfiltration, terrible for getting on site.

"I'm in, let's have a look."

The interior cameras showed the workforce present had more than doubled.

"Fuck," I swore. "They're swapping their operations here—*today*." That was going to fuck up all our plans. I could picture Bones' expression right now. "They've got a full crew in there cleaning the tables, and sweeping out the main body of the warehouse. I'd imagine they are going to bring the trucks in to do the cutting here, then box it to send it back out."

They processed somewhere between ten and twenty million dollars in cocaine weekly in these factories. That was part of the reason we'd been brought in to remove them. Cartels were always jockeying for control and power. Cut off one head, another would rise up to take its place.

Remove the bones of their operations though? It could force them down a chute of the client's choosing and give us alternate ways of shutting them down. Right now, the only job we had was to destroy these factories.

"How soon do you think they'll have the drugs on site?" Bones asked, I could almost hear the wheels turning in his head.

"No clue. It could be five minutes or five hours, depending on when they got started." I checked the other factories. Both empty and unmanned.

The day before, they'd had a full complement and crew...

"Are we a go or do we scrub?" Lunchbox asked. Goblin glanced up from where he was sprawled, his tail thumping. Grace was back.

"Alphabet?" Bones prodded me.

"We've got two empty factories and a third now with a new staff. I'm guessing they are on the way to you."

"Or maybe they saw you guys were looking and are giving you something else to look at." The soft words from behind me might have made me jump if I hadn't seen Goblin's reaction.

"Maybe," I answered her.

"Tell her to take a walk," Bones said without any preamble and for now, I ignored him. He wasn't here and she couldn't hear him and they weren't shooting anything yet.

"We've got movement," Voodoo intervened. "Looks like a half-dozen vehicles about a mile out. If that's more security, we're fucked for real."

More security. I leaned forward and studied the screens. There were definitely women in the cleaning crew. They didn't look like soldiers or mercenaries. They also didn't look like they were under duress. They were laughing and teasing each other as they moved.

"Anyone get close enough to hear what they are saying?"

"They are bitching about some guy on the telenovela they are all watching. Saying he's unreal." Lunchbox's tone never varied from easy. "Nothing special, why?"

"Something is off," I said, but I couldn't put my finger on it.

"Are they putting on a show?" Gracie asked and I cut a glance to the side to look at her. Our earlier conversation. Did the nudity actually sell? If it made you associate the vehicle or the product with why the woman was naked?

"What would be the point of this show?" To get us to pull the plug. "Guys, I'd advise withdrawing sooner rather than later. We can blow the other two locations, put some delayed timers here. We can blow it remotely when they are done."

"If we do that, we give them time to keep the product on the move." Bones didn't like either option.

"There's no good answer." If we'd moved the day before, we could have blown the factory with the product in it *after* the workers went home. "If we blow it while they are there, we're going to kill innocents. If we don't, we risk letting the drugs go and that makes all of this a moot point."

"Unacceptable," Bones muttered but I didn't think he was talking to me. The man hated when our options got slashed.

"These trucks are about to be on top of us," Voodoo warned.

"Hold," Bones said. "Hold position, stay low. Alphabet, get me IDs on the incoming. Going dark."

That shut them all off, they'd be able to hear me if I sent but they weren't transmitting. For now that would have to work. I checked my watch and then worked to switch my camera views.

A light hand feathered over my shoulder and I glanced up at Gracie. Hitting one button on the keyboard, I muted myself. "This could take a while..."

"Can I help?"

I blinked at her. It was a lovely offer, but...

"I can get you drinks, food, you can even have me read something to you if you need it. You have more than one laptop here. I'm not—" She waved a hand to my setup. "Whatever this is, but I can follow instructions."

"Not yet," I said. "But let's keep that in our back pocket. Water would be great, get some for you and drag a chair over here."

Her whole expression brightened. "On it."

Bones would be pissed, but he was there and what he didn't know wouldn't get me in trouble. I scratched at the scruff on my jaw. I really needed to shave. She settled into the chair next to me and I went to work. I got images of most of the people coming in.

It was definitely more security arriving. The world faded as I snapped screenshots. The cameras on their property weren't the best and enhancement would be impossible, but we should have enough to start an ID.

Two hours after their arrival, the larger trucks arrived. The soldiers were everywhere. So far the team had remained silent, but I didn't see any direction for this to go in that wasn't sideways.

The longer this dragged on, the more uneasy I became. Outside, the sun was going down. The schedule was out the window.

"Blow number two," Bones said, the hush on the order giving it a more ominous tone than if he'd yelled. That was definitely one way to test it.

"Standby," I said, answering in the same solemn tone. They'd been offloading pallets of product. Or at least it looked like product. The cleaners had all changed their clothes and wore plastic gowns over everything and face masks.

The guards were still thick around the edges of the room, they had all the angles covered in theory. Chances were they had eyes on the cameras too and I could see quite a bit.

Tabbing over to the second factory that they'd basically just abandoned, I sent the signal to the bombs they'd wired into place. The first detonation filled one of my camera views with fire. The second took out the camera.

I flicked my gaze back to the location with the full staff. The women were already working on breaking the bricks up...

Several men bolted and activity outside increased.

"They have enough here to field an invasion force," Lunchbox said in a softer whisper. "If we don't want to blow everything, we could always throw some bleach into the sprinkler system."

"I'm so glad you think their buildings are up to code and have sprinklers." I resisted the urge to snort. Pun intended. "The issue we have here is we still don't know what they are doing…"

"Making craft cocaine." Three words that I never thought I would hear from Gracie.

"What?" I asked at the same moment as Bones, though she couldn't hear him.

"Put her on," Bones said, but I ignored that order for the moment.

"Craft Cocaine. It's really popular in some circles. It's a high end business. You want the organic not the chemical-infused, although they call it petrol-infused. Some of the dealers fancy themselves to be like a sommelier for cocaine the way some are for wine. They'll tell you if it's earthy or salty or sometimes if it's just too stinky. The more chemicals it's cut with and the cheaper it is and you won't get much for it."

"It gets you high either way." I had to know, cause that just sounded about as stupid as the pharma-parties I'd heard about.

"In theory, I suppose. I've never used it."

"Good girl."

"Alphabet," Bones said, interrupting. "Stop flirting with the client and put her on the headset. *Now.*"

"The boss wants to talk to you," I said, then switched to the speakers. "She can hear you."

"Good." The snap in his voice made me frown. "Miss Black, I appreciate your expertise on designer drugs, but we're working. You need to find somewhere else to be. Perhaps in another room and stay out of matters that don't concern you."

I sighed.

"Bones, you and I are going to have a very long discussion when we're done," Voodoo warned. "Make time for it."

For her part, Grace pursed her lips. "Fine, I'll let you all *get to it*. I think I'm just going for a walk."

"Take Goblin," I told her, but he was planted with his head on my foot. Probably because my stress was up. "I'd rather you didn't go too far."

"As we already discussed," she said as she headed for the door. "Where am I going to go?"

Then she was out the door and it closed behind. Goblin lifted his head to look at the door then at me.

Fuck.

"Blow number one," Bones ordered.

"Just so you know," I said. "I'm with Voodoo, we're going to be having a talk. I don't know what your problem with her is, but get the fuck over it already. Blowing number one."

The incendiaries went off and it pulled away a couple more soldiers, but the majority of security stayed in place. They weren't leaving their product undefended. Our options were rapidly dwindling.

Goblin stood abruptly and went on point. I shifted in my seat and flicked to the cameras that gave me angles out front and back. They weren't the best, but they had night vision.

Nothing jumped out at me.

But Goblin didn't settle and Gracie wasn't back. "Guys, exfil. Blow it if you have to, but I don't think this is just about product. I think they are putting on a show."

"Why would they—" Bones stopped. "We're abandoning the vehicle here and getting something different. Shut it down, you three get on the move and head north. We'll catch up to you."

"We're on our way," Lunchbox promised, but I was already rising. If they'd tracked the van here, they could have used today as bait to hold the team there while they came here.

"Let's go, Goblin," I said, then tapped my leg. "Stay close." I already had my gun out and picked up the flashlight. Stepping outside, I let the door bang shut. Might as well let everyone know what was going on.

"Gracie!" I called and eased my way down the steps. Goblin moved right at my side as I left the lights from the porch and headed out back. I hadn't seen anything. Not even Gracie on the cameras.

There was one place we didn't have eyes and that was the barn.

"Come on, Gracie. I know you're pissed. I'd be pissed too. But this isn't the time to play these games."

Goblin let out a low sound, it wasn't quite a growl but his head was up and his tail had gone ramrod straight. Yes, we had company out here.

Hang on, sweetheart. "Gracie," I called again, trying to sound persuasive. "C'mon, I promise, I'll pin the dickhead down for you and you can pummel him."

That was a real promise, but I could prove that to her later. We were almost to the barn. There was no sign of vehicles or movement, but then I could smell it.

Son of a bitch.

"Gracie!"

I could smell blood...

The adventure will continue in LURE.

Afterword

Thank you so much for reading., we'll return to the chaos very soon. The preorder says April, but I have every intention of getting it out much sooner! If you enjoyed the read, be sure to leave a review and head over to the pack, we'd love to have you!

xoxo
Heather

Website:
heatherlong.net
Reader group:
facebook.com/groups/heatherspack
Spoiler group:
facebook.com/groups/teammadatheather

ABOUT HEATHER LONG

I *love* books. Not just a little bit, but a lot. Books were my best friends when I was growing up. Books didn't care if I was new to a town or to a class. They were always there, my trustiest of companions. Until they turned on me and said I had to write them.

I can tell you that my own personal happily ever after included writing books. I've always said that an HEA is a work in progress. It's true in my marriage, my friendships, and in my career. I am constantly nurturing my muse as we dive into new tales, new tropes, new characters and more.

After seventeen years in Texas, we relocated to the Pacific Northwest in search of seasons, new experiences, and new geography. I can't wait to discover what life (and my muse) have in store for me.

Maybe writing was always my destiny and romance my fate. After all, my grandmother wasn't a fan of picture books and used to read me her Harlequin Romance novels.

Follow Heather & Sign up for her newsletter:
www.heatherlong.net
TikTok

Also by Heather Long

82nd Street Vandals

Savage Vandal

Vicious Rebel

Ruthless Traitor

Dirty Devil

Shamelessly Loyal (Novella)

Brutal Fighter

Dangerous Renegade

Merciless Spy

Reckless Thief

Fierce Dancer

Dirty Dancer

Bay Ridge Royals

Shamelessly Loyal (Novella)

Battle Lines

Deceptive Truce

Wicked Surrender

Violent Chaos

Desperate Victory

BLOOD Brothers

Burn

Lure

Blue Ivy Prep

Problem Child

Mad Boys

Party Crashers

Money Shot

Bravo Team Wolf

When Danger Bites

Bitten Under Fire

Cardinal Sins

Kill Song

First Chorus

High Note

Last Word

Chance Monroe

Earth Witches Aren't Easy

Plan Witch from Out of Town

Bad Witch Rising

Fevered Hearts

Marshal of Hel Dorado

Brave are the Lonely

Micah & Mrs. Miller

A Fistful of Dreams

Raising Kane

Wanted: Fevered or Alive

Wild and Fevered

The Quick & The Fevered

A Man Called Wyatt

Heart of the Nebula

Queenmaker

Deal Breaker

Throne Taker

Lone Star Leathernecks

Semper Fi Cowboy

As You Were, Cowboy

Shackled Souls

Succubus Chained

Succubus Unchained

Succubus Blessed

Shackled Souls (Omnibus)

STANDALONES

Kiss of Fate (w/Blake Blessing)

Taste of Karma (w/Blake Blessing)

I'll Be Home... (w/Tate James)

Overexposed (w/Tate James)

Switchboard Duet

Talk to Me

Don't Let Go

Untouchable

Rules and Roses

Changes and Chocolates

Keys and Kisses

Whispers and Wishes

Hangovers and Holidays

Brazen and Breathless

Trials and Tiaras

Graduation and Gifts

Defiance and Dedication

Songs and Sweethearts

Legacy and Lovers

Farewells and Forever

Hellos and Happily Ever Afters

Wolves of Willow Bend

Wolf at Law

Wolf Bite

Caged Wolf

Wolf Claim

Wolf Next Door

Rogue Wolf

Bayou Wolf

Untamed Wolf

Wolf with Benefits

River Wolf

Single Wicked Wolf

Desert Wolf

Snow Wolf

Wolf on Board

Holly Jolly Wolf

Shadow Wolf

His Moonstruck Wolf

Thunder Wolf

Ghost Wolf

Outlaw Wolves

Wolf Unleashed

www.ingramcontent.com/pod-product-compliance
Lightning Source LLC
Chambersburg PA
CBHW021726190726
48289CB00008B/2707